THE PEOPLE OF THE RUINS

THE PEOPLE OF THE RUINS

by

EDWARD SHANKS

introduction by **TOM HODGKINSON**

—

HiLoBooks
powered by **Cursor**
Boston, MA *and* **Brooklyn, NY**
2012

Series Foreword © Joshua Glenn 2012
Introduction © Tom Hodgkinson 2012

This edition of *The People of the Ruins* follows the text
of the 1920 edition published by Frederick A. Stokes Co.,
which is in the public domain. We have excised a few
passages in order to arrive at a manageable length; an
unabridged version of the novel was serialized by HiLobrow.

Library of Congress Control Number: 2012939659
ISBN: 978-1-935869-58-0

Cover illustration © Michael Lewy 2012
Cover design by Tony Leone, Leone Design

Printed in the United States of America

HiLoBooks
A project of HiLobrow.com, a critical-culture website
founded by Matthew Battles and Joshua Glenn.
Series Editor: Joshua Glenn
For more information, visit HiLobrow.com/HiLoBooks
Follow us on Twitter: @HiLoBooks

HiLoBooks is grateful to Richard Nash for his vision
and publishing acumen.

Powered by Cursor

Distributed by Publishers Group West
10 9 8 7 6 5 4 3 2 1

TABLE *of* CONTENTS

Radium Age Science Fiction

Back to Freedom or Forward to Slavery

——

PEOPLE OF THE RUINS

RADIUM AGE SCIENCE FICTION
Series Foreword by **Joshua Glenn**

SEVERAL YEARS AGO, I read Brian Aldiss's *Billion Year Spree*—his "true history of science fiction" from Mary Shelley to the early 1970s. I admire Aldiss tremendously, and I found his account of the genre's development entertaining and informative… but something bothered me, after I'd finished reading the book. Something was missing.

Billion Year Spree is terrific on the topic of science fiction from *Frankenstein* through the "scientific romances" of Verne, Poe, and Wells— and also terrific on science fiction's so-called Golden Age, the start of which sf exegetes date to John W. Campbell's 1937 assumption of the editorship of the magazine *Astounding*. However, regarding science fiction published between the beginning of the Golden Age and the end of the Verne-Poe-Wells "scientific romance" era, Aldiss (who rightly laments that Wells's 20th century fiction after, perhaps, 1904's *The Food of the Gods*, fails to recapture "that darkly beautiful quality of imagination, or that instinctive-seeming unity of construction, which lives in his early novels") has very little to say.

Aldiss seems to feel that authors of science fiction after Wells but before the Golden Age weren't very talented. He certainly doesn't think much of the literary skills of Hugo Gernsback, sometimes called the "Father of Science Fiction," who founded *Amazing Stories* in 1926 and coined the phrase "science fiction" while he was at it. He's right: Gernsback's story-telling abilities were as primitive as his ideas were advanced. But does that justify skipping over the 1904-33 era? (By my reckoning, Campbell and his cohort first began to develop their literate, analytical, socially conscious science fiction in reaction to the 1934 advent of the campy *Flash Gordon* comic strip, not to mention Hollywood's "sci-fi" blockbusters that sought to ape the success of 1933's *King Kong*. In other words, sf's Golden Age began before 1937; if I had to pick a year, I'd say 1934.) Is Aldiss's animus against that era due solely to style and quality? I suspect not.

Aldiss's book is hardly alone in sweeping pre-1934 science fiction under the rug. During the so-called Golden Age, which was given that moniker not after the fact, but *at the time*, as a way of signifying the end of science fiction's post-Wells Dark Age, Campbellians took pains to distinguish their own science fiction from everything that had been published in the genre (with the sole exception of 1932's *Brave New World*) since 1904. In his influential 1958 critique, *New Maps of Hell*, for example, Kingsley Amis noted that mature science fiction first established itself in the mid-1930s, "separating with a slowly increasing decisiveness from [immature] fantasy and space-opera." And in his introduction to a 1974 collection, *Before the Golden Age*, editor Isaac Asimov apologetically notes that although it certainly possessed an exuberant vigor, the pre-Golden Age science fiction he grew up reading "seems, to anyone who has experienced the Campbell Revolution, to be clumsy, primitive, naive."

We should be suspicious of this Cold War-era rhetoric of maturity! I'm reminded of Reinhold Niebuhr's pronunciamento, at a 1952 *Partisan Review* symposium, that the utopianism of the early 20th century ought to be regarded as "an adolescent embarrassment." Perhaps Golden Age science fiction's stars—Asimov, Robert Heinlein, Ray Bradbury, and so forth—were regarded as an improvement on their predecessors because in their stories utopian visions and schemes were treated with cynicism. Liberal and conservative anti-utopians who point out that pre-Cold War utopian narratives often demonstrate a naive and perhaps proto-totalitarian eagerness to force square pegs into round holes via thought control and coercion are not wrong. I wouldn't want to live in one of those utopias. However, I strongly agree with those who argue that the intellectual abandonment of utopianism since the 1930s has sapped our political options, and left us all in the helpless position of passive accomplices.

Sure, some 1904-33 science fiction—Gernsback, Edgar Rice Burroughs, and E.E. "Doc" Smith, for example—is indeed fantastical and primitive (though it's still fun to read today). But many other authors of that period—including Olaf Stapledon, William Hope Hodgson, Karel Čapek, Charlotte Perkins Gilman, and Yevgeny Zamyatin—gave us science fiction that was literate, analytical, socially conscious... and also utopian. Utopian in the sense that whatever their politics, Radium Age authors found in the newly named "science fiction" genre a fitting vehicle to express their faith, or at least their hope, that another world is possible. That worldview may have seemed embarrassingly adolescent from the late 1930s until, say, the fall of the Berlin Wall. But today it's an inspiring vision.

—*Joshua Glenn*
  Cofounder, HiLobrow.com & HiLoBooks
  Boston, 2012

HiLoBooks
RADIUM AGE SCIENCE FICTION

2012

The Scarlet Plague
Jack London
Comment by Matthew Battles

With the Night Mail *and* "As Easy as A.B.C."
Rudyard Kipling
Comments by Matthew De Abaitua & Bruce Sterling

The Poison Belt
Arthur Conan Doyle
Comments by Joshua Glenn & Gordon Dahlquist

When the World Shook
H. Rider Haggard
Comments by James Parker & J.R. Bickley, M.R.C.S.

People of the Ruins
Edward Shanks
Comment by Tom Hodgkinson

2013

The Night Land
William Hope Hodgson
Comment by Erik Davis

Goslings
J.D. Beresford

& more to follow

BACK TO FREEDOM OR FORWARD TO SLAVERY
Introduction by **Tom Hodgkinson**

IT IS 1924 AND LONDON is in the grip of a proletarian uprising. Our hero, an earnest young physics lecturer named Jeremy Tuft, gets called a "dirty boorjwar" by a revolutionary truck-driver as he walks down the riot-torn streets of Whitechapel in East London. In his scientist friend's flat, a bizarre experiment is going on, involving a new kind of ray with untested properties. A bomb hits the house and Jeremy gets zapped by the ray. He falls into a deep sleep and wakes up in 2074 to find that society has reverted to a sort of pre-industrial state. The leader of post-apocalyptic England refers to the revolution of 1924 as "The Troubles" and looks back to the pre-revolutionary time as a golden age of knowledge and sophistication.

Such is the premise of *The People of the Ruins: A Story of the English Revolution and After* by poet and journalist Edward Shanks, written in 1920, just two years after the end of the horrifying Great War. Style-wise, it is fair to say that Shanks lacks the light touch. The reader needs to do a lot of wading. Having said all that, it is a very good and a very interesting novel, and the patient reader will be well rewarded.

The People of the Ruins has a certain gloomy charm to it. Tuft is delighted with some aspects of the ruined society. The noble families seem more interested in gardens than buildings. "Jeremy walked in a great shrubbery where Charing Cross Road had been and in a rose garden on the deep-buried foundations of Scotland Yard." That's an appealing image, almost Blakeian. Central government is very small, and the provinces govern themselves, which should cheer the anti-statist libertarians amongst us.

It's not all rosy. Some of the inhabitants live in squalor: "Jeremy saw in the fields bowed laborious figures wrapped in rags which forbade him to say whether they were men or women, and troops of dirty, half-naked children." Despite all this a new beauty opens up in London, and Jeremy sees in it a sort of Epicurean paradise: "You are happier than we were," he says to his pal, "though you are poorer. Your air is clean, you have room, you live at peace, you have time to live... I can remember how delicious it was to lie down in a field off the road, to let the business all go, not to care where one got to or when. It was this peacefulness we should have been aiming at all the time, only we never knew..."

He goes on to express anti-consumerist and anti-work sentiments that chime harmoniously with the writer of this introduction: "We wretched ants piled up more stuff than we could use, and though the mad people of the Troubles wasted it, yet the ruins are enough for this people to live in for centuries. And aren't they more sensible than we were? Why shouldn't humanity retire from business on its savings? If only it had done it before it got that nervous breakdown from overwork!"

Just as today, the anxiety culture and alienation were pressing issues in the Twenties, particularly to thoughtful young men who had seen close up the slaughter of the First World War. And like today's Thoreaus, Jeremy approves of the lack of machines. Somehow without them there is more time for living rather than less. "The trains were few and uncertain, and, from the universal decay of mechanical knowledge, were bound in time to cease all together; but England, so far as Jeremy could see, would get on very well without any trains at all. There was no telephone; but that was in many ways a blessing. There was no electric light... But it was certainly possible to regard candles and lamps as more beautiful. The streets were dark at night and not over-safe; but no man went out unarmed or alone after sunset, and actual violence was rare."

Another appealing feature of the new world, to those of us who are saddened by the rise of the megalopolis, is a sort of deurbanization: "He gathered that [the countryside] was richer and more prosperous than he had known it, and that the small country town had come again into its own." The social life, though, seems distinctly dismal: at a party Jeremy attends, aloofness, small talk and indifference seem to be the order of the day. Manners appear to have reverted to a courtly formality. No one seems to have any fun: where is the maypole dancing and music? Jeremy finds the clothing garish and gaudy, and compares the women's dresses to "a wallpaper of the 19th century", probably a dig at the medievalism of William Morris.

The reader at this point starts to wonder whether or not he would prefer this new world to our own. I suppose it is a strength of the book that the answer is not clear. One man who does not share Jeremy's enthusiasm for this world is its leader, a sinister figure called The Speaker. While Jeremy finds much to commend, the Speaker regrets its loss of technical knowledge. In particular he wants guns, and sets Jeremy to work in manufacturing cannons for a forthcoming showdown with enemies from the North. Demonstrating a lack of awareness of political correctness, he hints that if Jeremy is successful in this project he'll get to shag his daughter, the feisty Lady Eva: "You shall have your reward. I have no son and I have a daughter."

Jeremy is profoundly uncertain about the wisdom of getting back with the military-industrial programme. "He was sometimes far from sure that a regeneration which began by the manufacture of heavy artillery was likely to be a process of which he could wholly approve. He found this age sufficiently agreeable not to wish to change it. It was true that innumerable conveniences had gone. But on the other hand most of the people seemed to be reasonably contented, and no one was ever in a hurry."

Despite such misgivings, he finds himself the reluctant leader of a raggle-taggle band of soldiers, and there is a terrific showdown with the men from Yorkshire. Well, without wanting to spoil the plot, Jeremy Tuft does get the girl, hooray! There is a moment of joy amid the darkness. And we are treated to a fine image of soldiers bedecked in flora: "The troops marched off down Oxford Street and along the winding valley-road, covered again with flowers, which they stuck in their hats or in the muzzles of their rifles." But you couldn't say that the book has a happy ending.

As dystopian fantasies go, Shanks was later outshone by Aldous Huxley in *Brave New World* and George Orwell in *1984*. And Shanks's premise seems lifted from *News From Nowhere* by William Morris, in which a young hero returns home gloomily from a political meeting in the late 19th century and wakes to find himself transported into a future utopia where money has been abolished and a craft economy thrives. However, we must credit Shanks for creating a ground-breaking and very widely read book that may well have influenced the later experiments of Huxley and Orwell. And it could be argued that his gloom was a riposte to the perhaps naive optimism of Morris's fantasy.

So, while not a masterpiece, *The People of the Ruins* can be read with pleasure both as a curiosity item and for its own sake. Philosophically it occupies strange ground. It has none of the techno-utopianism of H.G. Wells, but then none of the revolutionary zeal of William Morris either. The socialists of the time would have found it too pessimistic with its vision of an apathetic state structure. But it has no 'good old days' nostalgia either. It is bleak and uninspiring, and its only conclusion as far as society goes appears to be: you can't win!

Most readers though would find a lot to agree with here. Like Shanks and like Morris, I think that the modern world leaves a lot to be desired, because of the state of anxiety it produces in many of us, the *ennui*, the sense of being perpetually unsatisfied. In chasing a technological utopia something has been lost. We don't quite feel in control of our own world. We work for the machine and not for ourselves. A part of us longs to connect with nature and with our own creativity. But despite these difficulties, I would remain optimistic, because it is not impossible to create little patches of paradise amid the hurly-burly: a shed, a study, a back yard, a contemplative space.

A measure of freedom can certainly be found in every day life by simply turning the clock back to the Middle Ages, when life was less comfortable, to be sure, but when we were not separated from the means of production by the factory system. G.K. Chesterton, the great English essayist of the early 20th century, wrote: "We must go back to freedom or forward to slavery," and this paradox is well worth exploring.

CHAPTER 1

Trouble

1

MR. JEREMY TUFT BECAME aware with a slight shock that he was lying in bed wide awake. He raised his head a little, stared around him, found something vaguely unfamiliar, and tried to go to sleep again. But sleep would not come. Though he felt dull and stupid, he was yet invincibly awake. His eyes opened again of themselves, and he stared round him once more. It was the subdued light, filtered through the curtains, that was strange; and as intelligence flowed back into his empty mind, he realized that this was because it was much stronger than it should have been at any time before eight o'clock. Thence to the conclusion that it was very likely later than eight o'clock was an easy step for his reviving faculties. Energy followed the returning intelligence, and he sat up suddenly, his head throbbing as he did so, and took his watch from the table beside him. It was, in fact, a quarter to ten.

Arising out of this discovery a stream of possibilities troubled the still somewhat confused processes of his mind. Either Mrs. Watkins for some unaccountable reason had failed to arrive, or else, contrary to his emphatic and often repeated instructions, she had been perfunctory in knocking at his door and had not stayed for an answer. In either case it was annoying; but Mrs. Watkins' arrival at half-past seven was so fixed a point in the day, she was so regular, so trustworthy, and, moreover, life without her ministrations was so unthinkable that the first possibility seemed much the less possible of the two. When Jeremy had thus exhausted the field of speculation he rose and went out of his room to speak sharply to Mrs. Watkins. His intention of severity was a little belied by the genial grotesqueness of his short and rather broad figure in dressing-gown and pyjamas; but he hoped that he looked a disciplinarian.

Mrs. Watkins, however, was not there. The flat was silent and completely empty. The blinds were drawn over the sitting-room windows, and stirred faintly as he opened the door. He passed into the kitchen, but not hopefully, for as a rule his ear told him without mistake when the charwoman was to be found there. As he had expected, she was not there, nor yet in the bathroom. There was a quite uncanny silence everywhere, so strange and yet at the same time so reminiscent of something that eluded his memory, that Jeremy paused a moment, head lifted in air, trying to analyze its effect on him. He ascribed it at last to the obvious cause of Mrs. Watkins' absence at this unusually late hour; and he went further into the bathroom, whence he could see, with a little craning of the neck, the clock on St. Andrew's Church in Holborn. This last testimony confirmed that of his watch. He returned to the sitting-room, struggling half-consciously in his mind with a quite irrational feeling, for which he could not account, that it was a Sunday. He knew very well that it was a Tuesday—Tuesday, the 18th of April, in the year 1924.

When he came into the sitting-room he drew back the blinds and let in the full morning light, and by its aid he surveyed unfavorably his overcoat lying where he had thrown it the night before, coming in late from a party. He looked also with some disgust at the glass from which he had drunk a last unnecessary whisky and soda previous to going to bed. Then he paddled back wearily with bare feet to the narrow kitchen (a cupboard containing a gas-stove and a smaller cupboard), set a kettle on to boil, and began the always laborious process of bathing, shaving, and dressing. At the end he shirked making tea, or boiling an egg, and he sat down discontentedly to another whisky, in the same glass, and a piece of stale bread.

As he consumed this unsuitable meal he remembered his appointment for one o'clock that day, and hoped with a sudden devoutness that the 'buses would be running after all. It was no joke to go from Holborn to Whitechapel High Street on foot. But a young and rather aggressive Socialist whom he had unwillingly met at that party had predicted with confidence a strike of 'busmen some time during the evening. Certainly Jeremy had had to walk all the way home from Chelsea, a thing he much disliked, but then perhaps by that time the 'buses had stopped running in the ordinary course... They *did* stop running, those Chelsea 'buses—a horrid place—at an ungodly early hour, he was not quite sure what. But then he was not quite sure at what time he had started home… he was not really sure of anything that had happened towards the end of the party. He remembered long, devastating arguments in the earlier part about Anarchism, Socialism, Syndicalism, Bolshevism, and some other doctrines, the names of which were formed on the same analogy, but which were too novel to him to be readily apprehended.

These discussions were mingled with more practical but equally windy disputes on the questions whether the railwaymen would come out, whether the miners were bluffing, what Bob Hart was going to do, and much more besides on the same level of interest. There had been also a youth with great superiority of manner, who seemed as tedious and irritating to the politicians as they were to Jeremy—a sort of super-bore who stated at intervals that the General Strike was a myth, but praised all and sundry for talking about it and threatening it. It had been—hadn't it?—a studio party. At least, Jeremy had gone to it on that understanding; but the political push had rushed it somehow, and had bored everybody else to tears. Jeremy, who did not very much relish political argument, had applied himself to a kind of pleasure he could better understand. He now remembered little enough of those long, muddling disputations, punctuated by visits to the sideboard, but he knew that his head ached terribly. Aspirin tablets washed down with whisky would probably not be much good, but they would be better than nothing. He took some.

In the midst of these difficulties and discomforts he began obscurely to miss something; and at last it flashed on him that he had no morning paper—because there had been no Mrs. Watkins to bring it in with her and put it on his table. He realized at the same time that the morning paper would tell him whether he had to walk to Whitechapel High Street, and that it was worth a journey to the street door from his flat at the top of the building to know the worst. But when he had made the journey there was no paper. While he was reflecting on this disagreeable fact an envelope in the letter box caught his eye. It was addressed to him in a somewhat illiterate script, and appeared to have been delivered by hand, since it bore no stamp. When he opened it he found the following communication:

"DERE SIR,—Ime sorry to tell you I shal not be able to come in to-morro as we working womin have gone on stricke in simpathy with husbands and other working men the buses are al out and the railways and so are we dere Mr. Tuft I dont know Ime sure how you will get on without me but do youre best and dont forget today is the day for your clean underclose they are in the chest of draws there is a tin of sardins in the larder so no more at present from your truely.

"MRS. WATKINS."

"Well, I'm damned..." said Mr. Tuft, staring at this touching epistle; and for a moment he was filled with annoyance by the recollection that he had not put on his clean clothes. Presently, however, he trailed upstairs again; and when he had found the sardines in the larder the effort thus endured strengthened him for the task of making tea. Eventually he got ready a quite satisfactory breakfast, in the course of which his mind cleared to an exhausted and painful lucidity.

"That's what it is!" he cried at last, thumping the table; and in his excitement, he let the last half sardine slide off his fork and on to the floor. He groped after it, wincing and starting up when his head throbbed too badly, retrieved the rather dusty fish, wiped it carefully with his napkin, and slowly ate it. The strange silence and the odd feeling that this was Sunday morning were at last explained. The printing works across the narrow street were empty, and through the grimy windows Jeremy could see the great machines standing idle. Below there were no carts, where usually they banged and clattered through the whole working day. The printers were out on strike. Very possibly everybody had struck; for surely nothing short of a national upheaval could have deterred the industrious Mrs. Watkins from her work.

He went to his window and threw it wide open to make a nearer inspection. The traffic which usually thronged the noisy little street, the carts and cars which stood outside the newspaper offices and printing works, were absent. A few of the tenement-dwellers lounged at their doors in such groups as were commonly seen only at night or on Saturday afternoons or Sundays. Jeremy felt a faint thrill go through him. This looked like being exciting. He had seen upheavals before, but never, even in the worst of them, had he seen this busy district in a state of idleness so Sabbatical. There had been 'bus strikes and tube strikes in 1918 and 1919, and since. The railwaymen and the miners had come out together for two days late in 1920, and had made a paralyzing impression. But throughout these affairs somehow printing had gone on, and newspapers had continued to be published, getting at each crisis, according to the temperaments of their proprietors, politer or more abusive towards the strikers. At the end of the previous year, 1923, when a very serious situation had arisen, and a collapse had been narrowly averted, there had been a distinct and arresting note of helpless panic in both politeness and abuse. During the last few days, while the present trouble was brewing, neither had much appeared in the papers, but only an exhibition of dithering fright.

But Jeremy had grown on the whole accustomed to it. He had ceased to believe in the coming of what some of the horrible people he had met at that studio referred to caressingly as the "Big Show." The Government would always arrange things somehow. The wages of lecturers and investigators in physics (of whom he was one) never went up, because they never went on strike, and because it was unlikely that any one would care if they did. He had not been able to believe that a time would ever come when there would be no Government, no Paymaster-General, no Ministry of Pensions, to pay him his partial disability pension. But this morning unexpected events seemed much more probable. There was not much of the world to be perceived from his window looking down the street, but what there was smelt somehow remarkably like real trouble.

2

Jeremy Tuft was not unused to "trouble" of one sort and another. When the Great War began in 1914 he was a lecturer on physical science in one of the modern universities of Northern England. He had published a series of papers on the Viscosity of Liquids, which had gained him a European reputation—that is to say, it had been quoted with approval by two

Germans and a Pole, while the conclusions had been appropriated without acknowledgment by a Norwegian—and he received a stipend of £300 per annum, to which he added a little by private coaching in his spare time. With what was left of his spare time he tried to make the liquids move faster or slower or in some other direction—in view of his ultimate destiny it matters very little which—and at all events to gather such evidence as would blow the Norwegian, for whom he had conceived an unreasonable hatred, quite out of the water.

War called him from these pursuits. He did not stand upon his scientific status or attainments; but concluding that the country wanted MEN to set an example, he hastened to set an example by applying for a commission in the artillery, which, after some difficulty, he obtained. When the first excitement and muddle had been cleared away, so he supposed, no doubt the specialists would be sorted out and set to do the jobs for which they were best fitted. He was a naturally modest man; but he could think of two or three jobs for which he was very well fitted indeed.

He passed through Woolwich in a breathless rush, and learnt to ride even more breathlessly. As the day for departure overseas drew near he congratulated himself a little that the inevitable sorting-out seemed to be postponed. He would get a few weeks more of this invaluable experience in a sphere which was completely unfamiliar to him; he would perhaps even see some of the fighting which he had never really expected. When, five days after his arrival in the Salient with the battery of sixty-pounders to which he was attached, one of the guns blew up with a premature explosion and drenched him in blood not his own, he felt that his experience was reasonably complete, and began to look forward to the still deferred sorting-out. Unfortunately, it continued to be deferred; but after a little while Jeremy settled down with the battery, and rose in it to the rank of captain.

His companions described him as the most consistent and richly eloquent grumbler on the British front; and he filled in his spare time by poking round little shops in Béthune and such towns, and picking up old, unconsidered engravings and some rather good lace. In the early part of 1918, his horse, in a set-to with a traction-engine, performed the operation of sorting-out which the authorities had so long neglected; and Jeremy, when his dislocated knee was somewhat recovered, parted forever from the intelligent animal, and went to use his special attainments as a bottle-washer in the office of Divisional Headquarters. The armistice came; and he was released from the army after difficulties much exceeding those which he had encountered in entering it.

In April, 1922, he was again a lecturer in physics, this time at a newly-instituted college in London, receiving a stipend of £350 per annum, to which he was luckily able to add a partial disability pension of £20. In his spare moments he pursued the Viscosity of Liquids with a movement less lively than their own; but he had forgotten the Norwegian's name. He lived alone, not too uncomfortably, in his little flat in Holborn, a short distance from the building where it was his duty to explain to young men who sometimes, and young women who rarely, understood him, the difference between mass and weight, and other such interesting points. He was tended daily by the careful Mrs. Watkins, and he had a number of friends, mostly artists, whose tendency to live in Chelsea or in Camden Town he heartily deplored.

On this morning of April, 1924, the first day of the Great Strike or the Big Show, Jeremy set out at a few moments after eleven to keep his appointment with a friend who lived in a place no less inconvenient than the Whitechapel High Street. The streets were, as they had seemed from his windows, even emptier and quieter than on a Sunday, and most of the shops were closed. But there was, on the whole, a feeling of electricity in the air that Jeremy had never associated with that day. It was when he came into Fetter Lane and saw a patrol of troops lying on the grass outside the Record Office that he first found something concrete to justify this feeling.

"There *is* going to be trouble, then," he muttered to himself, admitting it with reluctance, as he walked on steadily into Fleet Street; and there his apprehensions were again confirmed. A string of lorries came rapidly down the empty roadway, past him from the West, and they were crowded with troops. Guards, he thought—carrying machine-guns in the first lorry.

Jeremy paused for a moment, staring after them, and then as he turned to go on he saw a small special constable standing as inconspicuously as possible in the door of a shop, swinging nervously the truncheon at his wrist. His uniform looked a little dusty and unkept, and there was an obvious moth-hole on one side of the cap. His whole appearance was that of a man desperately imploring Providence not to let anything happen.

"That man's face is simply asking for a riot," Jeremy grunted to himself; and he said aloud, "Perhaps you can tell me what it's all about?"

"The railwaymen came out yesterday, and the busmen last night. All the miners are out now. And the printers, too. They say the electrical men are out, too, but I don't know about that."

"Looks like almighty smash, don't it?" Jeremy commented. "Where are all those troops going?"

"I don't know," said the special constable. "Nobody really knows anything for certain."

"Cheerful business," Jeremy grumbled, mostly to himself. "And how the devil am I going to get to Whitechapel High Street, I wonder?"

"To Whitechapel High Street?" the special constable cried. "Down in the East End? Oh, *don't* go down there! It'll be *frightfully* dangerous there!"

"That be damned," said Jeremy. "I can't say you look as though you were feeling particularly safe yourself, do you?" And with a wave of his hand he passed down Fleet Street in an easterly direction.

It was only a few hundred yards farther on that he received his first personal shock of the day. As he came to Ludgate Circus he heard an empty lorry, driven at a furious rate, bumping and clanging down the street behind him. At the same time a large gray staff car, packed with red-tabbed officers, shot into the Circus out of Farrington Street, making for Blackfriars Bridge. His heart was for a moment in his mouth, but the driver of the lorry pulled up abruptly and let the car go by, stopping his own engine as he did so. Jeremy saw him descend, swearing softly, to crank up again; and the sight of the empty vehicle revived in him glad memories of the French and Flemish roads. He therefore stepped into the street, and said with a confidence that returned to him naturally from earlier years:

"Look here, my lad, if you're going east, you might give me a bit of a lift."

The soldier had got his engine going again, and rose from the starting handle with a flushed and frowning face.

"'Oo are you talkin' to?" he asked sullenly. "'Oo the 'ell do you think this lorry belongs to, eh? Think it belongs to *you*?" And as Jeremy was too taken aback to answer, he continued: "This lorry belongs to the Workmen's and Soldiers' Council of Southwark, that's 'oo it belongs to." He climbed slowly back into his seat, and, as he slipped the clutch in, leant outwards to Jeremy and exclaimed in a particularly emphatic and vicious tone, "Dirty boorjwar!" The machine leapt forward, swept round the Circus, and disappeared over the bridge.

Jeremy, a little perturbed by this incident, pursued his journey, unconsciously grasping his heavy cane somewhat tighter, and glancing almost nervously down every side street or alley he passed, hardly knowing for what he looked. His notion of the way by foot to Whitechapel High Street was not very clear, but he knew more or less the way to Liverpool Street, and he supposed that by going thither he would be following the proper line. He therefore trudged up Ludgate Hill and along Cheapside, cursing the Revolution and all extremists from the bottom of his heart. The lorry driver's parting shot still rankled in his mind. He felt that it was extremely unjust to accuse him of being a member of the bourgeoisie, and he was quite ready to exchange all his vested interests in anything whatever against a seat in a 'bus.

Close to Liverpool Street Station he came out of deserted and silent streets, whose silence and emptiness had begun to have an effect on his nerves, into a scene of activity and animation. A string of five lorries, driven by soldiers, but loaded with something hidden under tarpaulins instead of troops, was drawn up by the curb, while a large and growing crowd blocked its further progress. The crowd was held together apparently by an orator mounted on a broken chair, who was lashing himself into a fury which he found difficult to communicate to his audience. Jeremy pushed forward as unobtrusively as he could, but eventually found himself stayed, close to the foremost lorry, on the skirts of the crowd. The orator, not far off, was working himself into ever wilder and wilder passions.

"The hour has come," he was saying. "All over the country our brothers have risen—"

"And I and *my* brothers," Jeremy murmured to himself, "are going to get the dirty end of the stick."

But as he looked about him and examined the crowd in which he was involved, he found some difficulty in connecting it with the fiery phrases of the speaker or with the impending Revolution which, until this moment, he had really been beginning to dread. Now a sudden wave of relief passed over his mind. These honest, blunt, good-natured people had expressed the subtle influence of the day, which he himself had felt, by putting on their Sunday clothes. They were not meditating bloodshed or the overthrow of the State. But for a certain seriousness and determination in their faces and voices one might have thought that they were making holiday in an unpremeditated and rather eccentric manner. Their seriousness was not that of men forming desperate resolves. It was that of men who, having entered into an argument, intend to argue it out. They believed in argument, in the power of reason, and the voting force of majorities. They applauded the speaker, but not when he became blood-thirsty; and time and time again he lost touch with them in his violence. At the most frenzied point of the oration a thick-set man, with a startling orange handkerchief round his neck, turned to Jeremy and said disgustedly:

"Listen to 'im jowin'! Sheeny, that's what he is, no more than a —— Sheeny." Jeremy was neither a politician nor a sociologist. He did not weigh a previous diagnosis against this fresh evidence and come to a more cheerful conclusion; but he breathed rather more freely and relaxed his grip on his cane. He was not disturbed by the confused and various clamor which came from the crowd and in which there was a good admixture of laughter.

Just at this moment he saw on the lorry by which he had halted a face that was familiar to him. He looked again more closely, and recognized Scott—Scott who had been in the Divisional Office, Scott who had panicked so wildly in the 1918 retreat, though God knew he had taken a long enough start, Scott who had nearly landed him in a row over that girl in the estaminet at Bailleul, just after the armistice. And Scott, who never knew that he was disliked—a characteristic of his kind!—was eagerly beckoning to him.

He slid quietly through the fringe of the crowd and stood by the driving-seat of the lorry. Scott leant down and shook him by the hand warmly, speaking in a whisper:

"Tuft, old man," he said effusively, "I often wondered what had become of you. What a piece of luck meeting you here!"

"I could think of better places to meet in," Jeremy answered drily. He was determined not to encourage Scott; he knew very well that something damned awkward would most likely come of it. "This looks to me like a hold-up. What have you got in the lorries?"

"Sh!" Scott murmured with a scared look. "It's bombs for the troops at Liverpool Street, but it'd be all up with us if the crowd knew that. No—why I said it was lucky was because I thought you might help me to get through."

"I? How could I?" Jeremy asked defensively.

"Well, I don't know…. I thought you might have some influence with them, persuade them that there's nothing particular in the lorries, or…"

Jeremy favored him with a stare of bewildered dislike. "Why on earth should I have any influence with them?" he enquired.

"Don't be sick with me, old man… I only thought you used to have some damned queer opinions, you know; used to be a sort of Bolshevist yourself… I thought you might know how to speak to them." Scott, of course, always *had* thought that any man whose opinions he could not understand was a sort of Bolshevist. Jeremy shirked the task of explanation and contented himself with calling his old comrade-in-arms an ass.

"And, anyway," he went on, "I'll tell you one thing. There isn't likely to be any revolution hereabouts, unless you make it yourself. What are you stopping for? Did they make you stop?"

"Not exactly… don't you see, the General said…."

Jeremy heaved a groan. He had heard that phrase on Scott's lips before, and it was generally a sign that the nadir of his incapacity had been reached. Heaven help the Social Order if it depended on Scott's fidelity to what the General had said! But the voice above him maundered on, betraying helplessness in every syllable. The General had said that the bombs were at all costs to reach the troops at Liverpool Street. He had also said that on no account must the nature of the convoy be betrayed; and on no account must Scott risk any encounter with a mob. And the mob had not really stopped the convoy. They had just shown no alacrity in making room for it, and Scott had thought that by pushing on he would perhaps be risking an encounter. Now, however, he thought that by remaining where he was might be exciting curiosity.

Jeremy looked at him coolly, and spoke in a tone of restrained sorrow. "Scott," he said, "it takes more than jabberers like this chap here to make a revolution. They want a few damned fools like you to help them. I'm going on before the trouble begins." And he drew back from the lorry and began to look about for a place where the crowd might be a little sparser. The orator on the broken chair had now been replaced by another, an Englishman, of the serious type, one of those working-men whose passion it is to instruct their fellows and who preach political reform with the earnestness and sobriety of the early evangelical missionaries. He was speaking in a quiet, intense tone, without rant or excitement, and the crowd was listening to him in something of his own spirit. Occasionally, when he paused on a telling sentence, there were low rumbling murmurs of assent or of sympathetic comment.

"No, but look here—" came from the lorry after Jeremy in an agonized whisper. But he saw his opportunity, and did not look back until he was on the other side of the crowd round the speaker. He went on rapidly eastwards past the station, his mood of relief already replaced by an ominous mood of doubt. Once or twice, until the turn of the street hid them, he glanced apprehensively over his shoulders at the crowd and the string of motionless lorries.

CHAPTER 2
The Dead Rat

1

As he came closer to Whitechapel High Street, Jeremy found with surprise and some addition to his uneasiness, that this district had a more wakeful and week-day appearance. Many of the shops and eating-houses were open; and the Government order, issued two days before, forbidding the sale of liquor while the strike menace endured, was being frankly disregarded. This was the first use that had been made of the Public Order (Preservation of) Act, passed hurriedly and almost in secret two or three months before; and Jeremy, enquiring what his own feelings would have been if he had been in a like position to the restless workmen, had been stirred out of his ordinary political indifference to call it unwise. He might have been stirred to even greater feeling about the original Act if he had known that it was principally this against which the strikes were directed. But he had omitted to ask why the unions were striking, and no one had told him. The middle classes of those days had got used to unintelligible and apparently senseless upheavals. Now, as he passed by one public-house after another, all open, and saw the crowds inside and round the doors, conversing with interest and perceptibly rising excitement on only one topic, he rather wished that the order could have been enforced. There was something sinister in the silence which fell where he passed. He felt uncomfortably that he was being looked at with suspicion.

He turned out of the wide road, now empty of all wheeled traffic, except for a derelict tramcar which stood desolate, apparently where driver and conductor had struck work earlier or later than their fellows. In the side street which led to his destination, there were mostly women—dark, ugly, alien women—sitting on their doorsteps; and he began to feel even more afraid of them than of the men. They did not lower their voices as he passed, but he could not understand I what they were saying. But as he swung with a distinct sense of relief into the little narrow court where Trehanoc absurdly lived and had his laboratory, he heard one of them call after him, "Dir-r-rty bour-rgeois!" and all the rest laugh ominously together. The repetition of the phrase in this new accent startled him and he fretted at the door because Trehanoc did not immediately answer his knock.

"Damn you for living down here!" he said heartily, when Trehanoc at last opened to him. "I don't like your neighbors at all."

"I know… I know…," Trehanoc answered apologetically. "But how could I expect— And anyway they're nice people really when you get to know them. I get on very well with them." He paused and looked with some apprehension at Jeremy's annoyed countenance.

He was a Cornishman, a tall, loose, queerly excitable and eccentric fellow, with whom, years before, Jeremy had worked in the laboratories at University College. He had taken his degree—just taken it—and this result, while not abating his strange passion for research in physics, seemed to have destroyed forever all hope of his indulging it. After that no one knew what he had done, until a distant relative had died and left him a few hundreds a year and the empty warehouse in Lime Court. He had accepted the legacy as a direct intervention of providence, refused the specious offers of a Hebrew dealer in fur coats, and had fitted up the crazy building as a laboratory, with a living-room or two, where he spent vastly exciting hours pursuing with the sketchiest of home-made apparatus the abstrusest of natural mysteries. One or two old acquaintances of the Gower Street days had run across him here and there, and, on confessing that they were still devoted to science, had been urgently invited to pay a visit to Whitechapel. They had returned, half-alarmed, half-amused, and had reported that Trehanoc was madder than ever, and was attempting the transmutation of the elements with a home-made electric coil, an old jam-jar, and a biscuit tin. They also reported that his neighborhood was rich in disagreeable smells and that his laboratory was inhabited by rats.

But Jeremy's taste in acquaintances was broad and comprehensive, always provided that they escaped growing tedious. After his first visit to Lime Court he had not been slow in paying a second. His acquaintance ripened into friendship with Trehanoc, whom he regarded, perhaps only half-consciously, as being an inspired, or at any rate an exceedingly lucky, fool.

When he received an almost illegible and quite incoherent summons to go and see a surprising new experiment, "something," as the fortunate discoverer put it, "very funny," he had at once promised to go. It was characteristic of him that, having promised, he went, although he had to walk through disturbed London, arrived grumbling, and reassured his anxious host without once ceasing to complain of the inconvenience he had suffered.

"I ought to tell you," Trehanoc said, with increased anxiety when Jeremy paused to take breath, "that a man's dropped in to lunch. I didn't ask him, and he isn't a scientist, and he talks rather a lot, but— but— I don't suppose he'll be much in the way," he finished breathlessly.

"All right, Augustus," Jeremy replied in a more resigned tone, and with a soothing wave of his hand, "carry on. I don't suppose one extra useless object in one of your experiments will make any particular difference."

He followed Trehanoc with lumbering speed up the narrow, uncarpeted stairs and into the big loft which served for living-room and kitchen combined. There he saw the useless object stretched on a couch—a pleasant youth of rather disheveled appearance, who raised his head and said lazily:

"Hullo! It's you, is it? We met last night, but I don't suppose you remember that."

"No, I don't," said Jeremy shortly.

"No, I thought you wouldn't. My name's Maclan. You must have known that last night, because you told me twice that no man whose name began with Mac ever knew when he was boring the company."

"Did I?" Jeremy looked a little blank, and then began to brighten. "Of course. You were the man who was talking about the General Strike being a myth. I hope I didn't hurt your feelings too much?"

"Not at all. I knew you meant well; and, after all, you weren't in a condition to realize what I was up to. The secret of it all was that by boring all the rest of the company till they wanted to scream I was very effectually preventing them from boring me. You see, I saw at once that the politicians had taken the floor for the rest of the evening, and I knew that the only way to deal with them was to irritate them on their own ground. It was rather good sport really, only, of course, you couldn't be expected to see the point of it."

Jeremy began to chuckle with appreciation. "Very good," he agreed. "Very good. I wish I'd known." And Trehanoc, who had been hovering behind him uneasily, holding a frying-pan, said with a deep breath of relief: "That's all right, then."

"What the devil's the matter with you, Augustus?" Jeremy cried, wheeling round on him. "What do you mean, 'That's all right, then'?"

"I was only afraid you two chaps would quarrel," he explained. "You're both of you rather difficult to get on with."

Lunch was what the two guests might have expected, and probably did. The sausages would no doubt have been more successful if Trehanoc had remembered to provide either potatoes or bread; but his half-hearted offer of a little uncooked oatmeal was summarily rejected. Jeremy's appetite, however, was reviving, and Maclan plainly cared very little what he ate. His interest lay rather in talking; and throughout the meal he discoursed to a stolidly masticating Jeremy and a nervous, protesting Trehanoc on the theme that civilization had reached and passed its climax and was hurrying into the abyss. He instanced the case of Russia.

"Russia," he said, leaning over towards the Cornishman and marking his points with flourishes of a fork, "Russia went so far that she couldn't get back. For a long time they shouted for the blockade to be raised so that they could get machinery for their factories and their railways. Now they've been without it so long they don't want it any more. Oh, of course, they still talk about reconstruction and rebuilding the railways and so forth, but it'll never happen. It's too late. They've dropped down a stage; and there they'll stop, unless they go lower still, as they are quite likely to."

Trehanoc looked up with a fanatical gleam in his big brown eyes, which faded as he saw Maclan, poised and alert, waiting for him, and Jeremy quietly eating with the greatest unconcern. "I don't care what you say," he muttered sullenly, dropping his head again. "There's no limit to what science can do. Look what we've done in the last hundred years. We shall discover the origin of matter, and how to transmute the elements; we shall abolish disease… and there's my discovery—"

"But, my dear man," Maclan interrupted, "just because we've done this, that, and the other in the last hundred years, there's no earthly reason for supposing that we shall go on doing it. You don't allow for the delicacy of all these things or for the brutality of the forces that are going to break them up. Why, if you got the world really in a turmoil for thirty years, at the end of that time you wouldn't be able to find a man who could mend your electric light, and you'd have forgotten how to do it yourself. And you don't allow for the fact that we ourselves change… What do you say, Tuft? You're a scientist, too."

"The present state of our knowledge," Jeremy replied cheerfully with his mouth full, "doesn't justify prophecies."

"Ah! our knowledge… no, perhaps not. But our intuitions!" And here, as he spoke, Maclan seemed to grow for a moment a little more serious. "Don't you know there's a moment in anything—a holiday, or a party, or a love-affair, or whatever you like—when you feel that you've reached the climax, and that there's nothing more to come. I feel that now. Oh! it's been a good time, and we seemed to be getting freer and freer and richer and richer. But now we've got as far as we can and everything changes… Change here for the Dark Ages!" he added with a sudden alteration in his manner. "In fact, if I may put it so, this is where we get out and walk."

Jeremy looked at him, wondering vaguely how much of this was genuine and how much mere discourse. He thought that, whichever it was, on the whole he disliked it. "Oh! we shall go jogging on just as usual," he said at last, as matter-of-fact as he could.

"Oh, no, we sha'n't!" Maclan returned with equal coolness. "We shall go to eternal smash."

Trehanoc looked up again from the food he had been wolfing down with absent-minded ferocity. "It doesn't matter what either of you thinks," he affirmed earnestly. "There's no limit to what we are going to do. We—" A dull explosion filled their ears and shook the windows.

"And what in hell's that?" cried Jeremy.

2

For a moment all three of them sat rigid, staring instinctively out of the windows, whence nothing could be seen save the waving branches of the tree that gave its name to Lime Court. Maclan at last broke the silence.

"The Golden Age," he said solemnly, "has tripped over the mat. Hadn't we better go and see what's happened to it?"

"Don't be a fool!" Jeremy ejaculated. "If there really is trouble these streets won't be too pleasant, and we'd better not draw attention to ourselves." Immediately in the rear of his words came the confused noise of many people running and shouting. It was the mixed population of Whitechapel going to see what was up; and before many of them could have done so, the real fighting must have begun. The sound of firing, scattered and spasmodic, punctuated by the dull, vibrating bursts which Jeremy recognized for bombs, came abruptly to the listeners in the warehouse. There was an opening and shutting of windows and a banging of doors, men shouting and women crying, as though suddenly the whole district had been set in motion. All this gradually died away again and left to come sharper and clearer the incessant noise of the rifles and the bombs.

"Scott has set them going," Jeremy murmured to, himself, almost content in the fulfilment of a prophecy, and then he said aloud: "Have you got any cigarettes, Augustus? I can't say we're well off where we are, but we've got to stop for a bit."

Trehanoc produced a tin of Virginians which he offered to his guests. "I'm afraid," he said miserably, "that this isn't a very good time for asking you to have a look at my experiment." Jeremy surveyed him with a curious eye, and reflected that the contrast in the effect of the distant firing on the three of them was worth observation. He himself did not pretend to like it, but knew that nothing could be done, and so endured it stoically. Maclan had settled in an armchair with a cigarette and a very tattered copy of *La Vie Parisienne*, and was giving an exhibition of almost flippant unconcern; but every time there was a louder burst of fire his shoulders twitched slightly. Trehanoc's behavior was the most interesting of all. He had been nervous and excited while they were at table, and the explosion had obviously accentuated his condition. But he had somehow turned his excitement into the channel of his discovery, and his look of hungry and strained disappointment was pathetic to witness. It touched Jeremy's heart, and moved him to say as heartily as he could:

"Nonsense, old fellow. We'll come along and see it in a moment. What's it all about?"

Trehanoc murmured "Thanks awfully… I was afraid you wouldn't want…"—like a child who has feared that the party would not take place after all. Then he sat down sprawlingly in a chair and fixed his wild, shining eyes on Jeremy's face. "You see," he began, "I think it's a new ray. I'm almost certain it's a new ray. But I'm not quite certain how I got it. I'll show you all that later. But it's something like the ray that man used to change bacilli. He changed bacilli into cocci, or something. I'm no biologist; I was going to get in a biologist when you'd helped me a bit. You remember the experiment I mean, don't you?"

"Vaguely," said Jeremy. "It's a bit out of my line, but my recollection is that he used alpha rays. However, go on."

"Well, that's what I was after," Trehanoc continued. "I believe these rays do something of the same kind, and they've got other properties I don't understand. There's the rat… but I'll show you the rat later on. And then I got my hand in front of the vacuum-tube for half a second without any protection…"

"Did you get a burn?" Jeremy asked sharply.

"No," said Trehanoc. "No… I didn't… that's the strange thing. I'd got a little radium burn on that hand already, and a festering cut as well, where I jabbed myself with the tin-opener… Well, first of all, my hand went queer. It was a sort of dead, numb feeling, spreading into the arm above the wrist, and I was scared, I can tell you. I was almost certain that these were new rays, and I hadn't the least notion what effect they might have on living tissue. The numbness kept on all day, with a sort of tingling in the finger-tips, and I went to bed in a bit of a panic. And when I woke, the radium burn had quite gone, leaving a little scar behind, and the cut had begun to heal. It *was* very nearly healed!"

"Quite sure it's a new ray?" Jeremy interjected.

"Oh, very nearly sure. You see, I—" and he entered into a long and highly technical argument which left Jeremy both satisfied and curious. At the close of it Maclan remarked in a tone of deep melancholy:

"Tre, my old friend, if the experiment isn't more exciting than the lecture, I shall go out and take my turn on the barricades. I got lost at the point where you began talking about electrons. Do, for heaven's sake, let's go and *see* your hell-broth!"

"Would you like to go and see it now?" Trehanoc asked, watching Jeremy's face with solicitous anxiety; and receiving assent he led the way at once, saying, "You know, I use the cellar for this radio-active work. The darkness… And by the way," he interrupted himself, "look out how you go. This house is in a rotten state of repair." The swaying of the stairs down from the loft, when all three were upon them, confirmed him alarmingly.

As they went past the front-door towards the cellar-steps, Jeremy, cocking his head sideways, thought that every now and then some of the shots rang out much louder, as though the skirmishing was getting close to Lime Court. But he was by now deeply interested in Trehanoc's experiment, and followed without speaking.

When they came down into the cellar Trehanoc touched a switch and revealed a long room, lit only in the nearer portion, where electric bulbs hung over two great laboratory tables and stretching away into clammy darkness.

"Here it is," he said nervously, indicating the further of the two tables, and hung on Jeremy's first words.

Jeremy's first words were characteristic. "How you ever get any result at all," he said, slowly and incisively, "is more than I can make out. This table looks as though some charwoman had been piling rubbish on it."

"Yes, I know… I know. . ." Trehanoc admitted in a voice of shame. "That's where I wanted you to help me. You see, I can't be quite sure exactly what it is that *does* determine the result. There's the vacuum-tube, worked by a coil, and there's an electric magnet… and that tube on the other side has got radium-emanation in it…"

"And then there's the dead rat," Jeremy interrupted rather brutally.

"What about the dead rat? Does that affect the result?" He pointed with a forefinger, expressing some disgust, to a remarkably sleek and well-favored corpse which decorated the end of the table.

"I was going to tell you…" Trehanoc muttered, twisting one hand in the other. "You know, there *are* rather a lot of rats in this cellar—"

"I know," said Jeremy.

"And when I was making the first experiment that chap jumped on to the table and ran across in front of the vacuum-tube—"

"Well?"

"And he just dropped like that, dropped dead in his tracks… and… and I was frightfully excited, so I only picked him up by his tail and threw him away and forgot all about him. And then quite a long time afterwards, when I was looking for something, I came across him, just like that, just as fresh—"

"And when was that?" Jeremy asked.

"It must be quite six weeks since I made that first experiment."

"So he's one of the exhibits," Jeremy began slowly. But a new outbreak of firing, unmistakably closer at hand, broke across his sentence. Maclan, who was beginning to find the rat a little tedious, and had been hoping that Trehanoc would soon turn a handle and produce long, crackling sparks, snatched at the interruption.

"I *must* go up and see what's happening!" he cried. "I'll be back in a minute."

He vanished up the steps. When he returned, Jeremy was still turning over the body of the rat with a thoughtful expression and placing it delicately to his nose for olfactory evidence. Trehanoc, who seemed to have begun to think that there was something shameful, if not highly suspicious, in the existence of the corpse, stood before him in an almost suppliant attitude, twisting his long fingers together, and shuffling his feet.

Maclan disregarded the high scientific deliberations. "I say," he cried with the almost hysterical flippancy that sometimes denotes serious nerve-strain, "it's frightfully exciting. The fighting is getting nearer, and somebody's got a machine-gun trained down Whitechapel High Street.

There's nobody in sight here, but I'm certain there are people firing from the houses round about."

"Oh, damn!" said Jeremy uneasily but absently, continuing to examine the rat.

"And, I say, Tre," Maclan went on, "do you think this barn of yours would stand a bomb or two? It looks to me as if it would fall over if you pushed it."

"I'm afraid it would," Trehanoc admitted, looking as if he ought to apologize. "In fact, I'm always afraid that they'll condemn it, but I can't afford repairs."

"Oh, hang all that!" Jeremy suddenly interjected. "This is extraordinarily interesting. Get the thing going, Trehanoc, and let's have a look at your rays."

"That's right, Tre," said Maclan. "We're caught, so let's make the best of it. Let's try and occupy our minds as the civilians used to in the old air-raid days. Stick to the dead rat, Tre, and let politics alone." He laughed—a laugh in which hysteria was now plainly perceptible—but Trehanoc, disregarding him, went into a corner and began fumbling with the switches. In a moment the vacuum-tube began to glow faintly, and Jeremy and Trehanoc bent over it together.

Suddenly a loud knocking at the front door echoed down the cellar steps. Trehanoc twitched his shoulders irritatingly, but otherwise did not move. A moment after it was repeated, and in addition there was a more menacing sound as though some one were trying to break the door in with a heavy instrument.

"You'd better go and see what it is, Augustus," Jeremy murmured absorbedly. "It may be some one wanting to take shelter from the firing. Go on, and I'll watch this thing."

Trehanoc obediently but reluctantly went up the cellar steps, and Jeremy, with some idle, half-apprehending portion of his mind, heard him throw open the front door and heard the sound of angry voices coming through. But he remained absorbed in the vacuum-tube, until Maclan, who was standing at the foot of the steps, said in a piercing whisper:

"Here, Tuft, come here and listen!"

"Yes? What is it?" Jeremy replied vaguely, without changing his position.

"Come here quickly," Maclan whispered in an urgent tone. Jeremy was aroused and went to the foot of the steps to listen. For a moment he could only hear voices speaking angrily, and then he distinguished Trehanoc's voice shouting:

"You fools! I tell you there's no one in the upper rooms. How could any one be firing from the windows?" There was a shot and a gurgling scream. Jeremy and Maclan turned to look at one another, and each saw the other's face ghastly, distorted by shadows which the electric light in the cellar could not quite dispel.

"Good God!" screamed Maclan. "They've killed him!" He started wildly up the stairs. Jeremy, as he began to follow him, heard another shot, saw Maclan poised for a moment, arms up, on the edge of a step, and just had time to flatten himself against the wall before the body fell backwards. He ran down again into the cellar, and began looking about desperately for a weapon of some kind.

As he was doing so there was a cautious footstep on the stair. "Bombs!" he thought, and instinctively threw himself on the floor. The next moment the bomb landed, thrown well out in the middle of the cellar, and it seemed that a flying piece spun viciously through his hair. And then he saw the table which held the glowing vacuum-tube slowly tilting towards him and all the apparatus sliding to the floor, and at the same moment he became aware that the cellar-roof was descending on his head. He had time and wit enough to crawl under the other table before it fell. Darkness came with it.

Jeremy struggled for a moment against unconsciousness. Then something seemed to be going round and round, madly and erratically at first, finally settling into a regular motion of enormous speed. He was vaguely aware of the glowing vacuum-tube, and the dead rat, partly illuminated by it, close to his face; but he felt himself being borne away, he knew not whither. A sort of peace in that haste overtook his limbs and he slept.

CHAPTER 3

A World Grown Strange

1

WHEN JEREMY AWOKE at last it was to find only the change from darkness of the mind to darkness of the eyes. No dreams had stirred his sleep with memories or premonitions. At one moment that great engine had still been implacably and regularly revolving. At the next it slackened and stopped; and, without any transition, he found himself prone, staring into the blackness as he had hopelessly stared when he saw the cellar-roof coming down upon him. He felt no pain, nor was there any singing or dizziness in his head. There was only a sort of blankness, in which he had hardly begun to wonder where he was. He assumed for a moment that he was in his own bed and in his own flat. But two things persuaded him that he was not. He had been awakened by something soft and damp falling on his eyes, and when he tried to brush it away he found that he could not use his arms. Then he remembered.

But the memory brought for the moment a panic that made him dizzy. The bomb had been thrown, the roof had fallen, and, from then till now, there had been only darkness. What more certain than that in that catastrophe, which he now so clearly recalled, his back had been broken, so that he lay there with no more than an hour or two to live? The absence of pain made it only the more terrible, for had he been in agony he might have welcomed death, which now would approach, unmasked, in the most hateful aspect. He made a convulsive movement with his body, which showed him that he was held all along his length, and confirmed his fears. But, in the calmness of despair which followed, he became conscious that the air he was breathing was exceedingly close. Then he realized with a relief that again made him giddy that his back was not broken, but that he was unable to move because he was in some way pinned under the ruins of Trehanoc's crazy warehouse. He made a renewed effort to stir his body; and this time he was rewarded by an inch of difficult motion in each limb.

Fortified by this assurance, he lay still for a few seconds, and tried to make out his position. He was held tight at every point, but he was not crushed. Neither was he suffocated, nor, as it seemed, in any immediate danger of it. In these circumstances, to be buried alive was a comparatively small evil; it would be odd if he could not somehow dig himself out. The problem was merely how to do so with the least danger of dislodging the still unstable débris above him and so putting himself in a worse position than before. Apparently the ruins had formed a very constricted vault fitting closely to his body and raised a little over his face, where they seemed to admit the passage of air. It was obvious that his first step was to clear his face so that he might see what he was doing. But to do this he needed a free arm, and he could not move either of his arms more than an inch or two. Nevertheless he set to work to move his right arm to and fro in the cramped space that was possible.

The result delighted him. The roof of his grave was some hard substance, probably wood, so a splinter informed him; and he remembered the table under which he had crawled just in time. It must have buckled, so as to make a shield for him; and now, though he could not pick it away, it yielded—an infinitesimal distance at a time, but still it yielded. Presently, he was able to crook his elbow, and soon after that to draw his hand up to his face. Then he began to remove the roof which hung an inch or two from his eyes. The process was unpleasant, for as he plucked at the roof it crumbled between his fingers, and he was not able to protect his face from the dust that fell on it. In the darkness he could not trust his sense of touch, but otherwise he would have sworn that, with pieces of wood, which he expected, he was tearing up and pushing away damp clods of grass-grown earth. He had to keep his eyes closed while he worked. After a little while, when he judged that he had made an opening, he laboriously brushed his face clear of dust, opened his eyes, and looked anxiously up. There was darkness above him still, and a cool breath passed over his forehead. It was night. A single star hung motionless in the field of his vision.

A little exhausted by his efforts, Jeremy let his head sink down again, and reflected. Clearly the whole warehouse had come down with a surprising completeness, since he was able to look straight up into the sky. And there was another thing that engaged his attention, though he had not noticed it until now. His ears were quite free and his head lay at last in the open, but still he could hear nothing. Considering the circumstances in which he had been buried, he would certainly have expected to hear something going on. If there were not shots, there should at least have been shouting, movement, noise of some kind—any noise, he thought suddenly, rather than this uncanny, unbroken silence. But there was only a gentle, hardly perceptible rustling, like leaves in the wind… the old lime tree in the court he decided at last, which had escaped when the warehouse had fallen. He grew almost sentimental in thinking about it. He had looked at it with pleasure on that fatal day, leaning from the window, with MacIan and Trehanoc behind him; and now MacIan and Trehanoc were done for; he and the lime tree remained….

The fighting, he supposed eventually, when his thoughts returned to the strange silence, must have been brought to an end in some very decided and effective manner. Perhaps the troops had got the upper hand over the rioters, and had used it so as to suppress even a whisper of resistance. "Peace reigns in Warsaw," he quoted grimly to himself. But this explanation hardly satisfied him, and in a spasm of curiosity he renewed the effort to free himself from his grave.

When he did so, he made the discovery that the roof of his vault was now so far lifted that he might have drawn himself out, but for something that was gripping at his left ankle. He could kick his leg an inch or so further down, but he could not by any exertion pull it further out. Here a new panic overcame him. What might not happen to him, thus pinned and helpless, on such a night as this? The fighting seemed to have gone over, but it might return. The men who had killed Trehanoc and MacIan and had thrown a bomb at him might come this way again. Something might set fire to the ruins of the warehouse above him. The troops passing by might see him, take him for a rioter, and bomb or bayonet him on general principles of making all sure. As these thoughts passed through his mind he struggled furiously, and did not cease until his whole body was aching, sweat was running down his face, and his ankle was painfully bruised by the vise which held it. Then he lay panting for some minutes, like a wild animal in a trap, and in as desperate a state of mind.

But again the coolness of despair came to save him. He perceived that he had no hope save in lifting the heavy and solid timbers of the table which had closed about him. Only in this way could he see what it was that held his ankle; and, hopeless as it seemed, he must set about it. The effort was easier, and he was able to work more methodically than when he had given himself up for lost. But there was only an inch or two for leverage; and his labors continued, as it seemed to him, during fruitless hours. Certainly the small patch of sky which was visible to him had begun to grow pale, and the one star had wavered and gone out before he felt any result. Then, suddenly, without warning, the table top heaved up a good foot under his pressure and seemed much looser. He breathlessly urged his advantage, while the fabric of his grave shook and creaked reluctantly. He shoved once more with the last of his strength, and the coffin lid lifted bodily, and the invisible fetter on his ankle, with a last tweak, released it. He lay back again, fighting for breath, half in exhaustion, half in hysteria. He was free.

When at last he was a little recovered he drew himself gingerly out, looking anxiously into the vault lest it should close again and pin him. But when he knelt on the edge of the hole from which he had safely emerged, he paused in a frozen rigidity. The dawn was just breaking, and there was a little mist, with strange and unnatural shadows. In Whitechapel, as Jeremy knew it, dawn was usually apt to seem a little tarnished and cheerless. That neighborhood always seemed to him a more agreeable object for study when its inhabitants were hurrying about their business than when they were waking and first opening their doors. But this morning, as he knelt in an involuntary attitude of thanksgiving on the edge of his grave, Jeremy did not see Whitechapel at all, because it was not there. It had vanished overnight.

He was kneeling on short grass, and the crevice in the earth from which he had crept lay towards one end of a shallow depression, enclosed by low grassy banks. A young poplar in the middle of it moved its leaves delicately in the faint wind. All round were meadows of irregular and broken surface, with a few sheep grazing in them, and here and there patches of bramble and wild thorn. Farther off Jeremy could distinguish small groves of trees and the dark outlines of low houses or sheds. Farther off still he saw, black and jagged against the rising sun, something that resembled the tumbled ruins of a great public building. He turned giddy and could not rise from his knees. His muscles refused their service, though it seemed that he strained at them with all his strength, until his stomach revolted and he was seized with a dreadful nausea, which shook him physically and brought a sick taste into his mouth. He found himself looking down at his grave as though he wanted to crawl back into it; and then suddenly an inexplicable horror and despair overcame him, and he flung himself face downwards in the dew-laden grass.

2

What were Jeremy's thoughts while he lay face down in the grass he could not himself have told. They were not articulate, consecutive thoughts. The landscape that he had seen on emerging from his grave had pressed him back into the shapeless abysms that lie behind reason and language. But, when the fit had passed, when he raised his head again, and saw that nothing had changed, that he was indeed in this unfamiliar country, he would have given a world to be able to accept the evidence of his eyes without incurring an immediate self-accusation of folly.

The transition from the image in his mind to the image which his eyes gave him had been so violent and so abrupt that it had wrenched up all his ordinary means of thought, and set his mind wildly adrift. During a moment he would not have been surprised to hear the Last Trump, to see the visible world go up in flame, and the Court of Judgment assembled in the sky. He told himself that the next instant Maclan and Trehanoc might step from behind the nearest clump of thorn and greet him. But the new landscape continued stable and definite, as unlike the scene of an Apocalypse as the creation of a dream. Could this then be an hallucination of unusual completeness? And, if so, had those dreadful hours during which he had struggled in his tomb been also the result of an hallucination? He stooped absent-mindedly to the low grassy bank by which he was standing and plucked a confidently promenading snail from a plantain leaf. The creature hastily drew in its horns and retracted its body within the shell. Was that, too, delusion?

And yet, the day before, he had been in Trehanoc's warehouse in Lime Court in Whitechapel, there had been that sudden violence, and, as he still clearly remembered, he had crawled under the laboratory table before the cellar roof had fallen on him. While he had struggled through the night to free himself, a picture of the place had been perfectly distinct in his mind. On emerging he had turned without reflection to where he knew the door of the cellar stood. The table which had saved him had been at one end of the cellar, parallel to the shorter wall. Jeremy went back to his crevice and stood beside it. It lay in a depression which was roughly four-sided, and it was parallel to the shorter pair of sides. Jeremy bit his lips and looked about him vaguely. Over there should have been the cellar steps, and, going up them, one came to the front door... just over there... and beyond the front door there had been the flags of Lime Court. Jeremy followed this imaginary path with the absorbed care and exactitude which were his means of keeping in touch with reason. Where the flag-stones should have been there was now soft turf, dotted here and there with the droppings of sheep. And suddenly Jeremy saw a patch where something had rubbed away the turf and stone protruded... .

He stood above it, legs wide apart, teeth clenched, and hands gripped. He felt like a man whom a torrent carries down a dark cleft towards something he dares not conjecture. But when this fit, too, had passed away he felt nothing more acutely than the desire to be able to believe. Presently, as he stood and wrestled with himself, his scientific training and cast of mind came to his help. It was legitimate to form a hypothesis, provided that it accounted for all the facts and made no more assumptions than were necessary in order to do so. Illuminated by this thought, he took a few steps back to his crevice, sat down, grasped his jaw firmly between his hands, and began to enquire what hypothesis would be most suitable. That of an hallucination he immediately dismissed. It might be the true explanation; but as a working basis it led nowhere and required no thought. If he was living amid illusory shows the country round him might change at any moment to a desert or an ice-floe… or he might find himself pursued by snakes with three heads.

Well… The alternative theory assumed that the spot on which he now sat was the same which had formerly been occupied by Trehanoc's warehouse. His observations underground prior to his delivery, the shape of the depression, and the flag-stone where Lime Court should have been, all supported this assumption. In that case it followed irrefragably that he could not have been knocked on the head on the previous day. He must have been in that grave, covered by the table, and the rubble, and the turf for a considerable time. It therefore remained only to estimate a period sufficient for the changes he now observed to have taken place.

It was perhaps just as well that Jeremy had steadied his mind by exercising it in a mode of thought to which it was accustomed: for when he reached this point and looked round enquiringly at the material evidence his head began to whirl again. There was, in particular, a young poplar, about ten or twelve feet high, standing in the middle of the hollow…. Jeremy rose, went to it, and slapped the bole reflectively. It was still young enough to reply by a more agitated rustling of its leaves. Here was the problem compactly put. What was the shortest possible time in which the tree could have attained this growth?

If Jeremy knew that he would also indisputably know the shortest possible time he could have been underground. It was true that his estimate might still be too small by many years. He suspected that most of the much taller trees he could see round him at a greater distance must have been sown since the change; but still with the poplar he would have reached a firm minimum basis. Unfortunately, Jeremy did not know the answer to the question. He was not a botanist, but a physicist, and if he had ever known the rate at which a poplar grows, he had forgotten it. It could hardly be less than ten or fifteen years…. But if it was fifteen, what then? And if he could have lain entombed for fifteen years, why not for fifty? why not for five hundred? And the turf? How long would it be before the ruins of a house were covered with thick turf? That could hardly happen in fifteen years, even if the ruins were left quite undisturbed... And why had it been left undisturbed in what used to be a busy quarter of London? (The questions thronged now, innumerable and irrepressible.) What had been going on while he had been underground? Were any living men still left? As he asked the last question it was answered. In the distance a couple of figures walked leisurely across the meadows to one of the sheds which Jeremy had vaguely descried, fumbled with the door and went in. They were far too far off for Jeremy to see what manner of men they were; but were they never so gentle, never so kindly, he feared them. He crouched lower down by the entrance to his crevice, and for the second time that morning had half a mind to get back into it, as though it were a magic car that could transport him whence he had come.

The sun rose higher and began to grow hot, and the dew dried swiftly off the grass and the leaves. Very strangely sleep descended on Jeremy, not violently as before, but soft and unnoticed, as though some superior power, seeing his mind reach the limits of conjecture, had gently thrown it out of action. Before he even knew that he was drowsy he had collapsed on the soft turf, his head on the little mound which hid his table top, and there he slept for two or three hours, careless and defenseless in a novel and possibly hostile world. When he woke he found that in sleep his main perplexity had been resolved. He now believed without difficulty that he had been carried in a trance out of his own time, how far he did not know, and the admission of the fact gave him a curious tranquillity and courage to face whatever the consequences might be. It did not, however, alter the ineluctable truth that he was very hungry, and this truth made it plain to him that he must take up the business of living, and run even the risk of meeting the strange people from whom he instinctively shrank. He therefore stood up with a gesture of resolution, and determined to discover, if he could, the trace of Whitechapel High Street, and to follow it in the direction of what had once been London. He remembered having spent a toilsome morning in the South Downs following the track of an old Roman road, and he judged that this ought not to be much more difficult. He had a strange repugnance to throwing himself on the charity of the inhabitants of the new Whitechapel, and an equally strange desire to reach the ruins of Holborn, which had once been his home.

When he had made this resolution he went again into the ghost of Lime Court, took three steps down it, and turned to the left into what he hoped would be the side street leading to the main road. His shot was a lucky one. Banks of grass here and there, mounds crested with bramble, and at one point a heap of moldering brickwork, pointed out his road, and there was actually a little ribbon of a foot-path running down the middle of it. Jeremy moved on slowly, feeling unpleasantly alone in the wide silent morning, and watching carefully for a sign of the great street along which the trams used to run.

The end of the path which he was following was marked by a grove of young trees, surrounded by bushes; and beyond this, Jeremy conjectured, he would most likely find the traces of what he sought. He approached this point cautiously, and when the path dipped down into the grove he slipped along it as noiselessly as he could. When it emerged again he started back with a suppressed cry. Whitechapel High Street was not hard to find, for it was still in being. Here, cutting the path at right angles, was a road—one of the worst he had ever seen, but a road nevertheless. He walked out into the middle of it, stared right and left, and was satisfied. Its curve was such that with the smallest effort he could restore it in his mind to what it had been. On the side from which he came the banks and irregularities, which were all that was left of the houses, stretched brokenly out of sight. On the other side the rubble seemed for the most part to have been cleared, and some of it had been used to make a low continuous fence, which was now grass-grown, though ends of brick and stone pushed out of the green here and there. Beyond it cows were grazing, and the ground fell gently down to a belt of woods, which shut off the view.

Jeremy turned his attention again to the road itself. To a man who recollected the roads round Ypres and on the Somme, it had no new horrors to offer, but to a man who had put these memories behind him and who had, for all practical purposes, walked only yesterday through the streets of London, it was a surprising sight. Water lay on it in pools, though the soil at its side was comparatively dry. The ruts were six or seven inches deep and made a network over the whole surface, which, between them, was covered with grass and weeds. Immediately in front of Jeremy there was a small pit deeper than the ruts, and filled at the bottom with loose stones. It was below the worst of farm tracks, but it was too wide for that, and besides, Jeremy could not rid his vision of the great ghostly trams that flitted through it.

But, bad as it was, it meant life, and even apparently a degree of civilization. And Jeremy felt again an unconquerable aversion from presenting himself to the strange people who had inherited the earth of his other life. A road, to a man who comes suddenly on it out of open country, is always mutely and strangely a witness of the presence of other men. This unspeakable track, more than the path down which he had just walked, more even than the figures he had seen in the distance, filled him with a dread of the explanations he would have to make to the first chance comer he met. His appearance would no doubt be suspicious to them, and his story would be more suspicious still. Either they would not have the intelligence to understand it or, understanding, would not credit it. Jeremy tried to imagine his own feelings supposing that he had met, say, somewhere on the slopes of Leith Hill, a person in archaic costume who affirmed that he had been buried for a century or so and desired assistance. Jeremy could think of no method by which his tale could be made to sound more probable. He therefore, making excuses to himself, shrank back into the grove, and took shelter behind a bush, in the hope, as he put it, of thinking of some likely mendacity to serve instead of the truth. When he was settled there he broke off a young trailer of the hedge rose, peeled it, and ate it. It was neither satisfying nor nourishing, but it had been one of the inexpensive delights of his childhood, and it was something.

He was just consuming this dainty when a curious rattling and clanking round the curve of the road struck his ear. It rapidly approached, and he started forward to get a view through the leaves of his bush. To his astonishment he saw a young man propelling a bicycle of uncouth appearance, which leapt uncontrollably on the broken road, and threatened to throw its rider at every yard of progress. He peered at it as closely as he could, and had just decided that its odd look came from an unwieldy frame and most unusual tires when, after a last alarming stagger, its front wheel shot into a rut and its rider was deposited within a yard or two of Jeremy's feet.

Jeremy had then an opportunity of inspecting both at his leisure, and hardly knew which ought to engage his attention first. The machine was sufficiently remarkable, and reminded him of nothing so much as of some which he had seen in the occupied territories of Germany at the end of the war. Its frame was exceedingly heavy, as were all the working parts which could be seen; and it was covered, not with enamel, but with a sort of coarse paint. The spokes of the wheels were half the size of a man's little finger, and the rims were of thick wood, with springs in the place of tires. The rider, when he had wearily picked himself up and dusted his garments just under Jeremy's staring eyes, was by no means so unexpected. The dress, from which he was still brushing the dust with, reluctant fingers, consisted of a short brown coat like a blazer, brown breeches, and leather leggings, and on his head he wore a wide-brimmed brown soft hat. His shirt was open at the throat, but below the opening hung a loose and voluminous tie of green linen. His face, on which sat a plainly unwonted expression of annoyance, was mild, candid, and friendly. His voice, when he spoke, was soft and pleasant, and his accent had a strange rich burr in it, which vaguely reminded Jeremy of something he had heard before and could not quite name... something, it seemed, almost grotesque in this connection....

"I never," said the young man, solemnly but without rancor, to the inattentive universe, "I never will mount one of those devices again."

3

Jeremy had ample time to be certain of these details while the young man stood as it were for inspection. When he had dusted himself thoroughly and had looked three or four times round him and up into the sky, apparently to make sure that no celestial chariot was coming to rescue him, he dragged the bicycle from the middle of the road and began to examine it. First of all he tried to wheel it a pace or two, and when it refused to advance he discovered with a gesture of surprise that the chain was off. He slowly lowered the whole machine on to the grass by the roadside and squatted down to adjust the chain. After several fruitless attempts a renewed expression of annoyance crossed his tranquil features, and he sat back on his heels with a sigh.

Jeremy could bear it no longer. Dearer to him even than his European reputation for research into the Viscosity of Liquids was the reputation he had among his friends as a useful man for small mechanical jobs. He would soon have to introduce himself to one or another of what he vaguely supposed to be his descendants. This young man had an unusually calm and friendly appearance, and it was not unlikely that Jeremy might be able to help him in his trouble. He therefore came out of his hiding place, saying brusquely, "Let me see if I can do anything."

The young man did not start up in fear or even speak. He merely looked slightly surprised and yielded the bicycle without protest into Jeremy's hands. Jeremy turned it over and peered into it with the silent absorbed competence of a mechanic. Presently he looked up and made a brief demand for a spanner. The young man, still mutely, replied with a restrained but negative movement of his hands. Jeremy, frowning, ran through his own pockets, and produced a metal fountain pen holder, with which in a moment he levered the incredibly clumsy chain back into place. Then he raised the machine and wheeled it a few yards, showing the chain in perfect action. But the front wheel perceptibly limped. Jeremy dropped on one knee and looked at it with an acute eye.

"No good," he pronounced at last, "it's buckled. You won't be able to ride it, but at least you can wheel it." And he solemnly handed the machine back to its owner.

"Thank you very much," said the young man gently. Jeremy could still hear that odd, pleasant burr in his voice. And then he enquired with a little hesitation, "Are you a blacksmith?"

"Good Heavens, no!" Jeremy cried. "Why—"

The young man appeared to choose his words carefully. "I'm sorry. You see, you know all about the bicycle, and... and... I couldn't quite see what your clothes were....." He slurred over the last remark, perhaps feeling it to be ill-mannered, and went on hastily: "I asked because in the village I've come from, just a couple of miles down the road, the blacksmith is dead and..." He paused and looked at Jeremy expectantly.

Jeremy on his side realized that the moment had come when he must either tell his amazing story or deliberately shirk it. But while he had been bending over the bicycle a likely substitute had occurred to him, a substitute which, however, he would have hesitated to offer to anyone less intelligent and kindly in appearance than his new acquaintance. He hesitated a moment, and decided on shirking, or, as he excused it to himself, on feeling his way slowly.

"I don't know," he said with an accent of dull despair. "I don't know who or what I am. I think I must have lost my memory."

The young man gave a sympathetic exclamation. "Lost your memory?" he cried. "Then," he went on, his face brightening, "perhaps you *are* a blacksmith. I can tell you they want one very badly over there..." But he caught himself up, and added, "Perhaps not. I suppose you can't tell what you might have been." He ceased, and regarded Jeremy with benevolent interest.

"I can't," Jeremy said earnestly. "I don't know where I came from, or what I am, or where I am. I don't even know what year this is. I can remember nothing."

"That's bad," the young man commented with maddening deliberation. "I can tell you where you are, at any rate. This is called Whitechapel Meadows—just outside London, you know. Does that suggest anything to you?"

"Nothing... nothing... I woke up just over there"—he swung his arm vaguely in the direction of the ruins of the warehouse—"and that's all I know." He suppressed an urgent desire to emphasize again his ignorance of what year it was. Something told him that a man who had just lost his memory would be concerned with more immediate problems.

"Well," said the young man pleasantly at last, "do you think you came from London? If you do, you'd better let me take you there and see you safe in one of the monastery hospitals or something of that sort. Then perhaps your family would find you."

"I think so." Jeremy was uncertain whether this would be a step in the right direction. "I seem to remember… I don't know…." He paused, feeling that he could not have imagined a situation so difficult. He had read a number of books in which men had been projected from their own times into the future, but, by one lucky chance or another, none of them had any trouble in establishing himself as the immediate center of interest. Yet he supposed it would be more natural for such an adventurer to be treated as he was going to be treated—that is to say as a mental case. It would be tragically absurd if he in his unique position were to be immured in a madhouse, regarded as a man possessed by incurable delusions, when he might be deriving some consolation for his extraordinary fate in seeing how the world had changed, in seeing, among other things, what was the current theory of the Viscosity of Liquids, and whether his own name was remembered among the early investigators into that fascinating question.

While he still hesitated his companion went on in a soothing tone, "That will be much the best way. Come with me if you think you're well enough to walk."

"Oh, yes… yes…" distractedly. And as a matter of fact, his hunger and his increasing bewilderment aside, Jeremy had never felt so well or so strong in his life before. He was even a little afraid that the activity of his manner might belie the supposed derangement of his mind. He therefore attempted to assume a somewhat depressed demeanor as he followed his new friend along the road.

The young man was evidently either by nature not loquacious, or else convinced that it would be unwise to excite Jeremy by much conversation—perhaps both. As they went along he gave most of his attention to the conduct of his bicycle, and only threw over his shoulder now and again a kindly "Do you remember that?" or "Does that remind you of anything?" as they passed what would apparently be landmarks familiar to any Londoner in the habit of using that road.

But all were equally strange to Jeremy, and he gazed round him keenly to guess if he could what sort of people they were among whom he had fallen. Clearly, if he were to judge by the man who was walking at his side, they were not barbarians; and yet everywhere the countryside showed evidence of decay, which totally defeated all the expectations of the prophets of his own time. As they drew closer to London, which was still hidden from them by belts of trees, the broken meadows of Whitechapel gave place to cleared plots of garden, and here and there among them stood rude hovels, huts that no decent district council would have allowed to be erected. Jeremy, gazing at them as closely as he could without exciting the attention of his guide, thought that many of them seemed to have been built by piling roughly together fragments of other buildings. Presently a gang of laborers going out to the fields passed them, saluting Jeremy with a curious stare, and his companion, when they were able to transfer their gaze to him, with touched caps, whether because they knew him or merely out of respect for his appearance Jeremy could not decide. But it was surprising how familiar their look was. They were what Jeremy had encountered many hundreds of times in country lanes and the bars of country inns; and it was only vaguely and as it were with the back of his consciousness that he perceived their ruder dress and the greater respectfulness of their manner.

The transition from the fields to the town was abrupt. They reached and passed a little wood which bordered both sides of the road, and immediately beyond it the first street began. The houses were almost all of Jeremy's own day or before it, but though they were inhabited they were heavy with age, sagging and hanging in different directions in a manner which betokened long neglect. At the end of the street a knot of loiterers stood. Behind them the street was busy with foot passengers, and Jeremy stared along it to a tangle of houses, some old and some new, but nearly all wearing the same strange air of instability and imminent collapse. Their appearance affected him, as one is affected when one wakes in an unfamiliar room, sleepily expecting to see accustomed things and grows dizzy in substituting the real picture for the imagined. He caught his breath and paused.

"What's the matter?" asked the young man, instantly solicitous.

"Nothing," Jeremy replied, "only feel faint... must rest a minute." He leant against a mass of ruined and lichened brickwork, breathing shortly and jerkily.

"Here," cried his companion, dropping the bicycle, "sit down till you feel better." And, exerting an unsuspected strength, he took Jeremy bodily in his arms and lowered him gently till he reclined on the grass. Jeremy looked up, grateful for his kindness, which was reassuring, though he knew that it did not spring from sympathy with his real perplexities. But he immediately dropped his eyes and clenched his hands while he strove to master his doubts. Would it not perhaps be the wiser plan to confess his position to this young man and take the risk of being thought a madman? And a moment's reflection convinced him that he would never have a better opportunity. The face that now leant anxiously above him was not perhaps so alert or active in appearance as he could have wished; but it was extraordinarily friendly and trustworthy. If the young man could be made to believe in Jeremy's story, he would do all that was possible to help him. Jeremy made his decision with a leap, and looking up again said thickly:

"I say…. I didn't tell you the truth just now."

"What? Don't talk. You'll feel better in a moment."

"No, I must," Jeremy insisted. "I'm all right; I haven't lost my memory. I wish to God I had lost it."

The young man showed for the first time serious symptoms of surprise and alarm. "What," he began, "are you a—"

Jeremy silenced him with an imperative wave of the hand. "Let me go on," he said feverishly, "you mustn't interrupt me. It's difficult enough to say, anyway. Listen."

Then, brokenly, he told his story in a passion of eagerness to be as brief as he could, and at the same time to make it credible by the mere force of his will. When he began to speak he was looking at the ground, but as he reached the crucial points he glanced up to see the listener's expression, and he ended with his gaze fixed directly, appealingly, on the young man's eyes. But the first words in response made him break into a fit of hysterical laughter.

"Good heavens!" the young man cried in accents of obvious relief. "Do you know what I was thinking? Why, I more than half thought you were going to say that you were a criminal or a runaway!"

Jeremy pulled himself together with a jerk, and asked breathlessly, "What year is this? For God's sake tell me what year it is!"

"The year of Our Lord two thousand and seventy-four," the young man answered, and then suddenly realizing the significance of what he had said, he put his hand on Jeremy's shoulder, and added: "All right, man, all right. Be calm."

"I'm all right," Jeremy muttered, putting his hands on the ground to steady himself, "only it's rather a shock—to hear it—" For, strangely, though he had admitted in his thoughts the possibility of even greater periods than this, the concrete naming of the figures struck him harder than anything that day since the moment in which he had expected to see houses and had seen only empty meadows. Now when he closed his eyes his mind at once sank in a whirlpool of vague but powerful emotions. In this darkness he perceived that he had been washed up by fate on a foreign shore, more than a century and a half out of his own generation, in a world of which he was ignorant, and which had no place for him, that his friends were all long dead and forgotten…. When his mind emerged from this eclipse, he found that his cheeks were wet with tears and that he was laughing feebly. All the strength and activity were gone out of him; and he gazed up at his companion helplessly, feeling as dependent on him as a young child on its parent.

"What shall we do now?" he asked in a toneless voice.

But the young man was turning his bicycle around again. "If you feel well enough," he answered gently, "I want you to come back and show me the place where you were hidden. You know… I don't doubt you. I honestly don't; but it's a strange story, and perhaps it would be better for you if I were to look at the place before any one disturbs it. So, if you're well enough…?" Jeremy nodded consent, grateful for the kindness of his friend's voice, and went with him.

The way back to the little grove where they had first met seemed much longer to Jeremy as he retraced it with feet that had begun to drag and back that had begun to ache. When they reached it, the young man hid his bicycle among the bushes, and asked Jeremy to lead him. At the edge of the crevice he paused, and looked down thoughtfully, rubbing his chin with one finger.

"It is just as you described it," he murmured. "I can see the tabletop. Did you look inside when you had got out?" It had not occurred to Jeremy, and he admitted it. "Never mind," the young man went on, "we'll do that in a moment." Then he made Jeremy explain to him how the warehouse had stood, where Lime Court had been, and how it fell into the side-street. He paced the ground which was indicated to him with serious absorbed face, and said at last: "You understand that I haven't doubted what you told me. I felt that you were speaking the truth. But you might have been deluded, and it was as much for your own sake…"

Jeremy interrupted him eagerly. "Couldn't you get the old records, or an old map of London that would show where all these things were? That would help to prove the truth of what I say."

The young man shook his head doubtfully. "I don't suppose I could," he answered vaguely, his eyes straying off in another direction. "I never heard of such things. Now for this…" And turning to the crevice again he seized the tabletop and with a vigorous effort wrenched it up. As he did so a rat ran squeaking from underneath, and scampered away across the grass. Jeremy started back bewildered.

"You had a pleasant bedfellow," said the young man in his grave manner. Jeremy was silent, struggling with something in his memory that had been overlaid by more recent concerns. Was it possible that he was not alone in this unfamiliar generation? With a sudden movement he jumped down into the open grave and began to search in the loose dust at the bottom. The next moment he was out again, presenting for the inspection of his bewildered companion an oddly-shaped glass vessel.

"This is it!" he cried, his face white, his eyes blazing, "I told you I came to see an experiment—" Then he was checked by the perfect blankness of the expression that met him. "Of course," he said more slowly, "if you're not a scientist, perhaps you wouldn't know what this is." And he began to explain, in the simplest words he could find, the astonishing theory that had just leapt up fully born in his brain. He guessed, staggered by his own supposition, that Trehanoc's ray had been more potent than even the discoverer had suspected, and that welling softly and invisibly from the once excited vacuum-tube which he held in his hand, it had preserved him and the rat together in a state of suspended animation for more than a century and a half. Then with the rolling of the timbers over his head and the collapse of the soft earth which had gathered on them, the air had entered the hermetically sealed chamber and brought awakening with it.

As his own excitement began to subside he was checked again by the absolute lack of comprehension patent in his companion's face. He stopped in the middle of a sentence, feeling himself all astray. Was this ray one of the commonplaces of the new age? Was it his surprise, rather than the cause of it, which was so puzzling to his friend? The whole world was swimming around him, and ideas began to lose their connection. But, as through a mist, he could still see the young man's face, and hear him saying seriously as ever:

"I do not understand how that bottle could have kept you asleep for so long, nor do I know what you mean by a ray. You are very ill, or you would not try to explain things which cannot be explained. You do not know any more than I what special grace has preserved you. Many strange things happened in the old times which we cannot understand to-day." As he spoke he crossed himself and bowed his head. Jeremy was silenced by his expression of devout and final certainty, and stifled the exclamation that rose to his lips.

CHAPTER IV
Discoveries

1

How and when Jeremy's second unconsciousness overtook him he did not know. He remembered stumbling after his friend down the uneven road he had now begun to hate. He remembered that the heat of the day had grown intense, that his own dizziness had increased, and that he had been falling wearily over stones and from one rut to another. He had a dim recollection of entering the street he had seen before, and of noticing the odd effect produced by twentieth-century buildings sagging crazily forward over a rough cobbled roadway. But he did not remember his sudden collapse, or how his friend had secured a cart and anxiously bundled him into it. He did not remember the jolting journey that followed, as speedy as the streets of this new London would allow.

He came to himself in a bed in a little, bare, whitewashed room through the windows of which the westering sun was throwing a last golden flood. He sat up hastily, and saw that he was alone. At his side on a small table stood a metal dish holding a thick slice of bread and some leaves of lettuce; and by the dish there was a mug of rudely glazed earthenware. His mouth was dry and his tongue swollen; and he investigated the mug first. He was rewarded by a draught of thin but, as he then thought, delicious ale. He immediately set to on the bread and lettuce, and thought of nothing else till he had finished it. When he had scraped together the last crumbs and his first ravenousness had given way to a healthy and normal hunger, he looked about him with more interest.

The room, his first glance told him, was bare even to meanness. It held nothing but the bed in which he lay, the table and a large, cumbrously-made wooden chest which stood in the further corner. The walls, as well as the ceiling, were covered with a coarse whitewash which was flaking here and there; and there was a square of rough matting on the boards of the floor. Jeremy, quite awake and alert now, wondered whether, after all, he had not been taken to an asylum, perhaps—and this seemed most probable—to the infirmary of a workhouse. The sheets on the bed and the night-shirt in which he found himself, clean but of very coarse linen, seemed to support this theory. On the other hand, if it were correct, ought he not to be in a ward with the other patients? And was it usual in the workhouses of this age to have mugs of ale by the bedside of unconscious men?

Curiosity soon stirred him farther, and he put one foot cautiously to the ground. He was reassured at once by a sensation of strength and health; and he slipped out of bed and went to the window. Here he met with another surprise; for it was glazed with small leaded panes of thick and muddy glass, such as was becoming rare in his own time even in the remotest and most primitive parts of the country. And a brief examination showed that the window was genuine, not merely a sheet of glass cut up by sham leads to give a false appearance of antiquity. Puzzling a little over this, and finding that he could not see clearly through the stains and whorls in the glass, he undid the window, and thrust his head out. Below him stretched spacious gardens with lawns and shrubberies, fading in the distance among tall trees, through which buildings could just be discerned.

As he leant out he could hear the voices of persons hidden somewhere beneath; and he was straining forward to catch their meaning when a hand fell on his shoulder. He looked round with a start, and saw his friend carrying a pile of clothes over one arm, and smiling at him pleasantly.

"Well," said the young man, "I'm relieved to find you awake again. Do you know that you've lain there since before noon, and that it's now nearly six o'clock? I began to think that you'd fallen into another trance."

"Where am I?" Jeremy asked bluntly.

And the young man replied with simplicity: "This is the Treasury. You know, I'm one of the Speaker's Clerks." And then seeing Jeremy's stare of bewilderment, he went on: "Or perhaps you don't know. We have apartments here in the Treasury during our term of service, and dine in the Great Hall. This room belongs to another of the Clerks. Luckily he's away on a journey, and so I've been able to borrow it for you. And that reminds me that though you told me a great deal about yourself, you never told me your name." Jeremy told him. "And mine's Roger Vaile. Now I think you ought to get dressed, if you feel strong enough."

But Jeremy's bewilderment was by no means dissipated. "The Speaker? The Treasury?" he inquired disconnectedly.

The young man whose name was Roger Vaile laughed in a good-humored way. "Didn't you have them in your time? It's not much use asking me, I'm afraid. I know so little about the old times that I can't tell what will be new to you, and what you know already. But you must know who the Speaker is?"

"Yes… I suppose so… the Speaker of the House of Commons," Jeremy began. "But—"

Roger Vaile looked perplexed in his turn. "N-no—I don't know… perhaps… he's… oh, he's the ruler of the country—like a king, you know."

"But why is he called the Speaker?" Jeremy persisted.

"Oh, I suppose because he speaks for the people, who know more about these things than I do. Now; that's evident, isn't it? But I'll find some one for you. You'd better dress," he concluded, making for the door, plainly anxious to avoid further questions. "Dinner's served at half-past six. I'll call for you." He escaped, but returned in a moment to say: "By the way, I've told no one anything about you. I've only said that I'm entertaining a friend from the country."

"Thanks… oh, thanks," Jeremy replied hastily and rather foolishly, looking up from his manipulation of the garments which Roger had disposed on the bed. They proved, however, on examination, to be the least of the problems at that moment confusing his mind. They were, in fact, exceedingly like the evening dress to which he was accustomed. A kind of dinner-jacket with coarsely woven silk on the lapels was substituted for the tail-coat, and the shirt was made of heavy, unstarched linen, and had a soft collar attached to it. The socks were of thick and heavy silk; but the cloth of the coat, waistcoat and trousers, which turned out, under closer inspection, to be dark purple instead of black, was as soft and fine as could be desired. The shoes were more unusual. They were of fine leather, long and pointed and intricately adorned, and their color was a rich and pleasing green.

Jeremy had no trouble in dressing; but when he had finished he was made a little uneasy by what he could see of the result. He supposed, however, that his costume was that of a well-dressed young man of the period, though it did not fit him at all points as he could have wished; and he sat down on the bed to wait as tranquilly as he could till Roger should call for him. Tranquillity, however, was not to be had for the asking. Too many questions beset his mind; and though he had a wealth of observations on which to reflect there seemed to be at once too many and too few. He certainly had never believed that the Millennium was somewhere just around the corner, waiting to be led in by the hand of Science. But he *had* held the comfortable belief that mankind was advancing in conveniences and the amenities of life by regular and inevitable degrees. Yet all that he had seen so far seemed to be preparing an overthrow of this supposition no less direct and amazing than the revelation he had received when he looked for the houses of Whitechapel and found that they were no longer there. The mere fact that a whole quarter of London had been destroyed and had never been rebuilt was in itself significant. The condition of the still inhabited houses which he had seen was strange. The clothes he wore, the sheets on his bed, the glazing of his window, pointed to an unexpected state of affairs. And Roger Vaile's attitude towards the scientific theories which Jeremy had so guilelessly spread before him was perhaps the most striking phenomenon of all. Jeremy sought vainly for words which would describe the impression it had made on him. Could a savage have looked otherwise if you had explained to him the theory of atomic weights? And the Speaker, who spoke for the people... and the Treasury? Jeremy thought suddenly, with a certain ingratitude, that Roger's easy acceptance of his own almost impossible story had something about it that was decidedly queer.

The course of his meditations led him to as many blind alleys as there were paths to be followed; and he was just staring down the eighth or ninth when Roger entered, dressed in garments closely resembling those he had given to Jeremy. Jeremy followed his beckoning finger and was led down a narrow staircase, along a passage and into a hall of some dimensions, which was lit partly by the sun still streaming through the windows, partly by a multitude of tall, thick candles. It contained three tables, two of which were long and stood in the body of the hall. The third was much smaller and was raised on a dais at the end, at right angles to the others. This was still unoccupied; but around the long tables sat or stood a number of men of varying ages, mostly young, talking desultorily, and waiting. These were also dressed like Jeremy; but some of them had been more adventurous in the colors of their jackets, and some displayed modest touches of lace on their breasts or at their wrists.

Jeremy was still staring covertly at these people and finding, a little to his surprise, that neither their costume nor his own looked odd, being naturally worn, when a trumpet rang out metallically, and at once all the lounging men sprang to their feet in rigid attitudes. A door on the dais was thrown open by a servant, and a tall, stooping figure walked in.

"The Speaker," Roger whispered softly in Jeremy's ear. Jeremy craned his neck to see the ruler of England. He caught a glimpse of a large, rather fleshy face, with deep folds, discernible in spite of the long white beard about the heavy, drooping mouth, and more than a touch of Jewish traits in the curve of the nose, and the heaviness of the eyelids. As the Speaker walked to his seat, another man, shorter, but spare, and more erect, with lean features and a bearing of almost barbaric pride, which was accentuated by the dull red of his jacket, followed him in.

"That damned Canadian!" Roger muttered, and Jeremy staring in some surprise found that the exclamation was not for him. Still no one sat. Even the Speaker and his guest remained standing by their chairs, until another trumpet sounded, and a second door on the dais was thrown open. Two women came through it. The first was middle-aged and stout, florid of coloring, and, even at that distance, obviously over-painted. The second, whom the first partially hid, seemed to be young, and to move with a carriage as robust and distinguished as that of the erect Canadian. Jeremy had seen no more than this when his gaze was diverted by the rising of a priest who intoned a grace and then by the bustle attendant on the whole company sitting down. He gathered from Roger's whisper that these were the Speaker's wife and daughter; but after dinner had begun, he could not clearly see the party of four on the dais because of the glare and the flickering of the candles between him and them.

<h2 style="text-align:center">2</h2>

Roger Vaile did more for Jeremy than provide him with food and lodging. He was also at the pains of finding out the wisest man he knew to answer Jeremy's questions and resolve his doubts. After a lengthy meal of huge and crudely spiced dishes they returned to Roger's own room, an apartment a little larger than that in which Jeremy had found himself, but not much less bare; and there they discovered, sitting on the bed and waiting for them, an elderly priest in a long black soutane, with a golden crucifix at his breast.

He rose as they entered, and surveyed Jeremy with intense curiosity. Jeremy returned the stare, but rather less intently. This, he found with little interest, was like any priest of any age. He was clean shaven and almost bald, with pouched and drooping cheeks, and a chin that multiplied and returned to unity as he talked and moved his head. But above these signs of age were two large and childlike blue eyes which shone on Jeremy with something like greed in their eagerness.

"This is the man," Roger said briefly to the priest, and to Jeremy he said: "This is my uncle, Father Henry Dean. He is writing the chronicle of the Speakers, and he knows more about the old times than any other man alive."

The priest took Jeremy's hand in a soft clasp without relaxing his eager stare. "There are few men alive who are older than I am," he murmured, "but you are one of them, if my nephew has told me the truth. Yes—more than a century older."

"I don't feel it," Jeremy answered aimlessly.

"No? No. That is miraculous. Ah, yes, I believe your story. I know well that the world is full of marvels. Who should know that better than I who have spent so many years searching the wonderful past? And there were greater marvels in those days than now. Young man—" he stopped and chuckled with a touch of senility. "Young man, you will be nearly two centuries old."

Jeremy nodded without speaking.

"Yes, yes," the old man went on, "so many strange things happened in those days that we have no call to be amazed at you. Why, there used to be a machine in those times that the doctors used to look right through men's bodies."

Jeremy started slightly. "You mean the Röntgen Rays?" he said.

"A wonderful light," said the old man eagerly, "you know it, you have seen it?"

"Why, yes," Jeremy turned to Roger. "You know that vacuum-tube I showed you—" But the old man was continuing his catalogue of wonders.

"Men used to cross to America in less than a week. Yes—and some even flew over in aeroplanes in a day."

"Uncle, uncle," Roger remonstrated gently, "you mustn't tell fairy tales to a man who has been to fairyland. He knows what the truth is."

"But that is true," Jeremy roused himself to say; "it was done several times—not regularly, but often." Roger bestowed on him a glance of covert doubt, and the priest leant forward in tremulous gratitude.

"I knew it, I knew it!" he cried. "Roger, like all the world to-day you are too ignorant. You do not know—"

But Jeremy interrupted again. "But have you aeroplanes now?" he asked. "Can you fly?"

"Not for many years now," the old man sighed, "Roger has never seen a man flying. I did when I was very young." He drew a deep breath and regarded Jeremy almost with reverence. "You lived in a wonderful time," he said. "Why, you were alive in the time of the great artists, when that was made." He turned, and indicated with a devout finger a little marble statue which stood on the mantelpiece behind him. Jeremy followed his gesture, and noticed for the first time that the room was not entirely without decoration. The statue to which his gaze was directed represented the body of a man from the waist upwards. The anatomy of the body was entirely distorted, the ribs stood out like ridges, and one arm, which was raised over the head, was a good third longer than the other.

"Yes," Jeremy said, surveying it with interest, "perhaps I did. That is what we used to call Futurist art."

"They were masters then," said the priest with a deep expulsion of his breath. Jeremy's eyes wandered round the room and fell on a picture, plainly a lithograph of the war-period, which, when he had regarded it long enough, resolved itself into a crane lifting a great gun into a railway wagon. But it was drawn in fierce straight lines and savage angles, with shadows like wedges, making a bewildering pattern which for a moment defeated him. He dropped his eyes from it, and again looked round the room. This time his gaze fell on the bed, which was wooden and obviously new. The flat head of it was covered with rude carving such as might have been executed by a child armed for the first time with a gouge and a mallet. It had none of the vigor and rhythm that commonly goes with primitive workmanship. The design was glaringly stupid and senseless.

"We are poor workmen to-day," said the priest, following and interpreting his glance.

Roger, who had stood by, silent but a little impatient, now intervened. "These are old family things," he explained, "that I brought with me from home. They are very rare. But the bed is new, and I think it very pretty. I had it made only a few months ago." He motioned his guests into chairs, and produced a large earthenware pot which he offered to Jeremy. Jeremy removed the lid, and saw, somewhat to his surprise, that it contained a dark, finely cut tobacco.

"It's Connemara," he said laconically. The old priest shook a long finger at him.

"Ah, Roger, Roger!" he chided. "When will you learn to be thrifty? Cannot you smoke the tobacco of your own country? Winchcombe is good enough for me," he added to Jeremy, bringing a linen bag and a cherrywood pipe out of the folds of his robe.

"I've no pipe," said Jeremy, fumbling mechanically in his pockets. Roger, without speaking, went to a chest, and produced two new, short clay pipes, one of which he handed to Jeremy, while he kept the other himself. All three were silent for a moment while they filled and lighted from a taper; and the familiar operation, the familiar pause, afflicted Jeremy with an acute memory of earlier days. Then while his palate was still savoring the first breath of the strong, cool Irish tobacco in the new pipe, the priest began again his rambling spoken reveries.

"Tell me," he demanded suddenly, "did you live in the time of the first Speaker?"

Jeremy, hampered by a grievous lack of historical knowledge, tried to explain that the Speaker was a functionary dating from centuries before his time. The old man jumped in his chair with childlike enthusiasm.

"Yes, yes!" he cried. "This generation has almost forgotten how he came by his name. But I meant the great-grandfather of our Speaker, the first to rule England. You know he was the only strong man when the troubles began. Do you remember him? Surely you must remember him?" Jeremy shook his head, considering. He did not even recall what had been the name of the Speaker when he fell asleep. But his mind caught at a word the priest had used.

"The troubles?" he repeated.

"Yes," the priest answered, a little taken aback, throwing a glance at Roger. "Don't you know? The wars, the fighting…"

"The war…" Jeremy began. He knew a great deal about what had been called by his generation, quite simply, The War.

But Roger interposed. "My uncle means the civil wars. Surely it was in the middle of the troubles that your trance began?"

3

It was by way of such stumblings and misapprehensions that Jeremy gained at last a partial and confused picture of the world into which he had fallen. He had been the first to tire, but the old priest had been very unwilling to let him go.

"No, no," he said again and again, as Jeremy strove to rise, "you must first tell me…"—while Roger sat watching them with an air of inalterable mildness. Roger had taken but a little part in the conversation. His notions of the twentieth century were extraordinarily vague and inaccurate; and when he had been rebuked once or twice for ignorance he had shrugged his shoulders, placidly observing that it mattered very little, and had said no more.

Jeremy crept into bed very late by the light of a flickering candle, desiring only to forget everything, to postpone all effort of thought until another day. But when he had blown out his candle, and nothing remained but a patch of moonlight thrown through the window on the opposite wall, his mind grew active again. It was indeed absurd to be lying there in the darkness with nothing to give him ocular evidence of his strange misfortune, nothing visible at all but the square of pale radiance, barred by the heavy leads of the pane.

He might have been in bed in some old-fashioned country inn, the chance lodging of a night, where there would have been just such a window, and where the sheets would have been as coarse and heavy as these were. But then, a mile, or two miles, or five miles away there would have been a railway station, whence sooner or later a train would have carried him back to the flat in Holborn, back to his lectures and the classes of intelligent young men and women eager for rational instruction in the mysteries of the universe. He thought of that station, and for a moment could see it as vividly as he desired it, could picture the fresh morning walk there, the little, almost deserted platform with a name picked out in white pebbles, the old porter.... He could conjure up the journey and even the smoky approach to London. But here, though as he had learnt there were still trains, there was certainly no train which could do that for him.

He shifted uneasily on to the other side, and recognized with a groan that this was an empty vision. It behooved him to make himself at home as much and as soon as he could in the year two thousand and seventy-four, to learn what this world was like, to adapt himself to it.

"We are a diminished people," was the burden of the priest's lament. "Our ancestors were wise and rich and strong, but we have lost nearly all they had, and we shall never regain it." And he had rehearsed the marvels of the twentieth century, trains leaving every town in constant succession, motors on the roads, aeroplanes overhead, steamers on the sea. But the steamship, owing to the difficulties of its construction, had practically ceased to exist. A rapidly growing percentage of accidents, due to faulty workmanship, had driven the aeroplane altogether out of use. There were still a few motors; but these had long been less reliable, and were now growing less speedy, than the horse. As for trains—there were still trains running to and from London. One went to Edinburgh every week, and two to Liverpool and Bristol. The trains to Dover, to the Midlands and to Yorkshire were even more frequent. The line from London to the West of England was still open, but that district had now little importance, and trains were dispatched there only when there was some special reason.

Roger treated his uncle's laments with gentle and reasonable sarcasm. "I think," he said weightily, "that you exaggerate. I'm not convinced that the old times were as wonderful as you think. Why, so far as railways go, I know something about railways. It's part of my duties. And I know this, that engines are always breaking down. I take it that even in the old times an engine that had broken down wouldn't go. And I imagine that our clever ancestors had just as much trouble as we have in keeping the lines up. Now this week the train from Edinburgh is two days overdue, because there's been a landslide in the Midlands. I suppose you'll agree," he added, turning to Jeremy, "that even in your time a train couldn't get through a landslide."

Jeremy had agreed. "I dare say," Roger went on, "that the railways aren't as good now as they were before the troubles. But we're going to improve them. The Speaker talks about repairing the old line that went out to the eastern counties. You know—you can still see parts of it near Chelmsford."

The old man on this had looked appealingly at Jeremy, who sought without success to convince Roger that the difference was really great. But his attention was chiefly concentrated on discovering how this and other differences had come about. It seemed incredible that the race could have forgotten so much and yet live. The "Troubles" were so often in the mouths of both uncle and nephew that Jeremy's mind came at last to give them their due in the shape of a capital letter. The "Troubles." … He supposed that his trance had begun with this beginning and indeed much of what the priest had told him was more vivid to him than to the teller when he remembered the soldier and the alien woman who had called him a dirty bourgeois, or Scott leaning down, pale and anxious from the lorry, or the man whom he had never seen, but who had thrown a bomb at him down Trehanoc's cellar steps.

Jeremy gathered that it had been a question not of one outburst of fighting, one upheaval and turning-point of time, but of numbers spread over many years.

"It is hard to say how it all came about," mused the old man, at one of the few moments when he was cajoled into telling instead of asking. "Some have said that the old life grew too difficult, and just ground itself to pieces. It began with the rich and the poor. When some accident brought them to blows it was too late to put the world right. After that they never trusted one another, and there was no more peace."

"When did the fighting stop at last?" asked Jeremy.

"It kept on stopping—it kept on stopping. And it kept on breaking out again, first in one country and then in another. For fifty years there was always war in some part of the world. And when they stopped fighting they couldn't settle down again. The workers idled, or smashed the machines. And at last a time came when the fighting didn't stop. It went on and on in England and all over the Continent. All the schools were closed, all the teachers were idle for more than twenty years. I have often thought that that was how we came to lose so much. A generation grew up that had never learnt anything. Only a few men knew how to do the things their fathers had done every day, and the rest were too stupid or too lazy to learn from them properly. Then everybody was tired out and more than half the people were dead; they had to begin again, and they were too weary to recover as much as they might have done."

Jeremy pondered over again the vision raised by these words. He could see the earth ravaged by exhausted enemies, too evenly matched to bring the struggle to an end until exhaustion had reached its lowest pitch. He could see all the mechanical wonders of his own age smashed by men who were too weak to prevail, but who were strong enough not to endure the soulless contrivances which had brought them into servitude. And he could see the gradual triumph of the Speaker over a weary and starving population. The first Speaker, who had really been Speaker of the House of Commons in the year when Jeremy had fallen into his trance, had been a man of unsuspected strength of character and a member of a great and wealthy Jewish house. Assisted by his kinsmen in all parts of the world, he had been a rallying-point for the rich in the early disorders; and he had established a party which had lasted, with varying fortunes, through all the changes of succeeding years. He it was who had arranged that compromise with the Church of Rome by which all southern England became again more or less Catholic without too violently alienating those parts of the country in which other sorts of religion were dominant. Not the least of his claims for greatness had been his perception of the real power still concentrated in the fugitive and changing person of that Bishop of Rome who was chased from his own ruined palace and his own city, up and down Europe from one refuge to another, as the forces of disorder veered and changed…subsided here and rose again there. One by one the countries of the earth had sunk, bloodless and impoverished, into quiescence, and when the turn of England came, the house of the Speaker, the house of Burney, in the person of his grandson, had been at hand to take the opportunity.

"And did all the people die off in the fighting?" Jeremy had wondered.

"In battle and disease and famine," the priest answered. "Towards the end of the Troubles came the Great Famine. And that was the cause of the worst of the wars. The people of the towns were starving, because they were fighting in America and sent us no food-ships, and the country people were nearly starving too, because their crops had failed. They struggled for what food there was… they died by millions… by millions and millions…."

"I must say I find it hard to believe all that," Roger interposed with an air of detachment. "My uncle is so enthusiastic about the old times that he believes whatever any one tells him or what he reads in a lot of old books—books you couldn't imagine if you hadn't seen them, filthy, simply dropping to pieces…. The more improbable the story the better he likes it. Well, in the first place, why should those people have wanted food from other countries? What did they do if they didn't grow it for themselves? And why should so many of them be living in towns?"

"You are very ignorant, my boy," said the old man calmly. "Look at

London now; look at the miles of houses that no one has lived in for a hundred years. Who did live in them but the people who died of famine?"

"It isn't a very great matter after all, is it?" Roger muttered, suppressing a yawn.

"Before the Troubles," the priest continued, half to himself, "there were nearly fifty millions of people in England alone. Do you know what the census was?" he asked sharply, turning to Jeremy. Jeremy replied that he did. "Ah, Roger wouldn't know what the word meant. Well, I have read the report of the census of 1921, and then there were nearly fifty million people in England alone. Where are they now? We have not more than ten or twelve millions, and we have never counted them—never counted them. But Roger and the young men of his age think that nothing has happened, that we are not much worse off than we were, that there is no need for us to bestir ourselves."

"And is it like this all over the world?" Jeremy had asked, stunned by the implications of this fact.

"All over the world—so far as we know."

"All over the world—all over the world." The words rang again in Jeremy's ears as he tossed uneasily in bed. The old world had collapsed, and the falling roof had crushed and blotted, out forever most of what he had thought perpetually established. And then, amazingly, the stones and timbers had not continued in their fall to utter ruin. They had found their level and stayed, jammed together, perhaps, fortuitously, to make a lower and narrower vault, which still sufficed to shelter the improvident family of men. The human race had not perished, had not even been reduced to utter barbarism. Its glissade into the abyss had been arrested, and it remained on the ledge of ground where it had been thrown. So much was left. How much?

He realized with a slight shock that he was lying on his back, beating feverishly with his hands on the bedclothes, and muttering half aloud as though in a delirium, "What is left? What can be left?" He dragged himself back abruptly from what seemed for a moment to be the edge of madness. Still his mind obstinately demanded to know what was left that was tangible, that he had known and could recognize. He could not get beyond the landmarks of his childhood. Was Westminster Abbey still standing? Was the Monument? He knew that St. Paul's was gone. It had been lost by a generation which had been careless of the warnings given by its groaning arches and leaning walls; it had fallen and crushed some hundreds of the negligent inheritors. Was Nelson's column still in Trafalgar Square? Jeremy, with a childish unreason, was eager to have an answer to this question.

Now his thoughts abruptly abandoned it and fled back to pictures of the Troubles. He could see very vividly, more vividly than anything else, the classroom in which he had been accustomed to deliver his lecture empty and deserted, benches torn up to make bonfires or barricades, dust sifting in through the broken windows and lying thick on the floor. He remembered with a painful laugh that he had left the first written sheets of a paper on the Viscosity of Liquids in a drawer in the lecturer's table. Burnt, too, no doubt…. That knowledge had perished. But most knowledge had perished in another way, had merely faded from the mind of man, because of his growing incapacity for acquiring it. There flashed upon him the vision of a changed world, in which there was no fellow for him, save only a few, and those among the very old.

For a moment his mind paused, as though a cold finger had intervened and touched it. During the hours of the night his eyes had been growing used to the darkness, but, so much were his thoughts turned inwards, he had not noticed it. Now, in the sudden cessation of thought, he saw clearly the bed in which he was lying, the matting on the floor, the rough walls and ceiling, and every detail of the little room. He started up, went to the window and thrust his head out into the night air. The bushes below murmured faintly under the touch of a breeze he could not feel. All around was perfectly quiet; and where that evening he had seen buildings through the farthest trees, no lights were to be descried. He pushed his head farther out and looked to left and right. There were no lights in the Treasury: no sound came from any of the rooms. Jeremy stayed thus for a little, helpless in one of those fits in which every physical faculty is capable while the mind is dizzied by the mere power of a thought.

He knew that, by reason of his strange fate, he was alone in this generation. But he had only just begun to realize how much alone he was. Now he felt he had no community with any of these creatures, that not only the face of the earth but the spirit of its dwellers had been changed while he slept. They looked at the world and at themselves in a manner which was not familiar to him. They were ignorant of things he could never explain to them. They believed things which to him could never be credible. There was a gap between him and them which nothing could ever bridge.

Tears came into his eyes as he pondered numbly over his tragedy. It seemed to him that he could look back and see his own world, full of familiar men and places, friendly and infinitely desirable. He began to believe that all things which had happened and are to happen exist simultaneously somewhere in the universe. And then, shaking himself free from this absurd homesickness in time, he began to consider the immediate future. The rest of his life was perhaps a negligible piece of eternity compared with that through which he had already lived; but it would have to be passed somehow. The more he thought about it the more ridiculously impossible it seemed that he should now see out the reasonable span of human life.

Could he adjust himself to this new world, find a place in its business, earn a living, make friends, perhaps marry and beget children? The idea was preposterous; he ought rather to be in a museum. Could it be possible that one day his youth in the twentieth century would be as dim a recollection to him as must be, he supposed, the youth of most old men to them? There passed before his eyes, sudden and uncalled for, a procession of solemn persons, parents, and even aunts, schoolmasters, the principal of the college in which he lectured, the professor under whom he had worked. All, in that distant youth, when he had seemed rash and impatient, had advised him, had adjured him to consider his future. Well, here it was.... He laughed loudly and harshly.

4

In another room, not far off in that diminished city, candles were burning while Jeremy tossed to and fro in the darkness. At a great mahogany table—the dining-table of some moldered Victorian gentleman—Father Henry Dean sat down long after midnight, and, with the sleepless industry of a very old man, began to turn over the pages of his chronicle. All around the lighted circle in which he sat soft shadows filled the room, obscuring the great oak dresser, a now worn and mellowed relic of the Arts and Crafts Movement, and the bookcase, which was modern work, covered with crude and tasteless arabesques, and offended its owner whenever he saw it.

His labors in the composition of his history were immense and were bewildering to the younger men of his time. It had been a blissful experience to meet, in Jeremy, one who understood the pains he took in order to arrive at a seemingly useless truth. The pages through which he was now glancing represented a lifetime of devotion. They represented also an enduring and a passionate regret. Father Henry deserved whatever condemnation properly falls upon the praiser of the past.

In the pursuit of his object he had lavished his youth and his middle age; and he was still spending his last years in the discovery and study of the books that were now slowly vanishing from the world. He alone in his generation had made many journeys to the great deserted repository where, before the Troubles, the authorities of the British Museum had stored the innumerable and bewildering periodicals of a time that had been, if anything, too well informed. A satirical poet might have found a theme in that dark, dejected, and rat-ridden building, whose windows and doors had long since vanished and where man's neglect had conspired with the weather and the sheltering beasts to disperse the knowledge it contained.

The priest's youth had gone before he heard of this storehouse. When he found it, the stooping, patient figure, turning over the pages of long-forgotten newspapers, which were brown and ragged, dropping in pieces, covered with mildew, sodden with rain or eaten away by rats, might have offered the same poet a spectacle too pathetic for the exercise of his fancy. Father Henry did his best; but the ravages of time had been enormous.

For the whole of 1920 and part of 1921 he could find no connected authority but the files of an illustrated Sunday paper.

It had been almost the same in the British Museum itself, which he had discovered in earlier life and where his strange passion was first nurtured. There was only the tragic difference that here decay had not gone so far that it might not yet be repaired. Many of the treasures of the Museum had been destroyed, or spoilt, or stolen, and the library had suffered no less. Father Henry, when he was a young man, obtained a key to the rooms in which the books lay and wandered among the shelves, observing with tears the damage done here, too, by rain and the rats, so that here too many unique records were already wholly destroyed or rendered illegible. There was still a curator of the Museum, an official at the Speaker's court, who held the post as a sinecure and visited the building perfunctorily once or twice a year. In his very early and ardent youth the priest had addressed a petition to the Speaker, praying with some vehemence that the part of the Museum which held the library might be mended and made weatherproof. The Speaker was indifferent, the curator resentful; and Father Henry's foolish persistence had spoilt his own hopes of advancement and thrown him more deeply into his solitary enthusiasm for the recovery of knowledge.

Once again, in his middle years, on the succession of a new Speaker, he renewed his petition, and for a time his expectations had risen. But the new ruler had lost interest when he found that Father Henry's object was only the study of history, not the revival of mechanical inventions. Other things had intervened, and the project had been dropped. After that the priest began carrying to his own house such volumes as he most valued; but he dared not do this on a great scale, lest the curator should make it a convenient occasion for a display of zeal. He prophesied privately to acquaintances, who did not care, that in another generation the library would have been altogether lost.

Amid these difficulties he had almost completed the work through which he was now abstractedly rambling. Jeremy's appearance had filled him with homesickness for the past no less acute than Jeremy's own; and he looked at the crabbedly written pages through a film of tears. In an early chapter he corrected with pleasure his own doubt whether the Atlantic had ever really been crossed through the air. In the newspapers he had consulted by some odd chance, only allusions to this feat, but no direct record of it survived. He noted also that he must revise his estimate of one Bob Hart, a prominent Labor leader of the years in which the Troubles began. Relying on the illustrated Sunday paper, Father Henry Dean had depicted him as a great, corrupt, and sinister demagogue, who combined the more salient qualities of Robespierre and Heliogabalus. Jeremy happened to have met him once or twice, and affirmed confidently that he was a small, bewildered and timid man, with a stock of homely eloquence and no reasoning power.

The old priest turned on and reached his account of the ruin of St. Paul's, which had occurred after the Troubles and, indeed, during his own childhood. He had actually seen it standing, though he had not seen it fall. In the chronicle he described the catastrophe, the portents which preceded it, and the cloud of dust which hung for a few minutes over the settling ruins, and in which many had thought they had seen an avenging shape.

After this he had given a long and elaborate account of the wonderful building, supplementing his childish recollections from a rich and varied tradition. Father Henry remembered that the great dome of the cathedral had been gilded, and here tradition supported him. Jeremy, however, declared that this was not true. The old priest looked carefully through what he had written; and then, sitting back in his great chair and rattling his quill between his teeth, he considered Jeremy's evidence. At last he shook his head, put down his pen, and locked his papers away. Having done this, he blew out all the candles but one, took the last and dragged himself heavily away to bed.

CHAPTER V

The Speaker

1

WHEN JEREMY WOKE, the same panic terror of that transition seized him again for a moment and poised him on a razor's edge between consciousness and unconsciousness. It passed. The clear morning light falling on his bed revealed to him that his humdrum existence in the new world began with that day. The surprises and the anxieties were over. All that remained was a process of adaptation and settlement; and, feeling a certain eagerness to begin, he began by scrambling out of bed.

There was, as he might have remembered, no bath in the room; and he decided that to search for one along these unknown corridors would be an enterprise not less chimerical than embarrassing. He looked about the room rather helplessly and lit at last on what he had not seen the night before, a metal ewer of water with a basin, standing behind the wooden chest. There was no soap with them, and the chest turned out to be locked. He was still revolving this problem in his mind, while the nightshirt napped pleasantly round his legs in a light draught, when Roger came in, looking as placid and collected as he had been when he had shown Jeremy to bed.

"Are you well?" Roger asked; and, without waiting for a reply, he went on smoothly, "Of course you have nothing of your own for dressing. I've brought you my soap and a razor and a glass—and…" He hesitated a little.

"Yes?" Jeremy encouraged him.

"I thought perhaps it might be better if I were to lend you some of my clothes. You know, your own do look… If you don't mind…"

"Of course not," Jeremy assented with pleasure. It was the last of his desires to be in any way conspicuous. "I should very much prefer it."

When Roger had gone he examined with some interest the soap which had been given to him. It was a thin and wasted cake, very heavy, and of a harsh and gritty substance. But what was chiefly interesting was that it lay in a little metal casket which had a lock on it. This simple fact led Jeremy's mind down a widening avenue of speculation. He dragged himself away from it with difficulty, and was in the middle of washing and shaving when Roger returned. It was at least a relief to find that the razor had a practicable edge.

Roger sat on the bed and watched Jeremy in silence. There was nothing specially perplexing in these new clothes, which comprised a thick woolen vest, a shirt, breeches, and a loose coat, and were obviously the garments of a race, or a class, used to a life spent largely out of doors. Jeremy put them on without difficulty until he came to the shapeless bunch of colored linen which served as a tie. Here Roger was obliged to intervene and help him.

"How absurd!" Roger exclaimed with satisfaction, standing away and regarding him when the operation was completed. "Now you look like anybody else. And yet yesterday, when I found you, you looked like some one out of one of the old pictures. It's almost a pity…"

"That's all right," Jeremy sighed, still fidgeting a little with the tie and trying to see himself in a very small shaving-glass. "I want to look like anybody else. It's a great piece of luck that only you and your uncle know that I'm not. I feel somehow," he went on, with an increasing warmth of expression, "that I can rely on you. It would be unbearable if all these people here knew what I had told you." He paused, while the vision thus suggested took definite shape in his mind.

"You see," he ruminated, lost in speculation and half-forgetting his hearer, "I know that nothing would ever make *me* believe such a story. I know they would look at me out of the corners of their eyes and wonder whether there was anything in it. They'd begin to take sides and quarrel. The fools would believe me and the sensible people would laugh at me. I should begin to feel that I was an impostor, a sort of De Rougemont or Doctor Cook… only, of course, you don't know who they were—" He might have rambled on much longer without realizing that there was a certain ungracious candor in these remarks if his interest had not been attracted by a change of expression, a mere flicker of meaning in Roger's eyes.

"You haven't told any one?" Jeremy cried with a sudden gust of entreaty.

"No—well… no one of importance…" Roger answered, averting his glance. "But I didn't know—you didn't say— And there's my uncle—" He paused and considered.

"But—" Jeremy began, and stopped appalled.

The pressure of experience had taught him that it was not only an error but also gross ill-behavior to make large claims of any sort whatsoever. He strongly resented finding himself in the position of having to assert in public that he had lain in a trance for a century and a half. Surely Roger should have understood his feelings without warning, and should have respected his story as told in confidence under an obvious necessity. There flashed through his mind the question whether any newspapers still survived.

He burst out again wildly, fighting with a thickness in his throat. "Will your uncle have told any one? Isn't it much better to say nothing about me? At least, until I can prove—"

"But what do you mean—prove?" Roger interrupted. "Why shouldn't every one believe you as I did? There are some men who will believe nothing, but—" He shrugged his shoulders and dismissed them. "But, whatever you may wish, there's my uncle… He rises very early—I saw him here half-an-hour ago, after Mass."

Jeremy opened his mouth to speak and forebore.

"Consider, my dear friend," Roger went on persuasively, "we didn't know your wishes, and it's late in the day already. I've been up for some time; I've even begun my work. I didn't want to wake you, because—"

"Do you mean that you've been talking to every one about me?" Jeremy demanded, almost hysterically.

"You speak as though you had done something that you were ashamed of. I cannot think why you should want to hide so wonderful a matter."

Jeremy sat down on the wooden chest, unable to speak, but murmuring sullen protests in his throat. The face of the future had somehow changed since he had finished dressing; and he found himself unable to explain to Roger how important it was that his secret should be preserved, that he should slip into the strange world and lose himself with as little fuss as a raindrop disappearing in the sea. Besides, this young man was in a sort his savior and protector, to whom he owed gratitude, and on whom he certainly was dependent…. The anger which was roused in him by the placidly enquiring face opposite died away in a fit of hopelessness.

"What will happen to me then?" he muttered at last.

"You will be made much of," Roger assured him. "Crowds will flock round you to hear your story. The Speaker and all the great men of the country will wish to see you. Now come with me and eat something. Perhaps no one knows anything about you yet, I said nothing clear. You must come and eat."

"I don't want to eat," Jeremy mumbled, suffering from an intense consciousness of childish folly.

Perhaps Roger divined his feelings, for a slow, faint smile appeared on his face. "You must eat," he repeated firmly. "You are overwrought. Come with me." There was something in his serene but determined patience which drew Jeremy reluctantly after him.

The emptiness of the corridor outside did not reduce Jeremy's fears of the peopled house beyond. He dragged along a pace behind Roger, trying vainly to overcome the unwillingness in his limbs. When, as they turned a corner, a servant passed them, his heart jerked suddenly and he almost stopped. But there might have been nothing in the glance which the man threw at them. They went on. Presently they turned another corner and came to a broad staircase of shallow steps made of slippery polished wood.

When Jeremy was on the third step he saw below a group of young men, dressed like Roger and himself, engaged in desultory morning conversation. Again he almost stopped; but Roger held on, and the group below did not look up. Their voices floated lightly to him and he recognized that they were talking to pass the time. He steeled himself for self-possession and cast his eyes downward, because his footing on the polished wood was insecure.

Suddenly his ear was struck by a hush. He lifted his eyes and looked down at the young men and saw with terror that the conversation had ceased, that their faces were turned upwards, gazing at him. He returned the stare stonily, straining his eyes so that the eager features were confused and ran into a blur. The stairs became more slippery, his limbs less controllable.

Only some strange inhibition prevented him from putting out a hand to Roger for support. But Roger, still a step in front, his back self-consciously stiffened, did not see the discomfort of his charge. Somehow Jeremy finished the descent and passed the silent group without a gesture that betrayed his agitation. He fancied that one of the young men raised his eyebrows with a look at Roger, and that Roger answered him with a faint inclination of the head.

They were now in the wide passage which led to the dining-hall, and had almost reached the hall-door, when a figure which seemed vaguely familiar came into sight from the opposite direction. It was a man whose firm steps and long, raking stride, out of proportion to his moderate stature, gave him an ineffable air of confidence, of arrogance and superiority. He was staring at the ground as he walked; but when he came nearer, Jeremy was able to recognize in the lean, sharp-boned face, with the tight mouth and narrow nose, the distinguished person to whom Roger had alluded on the previous night as "that damned Canadian." He was almost level with them when he raised his head, stared keenly at Jeremy, turned his eyes to Roger, looked back again… Then with a movement almost like that of a frightened horse and with an expression of horror and dislike, he swerved abruptly to one side, crossed himself vehemently and went on at a greater pace.

Jeremy's sick surmise at the meaning of this portent was confirmed by Roger's scowl and exclamation of annoyance. Both involuntarily hesitated instead of going through the open door of the hall. At the tables inside four or five men were seated, making a late but copious meal. As Roger and Jeremy halted, a servant, dressed in a strange and splendid livery, came up behind them and touched Roger lightly on the shoulder. The young man turned round with an exaggeratedly petulant movement; and the servant, looking sideways at Jeremy, began to whisper in his ear. Jeremy, his sense of apprehension deepened, drew off a pace. He could see, as he stood there waiting, two other men, dressed in what seemed much more like a uniform than a livery, half concealed in the shadow of the further corridor.

The servant's whispering went on, a long, confused, rising and falling jumble of sound. Roger answered in a sharp staccato accent, most unlike the ordinary tranquillity of his voice, but still beneath his breath. Jeremy, with the stares of the breakfasting men on his shrinking back, felt that the situation was growing unbearable. Suddenly Roger raised and let fall his hands in a gesture of resigned annoyance.

"Then will you, sir…" the servant insisted with a deference that was plainly no more than formal.

Roger turned with unconcealed reluctance to Jeremy. "I am sorry," he said in the defensive and sullen tone of a man who expects reproach. "The Speaker has heard of you and has sent for you. I have asked that I may go with you, but I am not allowed. You must go with this man. I… am sorry…"

Jeremy faced the servant with rigid features, but with fear playing in his eyes. The man's back bent, however, in a bow and his expression betrayed a quite unfeigned respect and wonder.

"If you will come with me, sir," he murmured. Jeremy repeated Roger's gesture, and advanced a step into the darkness of the passage at the side of his conductor. He felt, rather than saw or heard, the two men in the shadow fall in behind him.

2

The way by which the servant led Jeremy grew darker and darker until he began to believe that he was being conducted into the recesses of a huge and gloomy castle. He had once or twice visited the Treasury, where one of his friends had been employed—nearly two hundred years ago!—on some minute section of the country's business. He could not, however, recognize the corridors through which they passed; and he supposed that the inside of the building had been wholly remodeled. All sensation of fear left him as he walked after his guide. His case was, at all events, to be settled now, and the matter was out of his hands. He felt a complete unconcern when they halted outside a massive door on which the servant rapped sharply three times. There was a pause; and then the servant, apparently hearing some response which was inaudible to Jeremy, threw open the door, held it, and respectfully motioned him in.

Jeremy was startled for a moment, after the darkness of the passages, to find himself in a full blaze of morning light. While he blinked awkwardly, the door closed behind him; and it was a minute or two. before he could clearly distinguish the person with whom he had been left alone. At last he became aware of a great, high-backed armchair of unpolished wood, which was placed near to the window and held the old man whom he had seen from a distance, indistinctly, the night before at dinner. This figure wore a dark robe of some thick cloth, which was drawn in loosely by a cord girdle at the waist and resembled a dressing-gown. His thick, wrinkled neck rising out of the many-folded collar supported a square, heavy head, which by its shape proclaimed power, as the face by every line proclaimed both power and age. The nose was large, hooked and fleshy, the lips thick but firm, the beard long and white; and under the heavy, raised lids the brown eyes were almost youthful, and shone with a surprising look of energy and domination. Jeremy stared without moving; and, as his eyes met those of the old man, a queer sensation invaded his spirit. He felt that here, in the owner of these eyes, this unmistakably Jewish countenance, this inert and bulky form, he had discovered a mind like his own, a mind with which he could exchange ideas, as he could never hope to do with Roger Vaile or Father Henry Dean.

The silence continued for a full minute after Jeremy had got back the use of his sight. At last the old man said in a thick, soft voice:

"Are you the young man of whom they tell me this peculiar story?" And before Jeremy could reply, he added: "Come over here and let me look at you."

Jeremy advanced, as if in a dream, and stood by the arm of the chair. The Speaker rose with one slow but powerful movement, took him by the shoulder and drew him close against the window. He was nearly a head taller than Jeremy, but he bent only his neck, not his shoulders, to stare keenly into the younger man's face. A feeling of hope and contentment rose in Jeremy's heart; and he endured this inspection for several moments in silence and with a steady countenance. At last the old man let his hand fall, turned away and breathed, more inwardly, almost wistfully: "If only it were true!"

"It is true," Jeremy said. There was neither expostulation nor argument in his voice.

The Speaker wheeled round on him with a movement astonishingly swift for his years and his bulk. "You will find me harder to persuade than the others," he said warningly.

"I know." And Jeremy bore the gaze of frowning enquiry with a curiously confident smile.

The Speaker's reply was uttered in a much gentler tone. "Come and sit down by me," he murmured, "and tell me your story."

Jeremy took a deep breath and began. He told his story in much more detail than he had given to Roger, dwelling on the riots and their causes, and on Trehanoc's experiment and his own interpretation of its effect. He did not spare particulars, both of the strikes, as well as he remembered them, and of the course of scientific investigation which had landed him in this position; and as he proceeded he warmed to the tale, and gave it as he would have done to a man of his own sort in his own time. The brown eyes continued to regard him with an unflickering expression of interest. When he paused and looked for some comment, some sign of belief or, disbelief, the thick voice murmured only:

"I understand. Go on."

Jeremy described his awakening, the terrors and doubts that had succeeded it and his eventual dismay when he was able at last to climb into the world again. He explained how he had gone back with Roger to the crevice, how they had seen the rat run out, and how he had found the vacuumtube. When he had finished, the Speaker was silent for a moment or two. Then he rose and walked slowly to a desk, which stood in the further corner of the room. He returned with an ivory tablet and a pencil which he gave into Jeremy's hands.

"Mark on that," he said, "the River Thames and the position of as many of the great railway stations of London as you can remember."

Jeremy suffered a momentary bewilderment, and stared at the intent but expressionless face of the old man, with an exclamation on his lips. But instantly he understood, and, as he did so, the map of old London rose clearly before his eyes. He drew the line of the river and contrived to mark, with reasonable accuracy, on each side of it as many of the stations as he could think of. He forgot London Bridge; and he explained that there had been a station called Cannon Street, which he had, for some reason, never had occasion to use, and that he did not know quite where it had stood.

The Speaker nodded inscrutably, took back the tablet and studied it. "Do you remember London Bridge!" he asked. Jeremy bit his lip and owned that he did. "Then can you say," the Speaker went on, "whether it was north of the river or south?"

Jeremy discovered, with a wild anger at his own idiocy, that he could not remember. It would be absurd, horribly absurd, if his credit were to be at the mercy of so unaccountable a freak of the brain. He thought at random, until suddenly there appeared before his mind a picture of the bridge, covered with ant-like crowds of people, walking in the early morning from the station beyond.

"It was on the south," he cried eagerly. "I remember because—"

The Speaker held up a wrinkled but steady hand. "Your story is true," tie said slowly. "I know very well, as you know, that nothing can prove it to be true; but nevertheless I believe it. Do you know why I believe it?"

"I think so," Jeremy began with hesitation. He felt that keen gaze closely upon him.

"It would be strange if you knew in any other way what only three or four men in the whole country have cared to learn. You could have learnt it, no doubt, from maps, or books. Such exist, though none now look at them. Yet how should you have guessed what question I would ask you? Do you know that of those stations only two remain? I know where the rest were, because I have studied the railways, wishing to restore them. But now they are all gone and most of them even before my time. They were soon gone and forgotten. When I was a boy I walked among the ruins of Victoria, just before it was cleared by my grandfather to extend his gardens. Did you go there ever when the trains were running in and out?"

The question aroused in Jeremy vivid memories of departures for holidays in Sussex, of the return to France after leave…. He replied haltingly, at random, troubled by recollections.

The same trouble was in the old man's eyes as he listened. "It is true," he said, under his breath, almost to himself. "You are an older man than I am." A long pause followed. Jeremy was the first to return from abstraction, and he was able, while the Speaker mused, to study that aged, powerful face, to read again a determination in the eyes and jaw, that might have been fanaticism had it not been corrected by the evidence of long and subduing experience in the lines round the mouth and eyes.

At last the Speaker broke the silence. "And in that life," he said, "you were a *scientist*?" He pronounced the word with a sort of lingering reverence, as though it had meant, perhaps, magician or oracle.

Jeremy tried to explain what his learning was, and what his position had been.

"But do you know how to make things?"

"I know how to make some things," Jeremy replied cautiously. Indeed, during the social disorders of his earlier existence he had considered whether there was not any useful trade to which he might turn his hand, and he had decided that he might without difficulty qualify as a plumber. The art of fixing washers on taps was no mystery to him; and he judged that in a week or two he might learn how to wipe a joint.

The Speaker regarded him with a growing interest, tempered by a caution like his own. It seemed as though it took him some time to decide upon his next remark. At last he said in a low and careful voice:

"Do you know anything about guns?"

Jeremy started and answered loudly and cheerfully: "Guns? Why, I was in the artillery!"

The effect of this reply on the Speaker was remarkable. For a moment it straightened his back, smoothed the wrinkles from his face, and threw an even more vivid light into his eyes. When he spoke again, he had recovered his self-possession.

"You were in the artillery?" he asked. "Do you mean in the great war against the Germans?"

"Yes—the great war that was over just before the Troubles began."

"Of course… of course… I had not realized—" It seemed to Jeremy that, though the old man had regained control of himself, this discovery had filled him with an inexplicable vivacity and excitement. He pressed Jeremy eagerly for an account of his military experience. When the simple tale was done, he said impressively:

"If you wish me to be your friend, say not one word of this to any man you meet. Do you understand? There is to be no talk of guns. If you disobey me, I can have you put in a madhouse."

Jeremy lifted his head in momentary anger at the threat. But there was an earnestness of feeling in the old man's face which silenced him. This, he still queerly felt, was his like, his brother, marooned with him in a strange age. He could not understand, but instinctively he acquiesced. "I promise," he said.

"I will tell you more another day," the Speaker assured him. And then, with an abrupt transition, he went on, "Do you understand these times?"

"Father Henry Dean—" Jeremy began.

"Ah, that old man!" the Speaker cried impatiently. "He lives in the past. And was it not his nephew, Roger Vaile, that brought you here?" Jeremy made a gesture of assent. "Like all his kind, he lives in the present. What must they not have told you between them? Understand, young man, that you are my man, that you must listen to none, take advice from none, obey none but me!" He had risen from his chair and was parading his great body about the room, as though he had been galvanized by excitement into an unnatural youth. His soft, thick voice had become hoarse and raucous: his heavy eyelids seemed lightened and transfigured by the blazing of his eyes.

Jeremy, straight from a century in which display of the passions was deprecated, shrank from this exhibition while he sought to understand it.

"If I can help you—" he murmured feebly.

"You *can* help me," the Speaker said, "but you shall learn how another day. You shall understand how it is that you seem to have been sent by Heaven just at this moment. But now, tell me what do you think of these times?"

"I don't know," Jeremy began uncertainly. "I know so little. You seem to have lost almost all that we had gained—"

"And yet?" the Speaker interrupted harshly.

Jeremy sought to order in his mind the confused and contradictory thoughts. "And yet perhaps you have lost much that is better gone. This world seems to me simpler, more peaceful, safer… We used to feel that we were living on the edge of a precipice—every man by himself, and all men together, lived in anxiety…."

"And you think that now we are happy?" the old man asked with a certain irony, pausing close to Jeremy's chair, so that he towered over him. "Perhaps you are right—perhaps you are right…. But if we are it is the happiness of a race of fools. We, too, are living on the edge of a precipice as terrible as any you ever knew. Do you believe that any people can come down one step from the apex and fall no further?" He contemplated Jeremy with eyes suddenly grown cold and calculating. "You were not, I think, one of the great men, one of the rulers of your time. You were one of the little people." He turned away and resumed his agitated pacing up and down, speaking as though to himself. "And yet what does it matter? The smallest creature of those days might be a great man to-day."

A profound and dreadful silence fell upon the room. Jeremy, feeling himself plunged again in a nightmare, straightened himself in his chair and waited events. The Speaker struggled with his agitation, striding up and down the room. Gradually his step grew more tranquil and his gestures less violent; his eyes ceased to blaze, the lids drooped over them, the lines round his mouth softened and lost their look of cruel purpose.

"I am an old man," he murmured indistinctly. His voice was again thick and soft, the voice of an elderly Jew, begging for help but determined, even in extremity, not to betray himself. "I am an old man and I have no son. These people, the people of my time, do not understand me. When my father died, I promised myself that I would raise this country again to what it was, but year after year they have defeated me with their carelessness, their indolence… If you can help me, if you understand *guns*… if you can help me, I shall be grateful, I shall not forget you."

Jeremy, perplexed almost out of his wits, muttered an inarticulate reply.

"You must be my guest and my companion," the Speaker went on. "I will give orders for a room near my own apartments to be prepared for you, and you shall eat at my table. And you must learn. You must listen, listen, listen always and never speak. I will teach you myself; but you must learn from every man that comes near you. Can you keep your tongue still?"

"I suppose so," said Jeremy, a little wearily. He was beginning to think that this old man was possibly mad and certainly as incomprehensible as the rest. He was oppressed by these hints and mysteries and enigmatic injunctions. He thought that the Speaker was absurdly, unreasonably, melodramatically, making a scene.

A change of expression flickered over the Speaker's face. "I have no son," he breathed, as though to himself, but with eyes, in which there was a look of cunning, fixed on Jeremy. And then he said aloud, "Well, then, you are my friend and you shall be well treated here. Now you must come with me and I will present you to my wife... and... my daughter."

3

In the sensations of that morning the last thing that troubled Jeremy was to find himself carrying on a familiar conversation with a prince. He accepted it as natural that his accident should have made him important; and he conducted himself without discomfort in an interview which might otherwise have embarrassed and puzzled him—for he was self-conscious and awkward in the presence of those who might expect deference from him. He was first recalled to the strangeness of the position by the Speaker's eager informality.

It was true that he was unacquainted with the habits of courts in any century. And yet should not the Speaker have called a servant or perhaps even a high official, instead of thus laying his own hand on the door and beckoning his guest to follow? Jeremy failed for a moment to obey the gesture, standing legs apart, considering with a frown the old man before him. It *was* nothing but an elderly Jew, by turns arrogant and supplicating, moved perhaps a little over the edge of sanity by his great age and by disappointed ambitions.

Then he started, recovered his wits and followed the crooked finger. They went out into the passage together. As they came into the gloom the old man suddenly put his arm round Jeremy's shoulders and, stooping a little to his ear, murmured in a manner and with an accent more than ever plainly of the East:

"My son, my son, be my friend and I will be yours. And you must be a little respectful to the Lady Burney, my wife. She will think it strange that I bring you to her without ceremony. She is younger than I am, and different from me, different from you. She is like the rest. But I do nothing without reason…"

Jeremy stiffened involuntarily under the almost fawning caress and muttered what he supposed to be a sufficient answer. The old man withdrew his arm and straightened his bent back; and they continued their way together in silence.

Presently they came into a broader and lighter corridor, the windows of which opened on to a garden. Jeremy recognized it as the garden he had seen from his room the evening before, and, looking aside as they passed, he caught a glimpse of a party of young men, busy at some game with balls and mallets—a kind of croquet, he imagined. They went on a few paces, and a servant, springing up from a chair in a niche, stood in a respectful attitude until they had gone by. At last the Speaker led the way into a small room where a girl sat at a table, languidly playing with a piece of needlework.

She, too, sprang to her feet when she saw who it was that had entered; and Jeremy looked at her keenly. This was the first woman he had seen at close quarters since his awakening, and he was curious to find he hardly knew what change or difference. She was short and slender and apparently very young. Her dress was simple in line, a straight garment which left the neck bare, but came up close to it and fell thence directly to her heels, hardly gathered in at all by a belt at the waist. Its gray linen was covered from the collar to the belt by an intricate and rather displeasing design of embroidery, while broad bands of the same pattern continued downward to the hem of the long skirt. Her hair was plaited and coiled, tightly and severely, round her head. Her attitude was one of submission, almost of humility, with eyes ostentatiously cast down; but Jeremy fancied that he could see a trace of slyness at the corners of her mouth.

"Is your mistress up, my child?" the Speaker asked In a tone of indifferent benevolence.

"I believe so, sir," the girl answered.

"Then tell her that I wish to present to her the stranger of whom she has heard."

She bowed and turned, not replying, to a further door; but as she turned she raised her eyes and fixed them on Jeremy with a frank, almost insolent stare. Then, without pausing, she was gone. The Speaker slipped into the chair she had left and drummed absently with his fingers on the table. When the girl returned he paid hardly any attention to her message that the Lady Burney was ready to receive them. A fit of abstraction seemed to have settled down on him; and he impatiently waved her on one side, while he drew Jeremy in his train.

Jeremy was doubtful how he ought to show his respect to the stout and ugly woman who sat on her couch in this room with an air of bovine dissatisfaction. He bowed very low and did not, apparently, increase her displeasure. She held out two fingers to him, a perplexing action; but it seemed from the stiffness of her arm that she did not expect him to kiss them. He shook and dropped them awkwardly and breathed a sigh of relief. Then he was able to examine the first lady of England and her surroundings, while, with much less interest and an expression of stupid aloofness, she examined him.

She was dressed in the same manner as the girl who waited in the anteroom, though her gown seemed to be of silk, and was much more richly as well as more garishly embroidered. It struck Jeremy that she harmonized well with the room in which she sat. It was filled with ornaments, cushions, mats and woven hangings of a coarse and gaudy vulgarity; and the woodwork on the walls was carved and gilded in the style of a florid picture-frame. The occupant of this tawdry magnificence was stout, and her unwieldy figure was disagreeably displayed by what seemed to be the prevailing fashion of dress. Her cheeks were at once puffy and lined and were too brilliantly painted; and the lashes of her dull, heavy eyes were extravagantly blackened. Jeremy hoped that his attitude, while he noted all these details, was sufficiently respectful.

It must have satisfied the Lady Burney, for, after a long pause, she observed in a gracious manner:

"I was anxious to see you. Why do you look like everyone else? I thought your clothes would have been different."

Jeremy explained that he had been clothed anew so that he should not appear too conspicuous. She assented with a movement of her head and went on:

"It would have been more interesting to see you in your old clothes. Do you—do you—" She yawned widely and gazed round the room with vague eyes, as though looking for the rest of her question. "Do you find us much changed?" she finished at last.

"Very much changed, madam," Jeremy replied with, gravity. "So much changed that I should hardly know how to begin to tell you what the changes are."

She inclined her head again, as though to indicate that her thirst for knowledge was satisfied. At this point the Speaker, who had been standing behind Jeremy, silent but tapping his foot on the ground, broke in abruptly.

"Where is Eva?" he said.

The lady looked at him with a corpulent parody of reserve. "She has just come in from riding. Shall I send for her?" The Speaker nodded, and then seemed to wave away a question in her eyes. She turned to Jeremy and murmured, "The bell is over there."

Jeremy stared at her a moment, puzzled; then, following the direction of her finger, saw hanging on the wall an old-fashioned bell-pull. Recovering himself a little he went to it, tugged at it gingerly, and so summoned the girl who sat in the ante-room. When she came in he saw again on her face the same look of frank but unimpressed curiosity. But she received her orders still with downcast and submissive eyes and departed in silence.

Then a door at the other end of the room opened abruptly and gustily inwards. Jeremy looked towards it with interest, saw nothing but a hand still holding it, and, dimly, a figure in the opening turned away from it. He heard a fresh, cheerful voice giving some parting directions to an invisible person. The blood rose suddenly to his head and he began to be confused. He waited in almost an agony of suspense for the Speaker's daughter to turn and enter the room.

He had indeed experienced disturbing premonitions of this sort before. Now and again it had happened in the life of his own lecture-rooms and of his friends' studios, that, without reason, he wondered why he had been so immune from serious love-sickness. Now and again, like a child with a penny to spend, he would take his bachelor state out of some pocket in his thoughts, turn it over lovingly, and ask himself what he should do with it. He had indeed a great fear of spending it rashly; but often, after one of these moods, the mention of an unknown girl he was to meet would set his heart throbbing, or he would look at one of his pupils or one of his friends with a new and faintly pleasant speculation in his mind. Yet there had never been anything in it. He had had one flirtation over test-tubes and balances, ended by his timely discovery of the girl's pretentious ignorance in the matter of physics. He would not have minded her being ignorant, but he was repelled when he thought that she had baited a trap for him with a show of knowledge. There had been another over canvases and brushes. But he had not been able to talk with enough warmth about the fashions of art; and, before he had made much progress, the girl had found another lover more glib than he—which was, he reflected, when he was better of his infatuation and considered the kind of picture she painted, something of a deliverance. Now his heart was absurdly beating at the approach of a princess—of a princess who was nearly two hundred years younger than himself!

She turned and came into the room, stopping a few paces inside and staring at him as frankly as he at her. She must have seen in him at that moment what we see in the house where a great man was born—a house that would be precisely like other houses if we knew nothing about it.

Or did her defeated curiosity wake in her even then extraordinary thoughts about this ordinary young man? Jeremy's mind had become too much a stage set for a great event for him to get any clear view of the reality. But he received an impression, ridiculously, as though the fine, blowing, temperate, sunshiny day he had seen through the windows had come suddenly into his presence. And, though this tall, straight-backed girl, with her wide, frank eyes and all the beauty of health and youth, had plainly her mother's features, distinguished only by a long difference of years, he guessed somehow in her expression, in her pose, something of the father's intelligence.

The pause in which they had regarded one another lasted hardly ten seconds. "I wanted so much to see you," she cried impulsively. "My maids have told me all about you, and when I was out riding—" She stopped.

The Lady Burney frowned, and the Speaker asked in a slow, dragging voice, as though constraining himself to be gentle, "Whom did you meet when you were out riding?"

"Roger Vaile," the girl answered, with a faint tone of annoyed defiance. "And he told me how he came to find this gentleman yesterday."

"I am very much in his debt," Jeremy said. "I suppose he saved my life."

"You should not be too grateful to him," the Speaker interposed, in a manner almost too suave. "Any man that found you must have done what he did. You are not to exaggerate your debt to him."

The girl laughed, and suppressed her laughter, and again the Lady Burney frowned. Jeremy, scenting the approach of a family quarrel and unwilling to witness it, spoke quickly and at random in the hope of relieving the situation: "I hope, sir, you will allow me to be grateful to Mr. Vaile, who was, after all, my preserver, and treated me kindly."

The girl laughed again, but with a different intention. "Mister?" she repeated. "What does that mean?"

Jeremy looked at her, puzzled. "Don't you call people Mister now?" He addressed himself directly to her and abandoned his attempt to embrace in the conversation the Speaker, who was trying to conceal some mysteriously caused impatience, and the Lady Burney, who was not trying at all to conceal her petulant but flaccid displeasure.

"No," said the girl, equally ignoring them. "We call Roger Vaile so because he is a gentleman. If he were a common man we should simply call him Vaile. Did you call gentlemen—what was it?—Mister, in your time?" Jeremy, studying her, admiring the poise with which she stood and noting that, though she wore the narrow, simply-cut gown of the rest, it was less tortured with embroidery, strove to find some way of carrying on the conversation and suddenly became aware that there was some silent but acute difference between the Speaker and his wife.

"Eva!" the Lady Burney broke in, disregarding her husband's hand half raised in warning. "Eva," she repeated with an air of corpulent and feeble stateliness, "I am fed up with your behavior!"

Jeremy started at the phrase as much as if the stupid, dignified woman had suddenly thrown a double somersault before him. But he could see no surprise on the faces of the others, only unconcealed annoyance and alarm.

"You may go, Eva," the Speaker interposed with evident restraint. "Jeremy Tuft is to be our guest, and you will see him again. He has much to learn, and you must help us to teach him."

The girl, as though some hidden circumstance had been brought into play, instantly composed her face and bowed deeply and ceremoniously to Jeremy. He returned the bow as well as he was able, and had hardly straightened himself again before she had left the room.

"I am fed up with our daughter's behavior," the Lady Burney repeated, rising. "I will go now and speak to her alone." Then she too vanished, ignoring alike her husband's half-begun remonstrance and Jeremy's second bow.

It was with some amazement that Jeremy found himself alone again with the old man. His brain staggered under a multitude of impressions. The astonishing locution employed by the great lady had been hardly respectable in his own day, and it led him to consider the strange, pleasant accent which had struck him in Roger Vaile's first speech and which was so general that already his ear accepted it as unremarkable. Was it, could it be, an amazing sublimation of the West Essex accent, which in an earlier time had been known as Cockney? Then his eye fell on the silent, now drooping figure of the Speaker, and recalled him to the odd under-currents of the family scene he had just beheld.

"My wife comes from the west," said the Speaker in a quiet, tired voice, catching his glance, "and sometimes she uses old-fashioned expressions that maybe you would not understand… or perhaps they are familiar to you…. But tell me, how would a father of your time have punished Eva for her behavior?"

"I don't know," Jeremy answered uncomfortably. "I don't know what she did that was wrong."

The Speaker smiled a little sadly. "Like me, she is… is unusual. She should not have addressed you first or taken the lead so much in speaking to you. I fear any other parent would have her whipped. But I—" his voice grew a little louder, "but I have allowed her to be brought up differently. She can read and write. She is different from the rest, like me… and like you. I have studied to let her be so… though she hardly thinks it… and I daresay I have not done all I should. I have been busy with other things and between the old and the young… I was already old when she was born— but now you…" His voice trailed away into silence, and he considered Jeremy with full, expressionless eyes. At last he said, "Come with me and I will make arrangements for your reception here. In a few days I shall have something to show you and I shall ask your help." Jeremy followed, his mind still busy. His absurd premonitions had been driven away by tangled speculations on all these changes in manners and language.

CHAPTER VI
The Guns

1

DURING THE DAYS THAT immediately followed, the Speaker left Jeremy to make himself at home as best he could in the new world. For a time Jeremy was inclined to fear that by a single obstinacy he had forfeited the old man's favor. He had been removed from the little room which he had first occupied to another, larger and more splendidly furnished, near the Speaker's own apartments. But he had pleaded, with a rather obvious confidence in his right to insist, that he should be allowed to continue his friendship with Roger Vaile. Some obscure loyalty combined with his native self-will to harden him in this desire; and the Speaker was displeased by it. He had evidently had some other companion and instructor in mind.

"The young man is brainless, like all his kind," he objected. "You will get no good from him."

"But he did save my life. Why would he think of me if I forgot him now?"

"No man could have done less for you than he did. You ought not to let that influence you."

The wrangle was short but too rapidly grew bitter. To end it Jeremy cried with a gesture of half-humorous despair, "Well, at least he is my oldest living friend."

The Speaker shrugged his shoulders and gave way without a smile; but he seemed from this moment to have abandoned him to the company he thus wilfully chose. For the better part of a day Jeremy was pleased by his deliverance from a dangerous and uncomfortable old fanatic. Thereafter he fell to wondering, with growing intensity, what were now his chances of meeting again with the Speaker's daughter.

When he rejoined Roger Vaile, that placid young man received him without excitement, and informed him that they might spend the next few days in seeing the sights of London. Jeremy's great curiosity answered this suggestion with delight; and in his earliest explorations with Roger he found many surprises within a small radius. The first were in the great gardens of the Treasury, which, so far as he could make out, in the absence of most of the familiar landmarks, took in all St. James's Park, as well as what had been the sites of Buckingham Palace and Victoria Station. Certainly, as he rambled among them, he came upon the ruins of the Victoria Memorial, much battered and weathered, and so changed in aspect by time and by the shrubs which grew close around it that for several moments it escaped his recognition.

Outside the walls of the Treasury such discoveries were innumerable. Jeremy was astonished to find alternately how much and how little he remembered of London, how much and how little had survived. Westminster Bridge, looking old and shaky, still stood; but the Embankment was getting to be disused, chiefly on account of a great breach in it, how caused Roger could not tell him, in the neighborhood of Charing Cross. On both sides of this breach the great men who owned houses in Whitehall and the Strand were beginning to push their gardens down to the water's edge. Indeed, as Jeremy learnt by his own observation and by close questioning of Roger, the growth of huge gardens was one of the conspicuous signs of the age.

There existed, it seemed, an aristocracy of some wealth descended mostly from those supporters of the first and second Speakers who had taken their part in putting down the Reds and restoring order more than a hundred years before. Where one of the old ruling families, great landowners, great manufacturers, or great financiers had possessed a member of resolute and combative disposition, it had survived to resume its place in the new state. The rest were descendants of obscure soldiers of fortune. This class, of which Roger Vaile was an inconsiderable cadet, owned vast estates in some, though not in all, parts of the country. Here and there, as Jeremy surmised, where small-holders and market-gardeners had taken a firm grip, the landowning class had little power. But elsewhere it was strong, and drew great revenues from the soil, from corn, from tobacco, and from wool.

These revenues were spent by the ruling families—Roger called them "the big men"—in enlarging the gardens of their houses in London. They cared little to build. Houses stood in plenty, many even now unclaimed. But gradually the deserted houses were pulled down, their materials carted away and their sites elaborately planted. Jeremy walked in a great shrubbery of rhododendrons where Charing Cross Station had been and in a rose-garden over the deep-buried foundations of Scotland Yard. He observed that this fashion, which was becoming a mania, was creating again the old distinction between the City of London, which was still a trading center, and the City of Westminster, which was still the seat of government, although a revolutionary mob of somewhat doctrinaire inclinations had burnt down the Houses of Parliament quite early in the Troubles.

These excursions fascinated Jeremy, and he endeavored to make them useful by cross-examining Roger, as they walked about together, on the condition of society. But that typical man of far from self-conscious age had only scanty information to give. Even on the government of the country he was vague and unsatisfactory, though, when he had nothing better to do, he worked with the other clerks on the Speaker's business. Jeremy sometimes saw him and his companions at work, copying documents in a laborious round-hand or making entries in a great leather-bound and padlocked ledger. He felt often inclined to re-introduce into a profession which had forgotten it the blessed principle of the card index; but, after consideration, he abstained from complicating this idyllically simple bureaucracy. Besides, there was no need for labor-saving devices. Clerks swarmed in the Treasury. A few years in the Speaker's service was the proper occupation for a young man of good family who was beginning life; and the tasks which it involved weighed on them lightly.

The business of government was not elaborate or complex. Apparently the provinces looked very much after themselves under the direction of a medley of authorities, whose titles and powers Jeremy could by no means compose into a system. He heard vaguely of two potentates, prominent among the rest and typical of them, the Chairman of Bradford, who seemed responsible for a great part of the north, and the President of Wales, who had a palace at Cardiff. Jeremy guessed that the titles of these "big men" had survived from all sorts of "big men" of his own time. The Chairman of Bradford for example might inherit his power from the chairman of some vanished revolutionary or reactionary committee, or perhaps even, since he was concerned in a peculiar way with the great weaving trade of Yorkshire, from that of an employers' federation or a conciliation board. The President of Wales, whose relations with his tough, savage, uncouth miners were unusual, Jeremy suspected of being the successor of a trade union leader. The names and figures of these men lingered obscurely, powerfully, menacingly in his mind. The Speaker rarely interfered with them so long as they collected his taxes regularly and with an approach to completeness. And his taxes were moderate, for the public services were not exigent.

Jeremy caught a glimpse of one of these public services one day when Roger was taking him on a longer expedition than usual, to see the great northwestern quarter of old London. This district was one of the largest of those which, by some freak of chance, had escaped fire and bombardment and had been merely deserted, left to rot and collapse as they stood. Jeremy was anxious to examine this curiosity, and pressed Roger to take him there. It was when they were walking between the venerable and dangerously leaning buildings of Regent Street that they passed a column of brown-clad men on the march.

"Soldiers!" cried Jeremy, and paused to watch them go by.

"Yes, soldiers," Roger murmured with a smile of good-natured contempt, trying to draw him along. But Jeremy's curiosity had been aroused. He suddenly remembered, and then closed his lips on an enigmatical remark which the Speaker had made about guns; and he insisted on staying where he was until the regiment had gone out of sight. Their uniforms, an approximation to khaki, yet of a different shade, their rifles, clumsy and antiquated in appearance, their feet wrapped in rags and shod with raw-hide sandals, combined with their shambling, half-ashamed, half-sulky carriage to give them the air of a parody on the infantry of the Great War.

"Whom do they fight?" he asked abstractedly, still standing and gazing after them.

"No one," Roger answered, with the same expression of contemptuous tolerance. "They are good for nothing; there has been no war in England for a hundred years."

"But are there no foreign wars?"

"None that concern us." And Roger went on to explain in an uninterested and scrappy manner that there was always fighting somewhere on the Continent, that the Germans and the Russians and the Polish were forever at one another's throats, that the Italians could not live at peace with one another or with their neighbors on the Adriatic, and that the peoples of Eastern Europe seemed bent on mutual extermination. "But we never interfere," he said. "It isn't our business, though sometimes the League tries to make out that it is. And we need no army. It's a fad of the Speaker's, though he could always get Canadians if he wanted them."

"The League? Canadians?" Jeremy interjected.

"Yes; the Canadian bosses hire out armies when any one wants them. They do say that that ruffian who is staying with the Speaker came over for some such reason. But I can't see why we should want Canadians."

"But you said… something… the League?"

"Oh, the old League!" Roger answered carelessly. "Surely that existed in your time, didn't it? I mean the League of Nations." And, as Jeremy said nothing, he continued: "You know, they sit at Geneva and tell every one how to manage his own affairs. We take no notice of them, except that we send them a contribution every year. And I don't know why we should do even that. The officials are always all Germans… so close, you know…"

Jeremy fell into a profound reverie, out of which he presently emerged to ask, "Does your army have any guns… cannon, I mean?"

Roger shook his head. "You mean the sort of big gun that used to throw exploding shells. No; I don't believe there's such a thing left in the world. I never, heard of one."

In order to draw Jeremy away from his meditations in Regent Street, Roger had taken him by the elbow, and from that had slipped his arm into Jeremy's own. They walked along together in an amicable silence. Unexpected and violent events had drawn these two young men into a friendship which otherwise they would never have chosen, but which was perhaps not more arbitrary and not less real than the love of the mother for the child. Though their minds were so dissimilar, yet Jeremy felt a sort of confidence and familiarity in Roger's presence; and Roger took a queer pride in Jeremy's existence.

The district into which they entered when they got beyond the wilderness that had been Regent's Park was a singular and striking reminder of the time when London was a great and populous city. Every stage of desolation and decay was to be seen in that appalling tract, which had lost the trimness and prosperity of its flourishing period without acquiring the solemn and awful aspect of nobler ruins. Every scrap of wood and metal had long been torn from these slowly perishing houses. Some had collapsed into their own cellars and were gradually being covered over. Some, which had been built of less enduring bricks, seemed merely to have melted, leaving only faint irregularities on the surface of the ground. Others stood gaunt and crazily leaning, with ragged staring gaps where the windows had been. Even as they passed one of these they heard the resounding collapse of a wall they could not see, while the outer walls heaved visibly nearer to ruin.

And here and there enterprising squatters had cleared large spaces, joining up the old villa-gardens into fair-sized fields. These people lived in rude huts, made of old timbers and rough heaps of brickwork, in corners of their clearings. Some distaste or horror seemed to keep them from the empty houses in the shadow of which they dwelt. Jeremy saw in the fields bowed laborious figures wrapped in rags which forbade him to say whether they were men or women, and troops of dirty, half-naked children. Roger followed the direction of his glance and said that the squatters among the deserted houses were people little better than savages, who could not get work in the agricultural districts or had mutinously deserted their proper employers.

Jeremy shuddered and went on without replying. The plan of these old streets was still recognizable enough for him to lead the way, as if in a dream, through St. John's Wood to Swiss Cottage. Here they had to scramble across a tumbled ravine, which was all that was left of the Metropolitan

Railway, and up the steep rise of FitzJohn's Avenue to the little village of Hampstead clinging isolated on the edge of the hill. As they came into the village, Jeremy drew Roger into a side-track which he recognized, from one drooping Georgian house standing lonely there, as what he had known under the name of Church Row. The church remained, and beyond it Jeremy could see a farm half-hidden among trees. But he went no further. He turned his face abruptly southwards and stayed, gazing across London in that moment of perfect clearness which sometimes precedes the twilight of early summer.

For a moment, what he saw seemed to be what he had always known. At this distance the slope below seemed still to be covered with houses, and showed none of the hideousness of their decay. Farther out, in the valley, rose the spires and towers of innumerable churches, and beyond them came the faint blue line of the Surrey hills. But as he gazed he realized suddenly the greater purity of the air, the greater beauty of the view. London blackened no longer all the heaven above it, and the green gaps in the waste of buildings were larger and greener. Almost he thought he saw a silver line where the Thames should have been; but perhaps he imagined this, though he knew that the river was no longer dark and foul.

In his joy and contentment at the lovely scene he began to speak to Roger in a rapt, dreamy voice, as though he were indeed the mouthpiece and messenger of a less fortunate time. "You are happier than we were," he said, "though you are poorer. Your air is clean, you have room, you live at peace, you have time to live. But we were forced to live in thick, smoky air; we fought and quarreled, and disputed. The more difficult our lives became, the less time we had for them. This age seems to me," he continued, warming to his subject and ignoring Roger's placid silence, "like a man who has been walking at full speed on a long dusty road, only trying to see how many miles he can cover in a day. Suddenly he grows exhausted and stops. I have done it. I can remember how delicious it was to lie down in a field off the road, to let the business all go, not to care where one got to or when. It was this peacefulness we should have been aiming at all the time, only we never knew…." Roger's silence at last stopped him, and he turned to see what his companion was thinking. The expression of trouble on Roger's face brought up a question on his own.

"It has just occurred to me," Roger said slowly and reluctantly, "that it will be quite dark before we can get through all those houses...." He paused and shivered slightly. "I don't quite like..."

They set off homewards, and darkness overtook them in the middle of Finchley Road. Roger did not speak again of his fears. Jeremy could not determine whether they were of violent men or of dead men. But he felt their presence. Roger, hardly spoke or listened until they were once again in inhabited streets.

It was on the following morning that the Speaker again sent for Jeremy.

2

Jeremy answered the second summons with a little excitement but with a heart more at rest than on the first occasion. He found the Speaker leaning at his open window, his head thrust out, his foot tapping restlessly on the ground. It was some moments before the abstracted old man would take any notice of his visitor. When he did so, he turned round with an air of restless and forced geniality.

"Well, Jeremy Tuft," he cried, rubbing his hands together, "and have you learnt much from your friend?"

Jeremy replied stolidly that Roger had answered one way or another all the questions he had had time to ask. Some instinct kept him to his not very candid stubbornness. He was not going to be bullied into deserting Roger, of whose intellectual gifts he had nevertheless no very high opinion.

But the Speaker nodded without apparent displeasure. "And now you know all about our affairs?" he enquired.

Jeremy, still stolidly, shook his head but made no other answer. The Speaker suddenly changed his manner and, coming close to Jeremy, took him caressingly by the arm. "I know you don't," he murmured in a voice full of cajolery. "But tell me—you must have seen enough of our people—what do you think of them? What do you think can be done with them?" He leant slightly back and regarded the silent young man with an expression of infinite cunning. Then, as he got no response, he went on: "Tell me, what would you do if you were in my place—you, a man rich with all the knowledge of a wiser time than this? How would you begin to make things better?"

"I don't know... I don't know..." Jeremy cried at last, almost pathetically. "I can't make these people out at all." And, with that, he felt restored in his mind the former consciousness of an intellectual kinship between him and the old Jew.

But the Speaker continued with his irritating air of a ripe man teasing a green boy. "You remember the time when the whole world was full of the marvels of science. We suffered misfortune, and all the wise men, all the scientists, perished. But by a miracle you have survived. Can you not restore for us all the civilization of your own age?"

Jeremy frowned and answered hesitatingly. "How can I? What could I do by myself? And anyway, I was only a physicist. I know something about wireless telegraphy.... But then I could do nothing without materials, and at best precious little single-handed." He meditated explaining just how much one man could know of the working of twentieth-century machinery, opened his mouth again and then closed it. He strongly suspected that the Speaker was merely fencing with him. He felt vaguely irritated and alone.

The old man dropped Jeremy's arm, spun his great bulk round on his heel with surprising lightness and paced away to the other end of the room. There he stood apparently gazing with intent eyes into a little mirror which hung on the wall. Jeremy stayed where he had been left, forlorn, perplexed, hopeless, staring with no expectation of an answer at those huge, bowed, enigmatic shoulders. He was almost at the point of screaming aloud when the Speaker turned and said seriously with great deliberation:

"Well, I am going to show you something that you have not seen, something that not more than twenty persons know of besides myself. And you are going to see it because I trust you to be loyal to me, to be my man. Do you understand?" He did not wait for Jeremy's doubtful nod, but abruptly jerked the bell-pull on the wall. When this was done they waited together in silence. A servant answered the summons; and the Speaker said: "My carriage." The carriage was announced. The silence continued unbroken while they settled themselves in it, in the little enclosed courtyard that had once been Downing Street. It was not until they were jolting over the ruts of Whitehall that Jeremy said, almost timidly:

"Where are we going?"

"To Waterloo," the Speaker answered, so brusquely that Jeremy was deterred from asking more, and leant back by his companion to muster what patience he could.

He had already been to Waterloo under Roger's guidance. It was the station for the few lines of railway that still served the south of England; and they had gone there to see the train come in from Dover. But it had been so late that Roger had refused to wait any longer for it, though Jeremy had been anxious to do so. They had seen nothing but an empty station, dusty and silent. At one platform an engine had stood useless so long that its wheels seemed to have been rusted fast to the metals. Close by a careless or unfortunate driver had charged the buffers at full speed and crashed into the masonry beyond. The bricks were torn up and piled in heaps; but the raw edges were long weathered, and some of them were beginning to be covered with moss. The old glass roof, which he remembered, was gone and the whole station lay open to the sky. Pools from a recent shower glistened underfoot. Here and there a workmen sat idle and yawning on a bench or lay fast asleep on a pile of sacks.

This picture returned vividly to Jeremy as he rode by the Speaker's side. It seemed to him the fit symbol of an age which had loosened its grip on civilization, which cared no longer to mend what time or chance had broken, which did not care even to put a new roof over Waterloo Station. He reflected again, as he thought of it, that perhaps it did not much matter, that the grip on civilization had been painfully hard to maintain, that there was something to be said for sleeping on a pile of sacks in a sound part of the station instead of repairing some other part of it. "We wretched ants," he told himself, "piled up more stuff than we could use, and though the mad people of the Troubles wasted it, yet the ruins are enough for this race to live in for centuries. And aren't they more sensible than we were? Why shouldn't humanity retire from business on its savings? If only it had done it before it got that nervous breakdown from overwork!"

He was aroused by the carriage lurching into the uneven slope of the approach. The squalor that had once surrounded the great terminus had withered, like the buildings of the station itself, into a sort of mitigated and quiescent ugliness. As, at the Speaker's gesture, he descended from the carriage, he saw a young tree pushing itself with serene and graceful indifference through the tumbled ruins of what had once been an unlovely lodging-house. A hot sun beat down on and was gradually dispelling a thin morning haze. It gilded palely the gaunt, harsh lines of the station that generations of weathering could never make beautiful.

The Speaker, still resolutely silent, led the way inside, where their steps echoed hollowly in the empty hall. But the echoes were suddenly disturbed by another sound; and, as they turned a corner Jeremy was enchanted to see a long train crawling slowly into the platform. It slackened speed, blew off steam with appalling abruptness and force, and came to a standstill before it had completely pulled in. Jeremy could see two little figures leaping from the cab of the engine and running about aimlessly on the platform, half hidden by the still belching clouds of steam.

"Another breakdown!" the Speaker grunted with sudden ferocity; and he turned his face slightly to one side as though it pained him to see the crippled engine. Jeremy would have liked to go closer, but dared not suggest it. Instead he dragged, like a loitering child, a yard or two behind his formidable companion and gazed eagerly at the distant wreaths of steam. But he only caught a glimpse of a few passengers sitting patiently on heaps of luggage or on the ground, as though they were well used to such delays in embarkation. He ran after his guide, who had now passed the disused locomotive rusted to the rails, and was striding along the platform and down the slope at the end, into a wilderness of crossing metals. Here and there in this desert could be seen a track bright with recent use; but it was long since many of them had known the passage of a train. In some cases only streaks of red in the earth or sleepers almost rotted to nothing showed where the line had been. They passed a signal-box: a man sat placidly smoking at the top of the steps outside the open door. They went on further; into the desolation that surrounds a great station, here made more horrible by the absence of movement, by the pervading air of ruin and decay.

When they had walked a few hundred yards from the end of the platform, they came to a group of buildings, which, in spite of their dilapidation, had about them a certain appearance of still being used. "The repairing sheds," said the Speaker, pointing through an open door to a group of men languidly active round what looked like a small shunting-engine. Then he entered a narrow passage between two buildings.

As they went down this defile, a noise of hammering and another noise like that of a furnace grew louder and louder; and at the end of the passage there was a closed door. The Speaker paused and looked at Jeremy with a doubtful expression, as though for the last time weighing his loyalty. Then he seized a hanging chain and pulled it vigorously. A bell clanged, harsh and melancholy, inside the building. Before the last grudging echoes had died away, there was a rattling of bolts and bars, and the door was opened to the extent of about a foot. An old man in baggy, blue overalls, with dirty, white hair, and a short, white beard, stood in the opening, blinking suspiciously at the intruders.

He stood thus a minute in a hostile attitude, ready to leap back and slam the door to again. But all at once his expression changed, he shouted something over his shoulder and became exceedingly respectful. As Jeremy followed the Speaker past him into the black interior of the shed he bowed and muttered a thick incoherent welcome in a tongue which was hardly recognizable as English, so strange were its broad and drawling sounds.

Inside, huge shapes of machinery were confused with thick shadows, which jerked spasmodically at the light from an open furnace. It was some moments before Jeremy got the proper use of his eyes in the murky air of the shed. When he did he received an extraordinary impression. A group of old men, all in the same baggy blue overalls as the first who opened the door, had turned to greet them and were bowing and shuffling in an irregular and comical rhythm. Round the walls the obscure pieces of mechanism resolved themselves into all the appurtenances of a foundry, hammers, lathes and machines for making castings, in every stage of neglect and disrepair, some covered with dust, some immovably rusted, some tilted drunkenly on their foundation plates, some still apparently capable of use. And behind the gang of old men, raised on trestles in the middle of the floor, were two long and sinister tubes of iron.

The Speaker stood on one side, fixing on Jeremy a look of keen and exultant enquiry. Jeremy advanced towards the two tubes, a word rising to his tongue. He had not taken two steps before he was certain.

"Guns!" he whispered in a tense and startled voice.

"Guns!" replied the Speaker, not repressing an accent of triumph.

Jeremy went on and the old men shuffled on one side to make way for him, clucking with mingled agitation and pride. He examined the guns with the eye of an expert, ran his fingers over them, peered down the barrels, and rose with a nod of satisfaction. They seemed to be wire-wound, rifled, breech-loading guns, of which only the breech mechanism was missing.

They resembled very closely the sixty-pounders of his own experience, though they were somewhat smaller. When the breech mechanism was supplied, they would be efficient and deadly weapons of a kind that he well knew how to handle.

CHAPTER VII
The Lady Eva

1

THE SPEAKER'S RECEPTION was a gorgeous and tedious assembly, held in the afternoon for the better convenience of a society which had but indifferent resources in the way of artificial light. A great hall in the Treasury had been prepared for it; and here the "big men," and their wives and sons and daughters, showed themselves, paid their respects to the Speaker and to the Lady Burney, paraded a little, gathered into groups for conversation, at last took their leave.

Jeremy walked through the crowd at the Speaker's elbow and was presented by him to the most important of the guests. This was a mark of favor, of recognition, almost of adoption. He had at first been afraid of it and had wished to avoid it. But the Speaker's determination was unalterable.

"If it were nothing more," he said, with a contemptuous smile on his heavy but mobile mouth, "I shall be giving them pleasure by exhibiting you. You are a show, a curiosity to them. They are all longing to see you— once…. Only you and I know that you are something more. And to know it pleases me; I hope it pleases you."

This explanation hardly reconciled Jeremy to the ordeal; but the Speaker had easily overborne his reluctance. They walked through the room together, a couple strangely unlike; and the old man showed towards the younger all the tenderness, all the proud complaisances of a father to a son.

From this post of vantage Jeremy could at least see all that was to be seen. The assembly seemed to be gay and animated. The men wore the dress of ceremony, the latter-day version of evening dress; and some of them, especially the more youthful, were daring in the colors of their coats and in the bravado of lace at throat and breast and wrist. The women wore more elaborate forms of the gown of every day, simply cut in straight lines, descending to the heel and tortuously ornamented with embroideries in violent colors. Jeremy saw one stout matron who was covered from neck to shoes in a pattern of blowsy roses and fat yellow butterflies, like a wall-paper of the nineteenth century, another whose embroidery took the shape of zigzag stripes of crimson, blue and green, adjoining on the bodice, separated on the skirt.

But he was impressed by a certain effect of good breeding which their behavior produced and which contradicted his first opinion, based on the strangeness of their dress. They nodded to him (for the shaking of hands had gone quite out of fashion), stared at him a little, asked a color-less question or two, murmured politely on his reply, and drifted away from him. Where he expected crudity and vulgarity, he found a prevailing vagueness, tepidity, indifference, almost fatigue…. He was forced to con-clude that the flamboyancy of their appearance was mild to themselves, that they had no wish to appear startling, and did so only as the result of a universal lack of taste.

He moved among them, steadfastly following the Speaker, but feeling tired and stiff and inert. His limbs ached with unaccustomed labor, his left hand was torn and bandaged, and he had still in his nostrils the thick, greasy smell of the workshops in which he had spent the morning. Here, after his first shock of surprise at the sight of the guns, he had soon under-stood that he was expected to do much more than admire and approve. These, the Speaker said, were by no means his first experiments in the art of gun-casting. And, after that, the old man had recounted to Jeremy, assisted by occasional uncouth ejaculations from the aged foreman of that amazing gang of centenarians, a story that had been nothing less than stupefying.

The last men in whose fading minds some glimmer of the art still re-mained had been gathered together, at the cost of infinite trouble, from the districts where machinery was still most in use, chiefly from Scotland, Yorkshire, and Wales. They had been brought thither on the pretense that their experience was needed in the central repairing-shops of the railways; and apparently it had been necessary in all possible ways to deceive and to reassure the principal men of their native districts. Once they had been obtained, they had slaved for years with senile docility to satisfy the de-mands which the Speaker's senile and half-lunatic enthusiasm made on their disappearing knowledge. Somehow he had created in them a queer pride, a queer spirit of endeavor. That grotesque chorus of ancients had become inspired with a single anxiety, to create before they perished a gun which could be fired without instantly destroying those who fired it.

They had had trouble with the breech-mechanism, the Speaker nonchalantly remarked; and Jeremy had a vision of men blown to pieces in the remote and lonely valley where the first guns were tried. The immediate purpose for which Jeremy's help was required was the adjustment of the process of cutting the interrupted screw-thread by which the breech-block was locked into the gun. He had toiled at it all the morning, surrounded by jumping and antic old men, whose speech he could hardly understand and to whom he could only with the greatest exertion communicate his own opinions. He had wrestled with, and tugged at, antiquated and dilapidated machinery, had cursed and sworn, had given himself a great cut on the palm of his left hand and had descended almost to the level of his ridiculous fellow-workers. And yet, when he had finished, the difficult screw-thread was in a fair way to be properly cut.

He came hot from these nightmare experiences to the Speaker's reception; and when he looked round and contrasted the one scene with the other, he had a sense of phantasmagoria that made him feel dizzy. It was almost too much for his reason… on top of a transition that would have overbalanced most normal men…. He was recalled from his bewildering reflections by the Speaker's voice, low and grumbling in his ear.

They had drifted for a moment away from the thickest of the crowd into a corner of the room, and the old man was able to speak without fear of being overheard. "It is as I have noticed for years," he said, "but it gets worse and worse. These are only from the south."

Jeremy started and replied a little at random: "Only from the south…?"

"Listen carefully to all I say to you. It is all useful. These people here are only from the south, from Essex, like that young Roger Vaile, and Kent and Surrey and Sussex and Hampshire. The big men from the north and west come every year less often to the Treasury. And yet these fools hardly notice it, and would see nothing remarkable in it if they did."

"You mean…" Jeremy began. But before he could get farther he-saw the Speaker turn aside with a smile of obvious falsity and exaggerated sweetness. The sinister little person, whom Jeremy knew from a distance as "the Canadian," was approaching them with a characteristically arrogant step and bearing.

The Speaker made them known to one another in a manner that barely concealed a certain uneasiness and unrest. "Thomas Wells," he explained in a loud and formal voice, "is the son of one of the chief of the Canadian Bosses, whom we reckon among our subjects and who by courtesy allow themselves to be described as such. But I reckon it as an honor to have Thomas Wells, the son of George Wells, for my guest in the Treasury."

"That's so," said the Canadian gravely, without making it quite clear which part of the Speaker's remark he thus corroborated. Then he stared keenly at Jeremy, apparently controlling a strong instinct of discomfort and dislike by an effort of will. Jeremy returned the stare inimically.

"I believe we have met before," he suggested, not without a little malice.

"That's so," the Canadian agreed; and as he spoke he sketched the sign of the cross in an unobtrusive manner that made it appear as though it might have been a chance movement of his hand. The Speaker hung over them with evident anxiety, and at last said:

"You two are both strangers to this country. You ought to be able to compare your impressions."

"I would much rather hear something about Canada," Jeremy answered.

Thomas Wells shrugged his shoulders. "It isn't like this country," he said carelessly. "We can't be as easy-going as the people are here. We have to fight—but we do fight and win," he concluded, momentarily baring his teeth in a savage grin.

"The Canadians, as every one knows, are the best soldiers in the world," the Speaker interpolated. "They are always fighting."

"And whom do you fight?" Jeremy asked.

"Oh, anybody… You see, the people to the south of us are always quarreling among themselves, and we chip in. And then sometimes we send armies down to Mexico or the Isthmus."

"But the people to the south…" Jeremy began. "Haven't you still got the

United States to the south of you? And I should have thought they'd be too many for you?"

"There are no United States now—I've heard of them." Thomas Wells's dislike of Jeremy seemed to have been overcome by a swelling impulse of boastfulness. "From what I can make out, they never did get their people in hand as we did. They've always been disturbed. Their leaders don't last long, and they fight one another. And we're always growing in numbers and getting harder, while they get fewer and softer. Why, they're easy fruit!"

Jeremy could find nothing for this but polite and impressed assent. Thomas Wells allowed his lean face to be split by a startling grin and went on: "I suppose you've never heard of me? No! Well, I'm not like these people here. I was brought up to fight. My dad fought his way to the top. *His* dad was a small man, out Edmonton way, with not more than two or three thousand bayonets. But he kept at it, and now none of the Bosses in Canada are bigger than we are. It was me that led the raid on Boston when I was only twenty."

Jeremy turned aside from the last announcement with a feeling of disgust. He thought that Thomas Wells looked like some small blood-thirsty animal, a ferret or a stoat, with pale burning eyes and thin-stretched mouth that sought the throat of a living creature. He, was saved from the necessity for an answer by the Canadian turning sharply on his heel, as though something had touched a spring in his body. Jeremy followed the movement with his eyes and saw the Lady Eva making her way towards them through the crowd.

Thomas Wells went to meet her with an air of exaggerated gallantry, and murmured something with his bow. She seemed to be to-day in a mood of modest behavior, for she received his salutation with downcast eyes and no more than a movement of the lips. As he watched them Jeremy again became aware of the Speaker standing beside him, whom he had for a moment forgotten. He stole a look at the old man and saw that his brow was troubled and that, though his hands were clasped behind his back in an apparently careless attitude, the fingers were clenched and the knuckles white. As he registered these impressions, the Lady Eva, still with downward glance, sailed past Thomas Wells and approached him. When he saw her intention, a faint disturbance sprang up in his heart and interfered with his breathing.

She had already halted beside him when he realized that now, in the presence of this company, her deportment being what it was, he must make the first speech. He stuttered awkwardly and said: "I have been hoping to see you again."

She raised her eyes a trifle, and he fancied that he saw the shadow of a smile in the corners of her mouth. Her reply was pitched in so low a tone as to be at first incomprehensible, and there followed a moment of emptiness before he realized that she had said, "You have been with Roger Vaile."

He interpreted it as in some sort of a reproach, and was about to protest when he saw the Speaker frowning at him. He did not understand the frown, but he moderated his vehemence. "I have been learning," he said in level tones. "I have been learning a great deal." And then he added more quietly, "Not but what you could teach me much more."

At this she raised her head and laughed frankly; and he, looking up too, saw that the Speaker had drawn Thomas Wells away and that the backs of both were disappearing in the throng. A strange, uncomfortable sense of an intrigue, which he could not understand, oppressed him. He glared suspiciously at the girl, but read nothing more than mischief and merriment in her face.

"I was well scolded the last time I spoke to you," she said, "but I have behaved well this time, haven't I?"

Exhilaration chased all his doubts away. He gazed at her openly, took in the wide eyes, the straight nose, the sensitive mouth, the healthy skin. Then he tried to pull himself together, to recover a dry, sane consciousness of his situation. It was absurd, he told himself—at his age!—to be unsettled by a conversation with a beautiful girl who might have been, if he had had any, one of his remote descendants. He felt unaccountably like a man glissading on the smooth, steep slope of a hill. Of course, he would in a moment be able to catch hold of a tuft of grass, to steady himself by digging his heels into the ground… But meanwhile the Lady Eva was looking at him.

"What do you think I could teach you?" she asked.

"I know so little," he answered haphazard. "I know nothing about any of the people here. I suppose you know them all?"

"They are the big men and their wives. What can I tell you about them?"

"What do you think of them yourself?"

She eyed him a little askance, doubtful but almost laughing. "What would you think... what would they think—if I were to tell you that?"

"But they will never know," he urged, in a tone of ridiculously serious entreaty.

"Don't you know that I am already considered a little... strange? I don't think I could tell you anything about our society that would be any use to you. My mother tells me every day that I don't know how to behave myself; and I daresay all these people would say the same."

"But why?"

"Oh, I don't know..." She half swung round, tapped the floor with her heel and returned to him, grown almost grave. "I hate the... the... the easiness of everybody. They all stroll through life, and the women do nothing and behave modestly—they're not alive. I suppose I am like my father. He is odd too."

"But I am like him," Jeremy said earnestly. "If you are like him, then I must be like you. But I don't know enough to be sure how different every one else is. They seem very amiable, very gentle...."

"I hate their gentleness," she began in a louder tone. But instead of going on, she dropped her eyes to the ground and stood silent. Jeremy, perplexed for a minute, suddenly became aware of the Lady Burney beside them, an expression of dull disapproval on her brilliantly carmined face. He had the presence of mind to bow to her very respectfully.

"I am glad to see you again, Jeremy Tuft," she said with a heavy and un-deceiving graciousness. As she spoke she edged herself between him and the Lady Eva; and Jeremy could quite plainly see her motioning her daughter away with a gesture that she only affected to conceal. He strove to keep an expression of annoyance from his face and answered as enthusiastically as he could. She spoke a few more listless sentences with an air of fighting a rearguard action. When she left him he sought through the room for the Lady Eva, disregarding all who tried to accost him; but he could not come at her again.

2

Roger Vaile was divided between disappointment and pride at Jeremy's favor with the Speaker, and expressed both feelings with the same equability of demeanor.

"I hope I shall see you again sometimes," he said; "but the Speaker has always disliked me."

"And what does the Lady Eva think of you?" Jeremy asked curiously.

"Oh, the Lady Eva's a wonder!" Roger said with more fervor than he usually displayed. "She's not like any one else alive. Why, do you know the other day, when she was out riding with her groom she beckoned to me and made me ride with her for ten minutes while I told her all about you."

Jeremy supposed that this must be unusually daring conduct for a young girl of the twenty-first century, and he acknowledged the impression it made on him by nodding his head two or three times.

"That's the chief reason why the Lady Burney hates me," Roger continued, a slight warmth still charging his voice. "But she doesn't understand her own daughter. The Lady Eva takes no particular interest in me. She merely can't bear being cooped up, like other girls, and not being able to talk to any one she wants to. And because I've gone to her once or twice when she has called to me, they think there's something between us. But there isn't: I wish there were."

Jeremy regarded with admiration this moderate and gentle display of passion. "But whom will she marry?" he ventured, feeling himself a little disturbed by his own question as soon as it was uttered.

"I believe the Lady Burney would like her to marry that horrible Canadian. And her father would marry her to any one if he saw his profit in it. It's lucky for her that the Chairman of Bradford is married already."

"What makes you say that?"

"He's the biggest man of the North and one of the men, so they say, that the Speaker is most afraid of. There's some kind of dispute going on between them now. But it's all nonsense," Roger concluded indifferently. "There's really nothing for them to quarrel about and nothing will come of it. But the Speaker always does excite himself about nothing and always has. He's a very strange old man; and the Lady Eva is like him in some ways. And then there's that Canadian… You will find yourself among a queer lot: I own that I don't understand them."

But in spite of Roger's wishes and Jeremy's protestations their meetings were, for some time after this conversation, casual and infrequent. The Speaker, as he grimly said, had a use for Jeremy, and was determined to see it accomplished. Day after day they went together to the guarded and mysterious workshop behind Waterloo Station. There, day after day, Jeremy painfully revived his rusty knowledge of mechanics, and, himself driven by the Speaker, drove the gang of old men to feats of astonishing skill.

He was astonished at the outset to see what they had actually done. To have made two rifled, wire-wound guns, with their failing wits and muscles and with the crazy museum of machinery which they showed him, had been truly an amazing performance. He learnt later that this was the eleventh pair that had been cast in fifteen years, and the first since they had mastered the art of properly shrinking on the case. They were still in difficulties with the screw-thread inside the gun that locked the breech-block; and as he set them time and time again at the task of remedying this or that fault in their workmanship, he understood why they had taken so long and why so many guns had blown up. What he could not understand was the Speaker's indomitable persistence in this fantastic undertaking, which, but for his own arrival in the world, might have taken fifteen years more and outlasted all the old men concerned in it.

But while he slaved, sweating and harassed, sometimes despairing because of a scrap of knowledge that evaded his memory or because of the absence of some machine that would have ensured accurate working, the Speaker hovered round him and, little by little, in long harangues and confessions, laid bare the mainsprings of his nature. These extraordinary scenes lasted in Jeremy's mind, moved before his eyes, echoed in his ears, when he had left the shed, when he sat at dinner or in the darkness when he was trying to sleep, until he found that he was gradually being infected with a dogged, unreasoning enthusiasm like that of his dotard fellow-workers. He even felt a little ashamed of himself for succumbing to the fanatical influence of an insane old Jew.

But the Speaker would stand at his elbow, when he was adjusting a decrepit lathe that ought to have been long ago on the scrap-heap, and rhapsodize endlessly in his thick muttering voice that rose sometimes to a shout, accompanied by lifted hands and flashing eyes.

"I was born too late," he would cry, "and I should perhaps have given up hope if I had not found you. But you and I, when this task is done, will regenerate the kingdom. How long I have labored and these easy-going fools have not once helped me or understood me! But now our triumph begins—when the guns are made."

Jeremy, standing up to ease his back and wiping his hands on an oily rag, would reflect that if it took so long to cut a screw-thread correctly, the regeneration of the whole kingdom was likely to be a pretty considerable task. Besides, when he was away from the Speaker or when his absorption in the machinery removed him from that formidable influence, his thoughts took a wider cast. He was sometimes far from sure that a regeneration which began by the manufacture of heavy artillery was likely to be a process of which he could wholly approve. He found this age sufficiently agreeable not to wish to change it.

It was true that innumerable conveniences had gone. But on the other hand most of the people seemed to be reasonably contented, and no one was ever in a hurry. The Speaker, Jeremy often thought, was principally bent on regenerating those vices of which the world had managed to cure itself. The trains were few and uncertain, and, from the universal decay of mechanical knowledge, were bound in time to cease altogether; but England, so far as Jeremy could see, would get on very well without any trains at all. There was no telephone; but that was in many ways a blessing. There was no electric light, except here and there, notably, so he learnt, in some of the Cotswold towns, which were again flourishing under the rule of the wool-merchants and where it was provided by water-power to illuminate their great new houses. But it was certainly possible to regard candles and lamps as more beautiful. The streets were dark at night and not oversafe; but no man went out unarmed or alone after sunset, and actual violence was rare. Jeremy was anxious to see what the countryside looked like, when the Speaker would allow him a tour out of London. He gathered that it was richer and more prosperous than he had known it, and that the small country town had come again into its own. He learnt with joy that the wounds made by the bricks and mortar of the great manufacturing cities had, save in isolated places, in parts of Yorkshire and Wales, long been healed by the green touch of time. He formed for himself a pleasant picture of the new England, and, when his mind was his own, he shrank from disturbing it.

But when the Speaker, with mad eyes and clawing gestures, muttered beside him, he turned again with an almost equal fanaticism to the hopeless business of restoring all that was gone and that was better gone. And, under this slave-driver's eye, he had little time for anything else. Even at night they generally dined alone together in the Speaker's own room; and Jeremy, drugged and stupefied with fatigue, sat silent while the old man continued his unflagging monologue. And every day his enthusiasm grew greater, his demands for haste more frequent and more urgent. Only never, in all the ramblings of his speech, did he once betray the use he intended to make of the guns, the reason for his urgency.

Jeremy looked out from this existence and saw a resting world in which he alone must labor. The strain began to tell on his nerves; and he sometimes complained weakly to himself that the nightmare, into which he had awakened, endured and seemed to have established itself as a permanency. He had none save fleeting opportunities of seeing the Lady Eva. On the few occasions when they met it had been in the presence of the Lady Burney; and the girl had conducted herself with silent, almost too perfect, propriety. Jeremy, much too tired and harassed to think out anything clearly, concluded that circumstances had, once again in his life, taken the wrong turn and that his luck was out.

One morning, about three weeks after his first visit to the workshop, he succeeded for the first time in fitting the already completed breech-block into the gun and satisfied himself that the delicate mechanism, though it left much to be desired and would not last very long, would do well enough. He looked up wearily from this triumph and saw the old gnomes, his colleagues, grotesquely working all around him. Gradually, as he became convinced of the Speaker's insanity, these uncouth creatures had grown more human and individual in his eyes and less like a chorus in one of Maeterlinck's plays. He had not been busy all the time with that infernal screw-thread. He had looked now and then into a smaller shed close by, where in the most primitive manner and with an appalling disregard of safety, an aged workman occupied himself with the production of explosives. This man was a little more intelligent than the rest, and had studied with devotion a marvelous collection of old and rapidly disintegrating handbooks on his subject. He was a small and skinny creature, with an alert manner and a curious skipping walk; and Jeremy had got used to seeing the hatchet face bobbing towards him with demands for help.

Now, as he rested for a moment, there was a noise that penetrated even his dulled consciousness; and, as he started up in alarm, Hatchet-face skipped in, bursting with inarticulate excitement. It appeared, when he was able to speak, that he had just missed blowing off his left hand with the first detonator to function in an entirely satisfactory way; and, while one of his fellows bandaged his hurts, he continued to rejoice, showing a praiseworthy absence of self-concern. The hubbub attracted the Speaker, who was not far away; and when he arrived he learnt with delight of its cause. Jeremy capped this news with his of the breech-lock; and for a moment the old man's terrifying countenance was lit up with a wholly human and simple happiness. Then he announced that they would not attend at the workshop that afternoon. Jeremy, from the bench on which he had laxly subsided, remarked that they deserved a holiday.

"It is not that," said the Speaker, frowning again. "It is a reception to which I must go, an affair of ceremony, and I wish you to come with me. There will be some kind of a show."

Jeremy was not sure what significance this variable word might by now have acquired, and he did hot much care. He looked forward to an afternoon's relaxation. He was thankful for so much; but he wondered at the back of his mind what the Speaker would want to start on now that the guns were nearly finished.

3

The reception was to be held at the house of one Henry Watkins, a big man with large estates near London and in Kent, whom Jeremy had met and had a little remarked. He seemed to be the most influential and the most consulted frequenter of the Treasury; and Jeremy observed that the Speaker commonly mentioned him with rather less than his usual contempt. His house was a large one, almost exactly on the site of Charing Cross, with gardens stretching down to the river; and here, when their carriage arrived, he came out and with easy respectfulness helped the Speaker to alight.

He was a tall man, with a long, narrow face and a slightly fretful expression. As he took the old man's arm Jeremy fancied that he whispered something, and that the Speaker shook his head. Then he turned to Jeremy and said perfunctorily, "I have had the happiness of making your acquaintance," wheeled back to the Speaker and went on: "We waited only for you, sir. The Lady Burney and the Lady Eva and Thomas Wells are already here."

"Then lead us to them," the Speaker replied. And as they were being conducted through a crowd of waiting guests, who made way for them with a quiet buzz of deferential salutations, he observed in a gracious tone, "I need not ask whether you have a good show for us, Henry Watkins."

"I trust that it will please you, sir," the host replied. "I have heard this troop very well spoken of."

Jeremy was prepared by this conversation for something in the way of a performance; and he was therefore not surprised when they were ushered into a large room, which had been rudely fitted up as a theater. At the front, standing by themselves, were four gilt armchairs, and on these Jeremy thought he recognized the backs of the Speaker's wife, of his daughter, and of Thomas Wells. They caught the Speaker's notice, too, and he halted suddenly, craning his head forward and peering at them.

"There are only four chairs," he said in a rasping voice. "I wish another chair to be brought for my friend, Jeremy Tuft." In a moment, after some confusion, Jeremy found himself sitting next to the Lady Eva and hearing her demure reply to his greeting, which was almost drowned by the noise of the guests behind them entering the hall.

Presently three loud raps were heard and a hush fell on the audience. Jeremy started in his seat when an invisible performer at the piano began to play what sounded like a mangled waltz, very loud, very crude and very vulgar. The strings of the piano were in indifferent condition, the skill of the executant was no better, and Jeremy, who was proud of having some sympathy for music, suffered a little. When he looked about him, however, he saw neither amusement nor annoyance on any face. Luckily the performance lasted only a few minutes. As soon as it was done, an actress tripped affectedly on to the stage from the right side and began to declaim in a voice so high pitched and theatrical and with so many gestures and movements of her head that Jeremy could hardly understand a word of what she was saying. He gathered that she had come to this wood to meet her lover; and his guess was confirmed when an actor strode on from the left, stamping his feet on the resounding boards as he came. Then both began to declaim at one another in voices of enormous power. Their stilted violence alarmed and repelled Jeremy. He ceased to look at the stage, wondering whether, under cover of the excitement which this scene must be causing, he dared steal a glance at the Lady Eva. He did so, and discovered that she was looking at him.

Both averted their eyes, and Jeremy sat staring at the floor, his heart beating and, he felt certain, his cheeks burning. Above his head the drama ranted along with a loud monotonous noise like the sea beating on rocks, and made a background to his thoughts. That single glance had precipitated his emotions, and he must now confess to himself, what had been before a mere toy for the brain, that he loved this girl. The admission carried his mind whirling wildly away, and he would have been content to brood on it with a secret rising delight until he was interrupted. But he could not help asking himself whether he had not discovered something else, whether there had not been at least a particular interest in the eyes of the Lady Eva. This second thought at first terrified him by its revelation of his own audacity in conceiving it. For a moment it stopped him still, and then suddenly there was silence on the stage.

The actor and the actress were departing, she to the right, he to the left, bowing as they went. The whole audience began clapping in a decorous and gentle manner. The Lady Eva leant slightly towards Jeremy as he sat stupefied and motionless, and whispered:

"You must clap. You will be thought impolite if you do not."

He obeyed in a dazed way, watching her and seeing how she brought the palms of her hands together, regularly but so softly that it made hardly any sound. While the applause still continued, servants came forward from the sides of the hall, sprang up on the stage and began removing the scenery, which they replaced with other flats, representing a street. And after an interval, and another performance on the vile piano, the play resumed its course.

Jeremy must have followed it with some part of his mind of the existence of which he was ignorant: for when it was all over he had a reasonably clear notion of what it had been about. If Jeremy's conscious mind had been active while the performance was going on he could not but have followed every point with amazement and indulged in some interesting reflections on the dramatic tastes of his new contemporaries. As it was, when it was over and he was able to look back on it, he could only wonder whether his unaccountable recollection of it was to be believed.

For after the end of the first scene, after the Lady Eva had spoken to him, he was plunged even more deeply into that delicious but alarming turmoil of feeling. His mind unbidden suggested to him sobering considerations only for the pleasure, as it appeared, of seeing them flung on one side. There was no certainty, no probability even, that the girl had loved him. In his story there was enough reason why she should look at him with interest, and he had learnt that her usual manner was frank and unstudied, not therefore to be too easily construed. Yet a mad certainty rose in his heart and overwhelmed this sensible thought.

At that moment he would perhaps have been unwilling to be awakened to speak to her, even to embrace her. That would come, must come; but this exquisite dreaming, hitherto unknown to him, filled the circle of his forces, satisfied all his desires. Then suddenly across the texture of his passionate meditation came a thought of himself. He shifted uneasily and felt cold. Who and what was he? He told himself—a sport of nature, a young man unnaturally old, an old man unnaturally young. Could he be certain yet what trick it was that Trehanoc's ray had played on him? Might he not, one day, to-morrow or a year hence, perhaps in her very arms, suddenly expire, even crumble into dust?

He woke. Mixed with the light clapping, in which from time to time he had mechanically joined, there was a stir and shuffle as though the audience was preparing to depart; and, looking up, he saw the whole cast on the stage, bowing with a certain air of finality, the hero and the villain holding each a hand of the heroine. The Speaker was rising from his seat, and at that sign all the other persons in the room rose, too, and waited. Jeremy, brought down out of dreams, searched in his mind for something to say to the Lady Eva and dared not look at her until he had found it. But when he turned to her he saw that she was staring in another direction. A servant had just reached the Speaker and had apparently given him a letter. The whole assembly stood hushed and immobile while he read it, and Jeremy, his breath caught by an inexplicable sense of crisis, saw that, half-way through, the old man's hand jerked suddenly and was steady again.

The interruption, the hushed seconds that followed, seemed to spread an impalpable sense of dismay through the hall. Henry Watkins, his fretful expression deepened to one of alarm, made his way to the Speaker's side and whispered something in an anxious voice; but the old man waved his hand impatiently and went on reading.

"What is it?" Jeremy whispered sharply to the Lady Eva.

"I don't know… I don't know…" she uttered; and then, so low that he could hardly catch it, "I am afraid for him…"

Jeremy stared all around in the hope that somewhere he might find some enlightenment. But there was no trace of understanding on the faces of any of the guests. The Lady Burney stood lumpishly by her husband in an attitude of annoyance and boredom. Beyond her Thomas Wells half-leant on his chair in a barbaric but graceful pose, like that of a hunting animal at rest. Jeremy fancied for a moment that he could read some sort of comprehension, some sort of satisfaction even, in those vulpine features, in the small eyes, the swelling nostrils, the thin, backward-straining mouth. And still the Speaker read on, motionless, without giving a sign, while Henry Watkins stood at his elbow as though waiting for an order; and still the Lady Eva gazed at them, crumpling restlessly with one hand a fold of her dress.

All at once the grouping broke up, and the Speaker's voice came, steady and clear but not loud. "I must go back to the Treasury," he said. "I am sorry I cannot stay to speak with your guests, Henry Watkins, but you must dismiss them. I wish you to come with me. And I need you, too, Jeremy Tuft; you must follow us at once. And—" he hesitated, "if you will give me the benefit of your counsel in this grave matter, Thomas Wells..." The Canadian bowed a little and grinned more thinly. Jeremy found himself in a state of confusion walking at the end of the Speaker's party towards the door. In front of him the old man had gripped Henry Watkins firmly by the sleeve and was talking to him quietly and rapidly.

Jeremy's passing by was the sign to the other guests that they might now leave; and as he went through the door he could feel them thronging behind him. He pressed on to keep the Speaker in sight, but slackened his pace when a hand fell lightly on his shoulder. It was Roger Vaile.

"Do you know what the matter is?" Roger asked.

Jeremy shook his head.

"Well, be careful of that Canadian. I saw him looking at you while the show was on, and he doesn't like you."

CHAPTER VIII
Declaration Of War

1

THE DARK AND UNDEFINED CLOUD which had fallen upon the reception seemed to have overshadowed the Treasury as well. The Speaker had precipitately driven thither, taking Henry Watkins with him in the carriage and not waiting for Jeremy, who reached the door only in time to see that he must follow on foot. The Speaker's unexpected return, coupled with the unusual expression on his face and perhaps some rumor already set afloat, had unsettled the household. When Jeremy arrived he found the clerks and even the servants, together with the attendants of the Lady Burney and the Lady Eva, standing about in little groups in the entrance hall. They were talking among themselves in low voices, and they all raised their eyes questioningly to his as he passed by. There was a universal atmosphere of confusion and alarm.

At the door which led from the entrance-hall towards the Speaker's room, Jeremy paused disconsolately, uncertain what he ought to do. The Speaker had asked for his help, but had not stayed for him. Perhaps he ought to go to the Speaker; but he was unwilling to intrude into what seemed to be a council of the first importance. His doubts were relieved by a servant, who came anxiously searching among the loiterers and appeared relieved when he caught sight of Jeremy.

"Here you are, sir!" he said. "The Speaker has been asking for you ever since he came back. Will you please go to his room at once?" Jeremy's sense of a moment of crisis was by no means lessened as he threaded the dark, empty corridors of the private wing.

When he entered he found himself unnoticed, and had a few seconds in which to distinguish the members of the little group clustered at the other end of the room. The Speaker was standing motionless, with his eyes turned upwards to the ceiling, in an attitude apparently indicating complete unconcern. Yet, to Jeremy he seemed to be controlling himself by an enormous effort of will, while his whole body quivered with suppressed excitement. Below him and, to the eye, dominated by him, five men sat around a table. Jeremy saw at once the Canadian and Henry Watkins and another chief notable, named John Hammond, with whom he was slightly acquainted. The others had their backs to him; but their backs were unfamiliar, somehow out of place, with something uneasy and hostile in the set of their shoulders. As he came into the room, Henry Watkins was leaning forward to one of these strangers and saying earnestly:

"I want to make certain that we understand what this sentence means." He tapped a paper in front of him as he spoke.

"T' letter meaans what it saays," the stranger replied gruffly. His words and the broad, rasping accent in which they were spoken came to Jeremy as a shock, as something incomprehensibly foreign to what he had expected. His colleague nodded vigorously, and signified his agreement in a sound between a mutter and a growl.

"Yes," Henry Watkins began again patiently; "but what I want to know—"

The Speaker suddenly forsook his rigid posture, with the effect of a storm let loose, and, striding to the table, struck it violently with his fist. It seemed, as if the last fetter of his restraint had given way without warning.

"That's no matter," he cried hoarsely. "What I want to know is this: if I make another offer, will you take it back to your master?"

The stranger squared his shoulders and thrust his chin forward with an air of dogged ferocity. "We caame to get yes or noa," he answered in a deep grumbling voice. "T' letter saays soa."

Henry Watkins started at this outburst in the negotiations and looked around him with an appearance of fright. In doing this he caught sight of Jeremy hesitating by the door, and whispered a word to the Speaker, who cried out, without moderating the violence of his tone: "There you are! Come here now, I want you." And turning again to the strangers, he added, with an odd note of triumph: "This is Jeremy Tuft. Maybe you've heard of him."

The strangers, who had not yet noticed Jeremy's arrival, slewed around together and stared at him; and one of them said: "Oh, ay, we've heerd on him, reet enough." The others at the table stared too, while Jeremy reluctantly advanced. But before he could speak, Henry Watkins sprang up and murmured importunately in the Speaker's ear. Jeremy could catch the words:

"Talk privately… before we decide…"

"Very well," said the Speaker roughly, aloud. "Have it your own way. But I won't change my mind."

Henry Watkins returned to the table and addressed the strangers suavely: "The Speaker will give you his answer in a very short time," he said. "Will you be so good as to withdraw while he considers it?" And, when they had uncouthly assented, he conducted them to the door, showed them into an ante-room, and returned, his face full of anxiety.

Jeremy stood apart in a condition of great discomfort. He realized that he was regarded by all, save the Speaker, as an intruder, the reason for whose presence none could conjecture. He was not relieved by the dubious glance which Henry Watkins threw at him before he began to speak. But the Speaker made no sign, and the anxious counselor proceeded, with an air of distraction and flurry.

"Think, sir," he pleaded, "before you refuse. It is so grave a thing to begin again—after a hundred years. And who can tell what the end of it may be? We know that they are formidable—"

"All this is nonsense to Jeremy Tuft," the Speaker interrupted harshly. "We must tell him what the matter is before we go any further." Henry Watkins, with a movement of his hands, plainly expressed his opinion that there was no good reason why it should not all remain nonsense to Jeremy; and Jeremy felt slightly less at ease than before.

But the Speaker had begun to explain, with the sharp jerkiness of impatience in his voice: "We've had a message from the people up north. Perhaps you could see for yourself what sort of men they are. They are very unlike any one you have ever met here—rough, fierce, quarrelsome men. They have kept some of their machinery still going up there—in some of the towns they even work in factories. They have been growing more and more unlike us for a hundred years, and now the end has come—they want to force a quarrel on us. Do you understand?"

Jeremy replied that he did, and thought that he was beginning to understand a great deal besides.

"Well, then," the Speaker went on, growing a little calmer, "I told you when first we met that we were standing on the edge of a precipice. Now these are the people that want to throw us over. The chief of them, the Chairman of Bradford, has sent me a message. I won't explain the details to you. It comes to this, that in future he proposes to collect the taxes in his district, not for me, but for himself. I must say he very kindly offers to send me a contribution for the upkeep of the railways. But he wants a plain yes or no at once; and if we say no, then it means WAR!" In the last sentence his voice had begun to run upwards: he pronounced the final word in a sudden startling shout, and then stood silent for a moment, his eyes burning fiercely. When he continued, it was in a quieter and more reasonable tone. "There has been no fighting in this country since the end of the Troubles, a hundred years or so ago. A brawl here and there, a fight with criminals or discontented laborers—I don't say; but no more than enough to make our people dislike it. Of all of us here in this room, only you and Thomas Wells know what war is. Now"—and here he became persuasive and put a curious smooth emphasis on each word—"now, *knowing all that you do know*, what advice would you give me?"

Jeremy stood irresolute. Henry Watkins and John Hammond seemed to throw up their hands in perplexed despair, and the Canadian's thin, supercilious smile grew a trifle wider and thinner. The Speaker waited, rocking hugely to and fro on his feet with a gentle motion.

"I think," Jeremy began, and was disconcerted to find himself so hoarse that the words came muffled and inaudible. He cleared his throat. "I think I hardly know enough about it for my advice to be of any use. I don't even know what troops you have."

The Speaker made a deep booming sound in his chest, clasped his hands sharply together, and looked as though he were about to burst out again in anger. Then he abruptly regained his self-command and said:

"Then you shall speak later. Henry Watkins, what do you say? Remember, we must make up our minds forever while we are talking now. It will not do to argue with them, or temporize or make them any other offer."

Henry Watkins got up from his seat and went to the Speaker's side as though he wished to address him confidentially. Jeremy had an impression of a long dark face, unnaturally lengthened by deep gloom, and two prominent eyes that not even the strongest emotion could make more than dully earnest.

"I beg of you, sir," he implored, low and hurried, holding out his hands, "to attempt to argue with them, to offer them some compromise. You know very well that they are forcing this quarrel on us, because they are sure that they are the stronger, as I believe them to be. And anything, anything would be better than to begin the Troubles again!"

The Speaker surveyed him as if from an immense height. "And do you think that we can avoid the Troubles again, and worse things even than that, in any way except by defeating these people? Am I to surrender all that my grandfather and my great-grandfather won? Do you not see that they have sent us just these two men, stupider and stubborner even than the rest, so that we shall not be able to argue with them? They have been told to carry back either our yes or our no. If we do not give them a yes, they will take no by default. There is no other choice for us. What do you think, John Hammond?"

"I agree with Henry Watkins," said the big man hastily. He had not spoken before, and seemed to do so now only with great reluctance.

"Then we need not hear your reasons. And you, Thomas Wells?"

"Why, fight," said the Canadian promptly; and then he continued in a deliberate drawl, stretching himself a little as he spoke: "These folks are spoiling for trouble, and they'll give you no peace until they get it. I guess your troops aren't any good—I've seen some of them—but I know no way to make them so except by fighting. And besides, I've an idea that there's something else you haven't told us yet."

Jeremy shot a suspicious glance at him, and received in return a grin that was full at once of amusement and dislike. The Speaker appeared to be balancing considerations in his mind. When he spoke again, it was in a tone more serious and deliberate than he had yet used.

"Gentlemen," he said, "my decision remains unaltered. I shall refuse and there will be war. But Thomas Wells is right. I have had something in my thoughts that I have not yet disclosed to you. But I will tell you now what it is, because I do not wish you to lose your spirits or to be half-hearted in supporting me. Only I must command you"—he paused on the word, looked around sternly, and repeated it—"I must command you not to speak a word of it outside this room until I give you leave." He paused again and surveyed them with the air of a man who delays his certain triumph for a moment in order the better to savor it. "Gentlemen, when our troops take the field against these rebels, they will have something that no other army in the world has got. They will have guns!"

The great announcement had come, had passed, and seemed to have failed of its effect. Silence reigned in the council. Henry Watkins shifted from one foot to the other and regarded the Speaker with gloomy intentness. Then Thomas Wells broke the hush, with a faint tone of disappointment in his voice:

"Is that it? Well, I don't know how that will work out. I thought that perhaps you had got some of the bosses up there in your pay."

Henry Watkins was as silent as his companion, bewildered, disturbed, apprehensive. But the Speaker continued, his air of jubilation increasing rather than diminishing.

"And not only have we guns, but we have also a trained artilleryman to handle them. Jeremy Tuft, I must tell you, fought in the artillery in the great war against the Germans before the Troubles began. And now, Jeremy Tuft, let us hear your opinion, remembering that we have guns and they have none. Do you think we should fight or surrender?"

Jeremy was hard put to it not to give way physically before the old man's blazing and menacing stare. His mind scurried hastily through half a hundred points of doubt. How could he know, when he had been in this world no more than a few weeks? And yet it seemed pretty clear, from what he had heard, that the-soldiers from Yorkshire would be better than those that the Speaker had at his disposal. He could see only too plainly that the Speaker was trusting to the guns to work a miracle for him. He remembered that the guns were only just finished, had not been tested, that no gun-crew to fight them had yet been trained or even thought of. He had a sick feeling that an intolerable responsibility rested on him, that he must explain how much the effect of two guns in an infantry battle would depend on luck. He remembered that time at Arras, when they had got properly caught in the enemy's counter-battery work, and he had sat in his dug-out, meditating on the people, whoever they were, that had started the war, and wondering how human beings could be so diabolical... He woke abruptly from this train of thought as he raised his eyes and saw the Speaker still regarding him with that terrible, that numbing stare. His strength gave way. He stammered weakly:

"Of course, the guns would make a great difference...."

The Speaker caught up his words. "They would make just the difference we need. That is why I have made up my mind to fight now. Let those two men come in again."

There was dead silence in the room for a moment, and Jeremy was aware of the progress of a breathless spiritual conflict. He could feel his own inarticulate doubts, the timidity of Watkins and Hammond, the cynical indifference of the Canadian, hanging, like dogs around the neck of a bull, on the old man's fanatical determination. Then something impalpable seemed to snap: it was as though the bull had shaken himself free. Without uttering a sound, Henry Watkins went to the door of the ante-room and held it open. The two envoys from the north again appeared. They seemed unwilling to come more than a pace into the room; perhaps they thought it unnecessary since they wished to hear only a single word.

The Speaker was as anxious as they to be brief. "I refuse," he said with great mildness.

"That's t' aanswer, then?" asked the first envoy with a kind of surly satisfaction.

"That's t' aanswer. Coom on," his companion said, before any one else could reply.

"Good daay to you then, sirs," the first muttered phlegmatically; and with stumping strides they lumbered to the door. Henry Watkins hurried after them to find a servant to bring them their horses.

2

No less than the rest the Lady Eva was disturbed and made uneasy in her mind by the unexpected end of Henry Watkins's reception. The short drive back to the Treasury, sitting beside her mother in the vast, lumbering carriage, was a torment to her. Involuntarily she asked questions, well aware that the Lady Burney neither knew, nor was interested in, the answers. She was obliged to speak to assuage her restlessness, and expected the reproof which she received.

"It's not your business," said the Lady Burney heavily. "You must not meddle in your father's affairs. It shows a very forward and unbecoming spirit in you to have noticed that anything happened out of the ordinary. What people would say of you if they knew as much of your behavior as I do, I simply cannot think. They must see too much as it is. Remember that we ought to set an example to other people."

The Lady Eva was silent, white with restraint and anxiety. But when they arrived at the Treasury and came into the atmosphere of expectancy which filled the entrance-hall, she again showed signs of excitement, and seemed to wish to stop and share in the general state of suspense. Her mother ordered her to her room in a thick intense whisper. She remembered herself and went on, sighing once sharply.

She found her room empty. It was a pleasant place, looking over the gardens, furnished in an awkward and mixed style which reflected her distaste for her mother's notions of decoration, combined with her own inability to think of any better substitute. A riding-whip and gloves were thrown down on a table, beside a half-finished piece of needlework. Writing materials and a book lay on another. One of her eccentricities, not regarded so severely by the Lady Burney as the nest, was her wish to retain such slight knowledge of the arts of reading and writing as the scanty education of the women of that time had given her. But it was a hard business, starting from so insecure a foundation and proceeding with so little encouragement. The old books that she was able to obtain were very dull, very hard to understand, and told her little of what she wanted to know. Her companions of her own age laughed at her heartily for reading with so much devotion, after she had been released from the school-room, the works of the great poet, Lord Tennyson, from which they had all been taught their own language. She desired vaguely to be able to help her father, whose loneliness she obscurely but poignantly felt. But when in order to understand the old times she struggled through ragged and mildewed books, she despaired at the little assistance she was able to get from them.

She once expressed a timid wish that she might be allowed to learn history from Father Henry Dean, of whose knowledge she had heard confused but marvelous stories. But on this occasion her father had unexpectedly joined her mother to prevent her. He had said bluntly that the priest was an addled old man, while the Lady Burney had said that the suggestion was both improper and dangerous. Between the two opinions, her wish was effectually frustrated. Indeed, she got little encouragement from her father, whose loneliness often seemed to her to be in great part purely wilful. Now and then he would listen to her for a few minutes, and then rhapsodize cloudily for a long time on his hopes and fears. But when he did this, after the first few sentences he was up and away from her; and she soon realized that he talked to her only instead of talking to himself, and did not for the purpose much alter his method of address.

A minute or two after she came into her room, two of her attendants followed her, asking, without much hope, for news. She shook her head sharply, with compressed lips. She had no news, she knew nothing of the danger that threatened her father and had shaken his steady old hand so abruptly while he was reading that mysterious letter. The two girls broke at once into a babble of rumors and conjectures. The plague had reached England again, or the Chinese had begun to invade Europe, or the Pope had done something or other that was unexpected, it was not clear what.

These attendants were daughters of good families who came to be half maids, half companions to the Lady Burney and the Lady Eva for a year or two, as a way of graduating in the world, much as young men came to be clerks to the Speaker. But the cases were not quite parallel. All young men of family entered the Speaker's service, or would do so if they could. There was a certain tradition of gentility in the work of government. But only the daughters of the poorer and smaller houses came to wait on the Speaker's wife and daughter. The rich families, though they obeyed the Speaker, would not accord him royal prestige or his wife and daughter the privilege of noble ladies-in-waiting. They treated him and his household with respect, not with deference. Only the lesser among them thought that something might be gained by their daughters holding positions at what they would fain regard as a court, or that they might perhaps make good marriages, a hope which now and then miscarried into something less gratifying. They maintained that it was an honor to serve the ruling family, and were sneered at by their greater fellows.

The Lady Eva, though she was often indolent and was pleased to be waited on, would have preferred to be attended by servants. These girls claimed some sort of equality with her, and, though she had no objection to that, she wished that she could prevent them speaking to her, unless she called on them: She found them tedious. Now she listened to them patiently, and said at last with a faint ironic smile:

"Do you really know anything about it?" They began to protest and to double their rumors, but she stopped them with a lifted hand. "There is a council in my father's room, is there not?" And when they had said that there was, she went on: "Can you tell me who has been called to it?"

"Jeremy Tuft was called to it just before we came to you," answered Rose, simpering a little and placing her head on one side. Jeremy did not know that among the young girls in the Treasury he was the object of some longings and the subject of some confessions. He drew attention because of the air of mystery which surrounded his short and rather commonplace person. It was fashionable to affect a deliciously shuddering attraction towards the elements of eeriness and terror in what was known of his story. But this fashion was not allowed to interfere with any more practical project of love-making that happened to be going.

"I saw him go," affirmed Mary with an even more pronounced simper.

"Is Thomas Wells there?" the Lady Eva shot at her quickly. Mary winced, looked guilty and said that she believed he was. Then she fell silent in a self-conscious attitude.

The Lady Eva frowned a little. These girls, though she despised them for their shallowness, led fuller lives than she. They conformed more easily than she did with the prevailing ideal of womanly conduct; and yet in the Treasury they were free to do much what they pleased, to choose lovers if they were foolish enough... as she guessed this girl had been. And the reflection had annoyed her, for she thought it likely that she would have to marry Thomas Wells. He and her father had been bargaining interminably about something, her father importunate but cozening, Thomas Wells smiling but obdurate. It might occur to her father at any moment to throw her person into the scale; and she would not like for a husband the lover of one of her attendants. Then, as she stood musing, it suddenly occurred to her with great force that she would not like to marry Thomas Wells in any circumstances. Strange! She had been long accustomed to the idea that she, her father's only child, must marry some one who would be chosen to become his heir; and she had quite calmly contemplated the likelihood of Thomas Wells being chosen. Only to-day did she perceive that the idea was distasteful to her, and she wondered why. A vague answer presented itself....

"Go back, both of you," she commanded, "and bring me the news when you hear any." They left her at once, Rose anxious to return to the center of excitement, and Mary glad to escape any further uncomfortable questions.

The Lady Eva, left alone, walked up and down her room with short, impatient steps. It was very difficult to wait thus for news, more difficult still in view of the fact that she might not get any. She conceived cloudy romantic notions of intervening in the council, of persuading her father in the middle of it that she understood him and was with him against all the rest of the world. She walked towards the door in an exalted fit, certain that now at least in this moment of anxiety she could convince him. Then she remembered other appeals, made when she was alone with him and when his mood had seemed to promise sympathy. But he had smiled at her, patted her head or her hand, and answered vaguely in words that meant nothing and humiliated her. Once, gathering from one of the soliloquies, in which he so evidently forgot her presence, that he was concerned by the state of the railways, she had brooded on the problem through sleepless nights, at last hitting on a plan, which she laid eagerly before him. It had seemed as crude and childish to her as to him, after his first comment. A flash of realism showed her the injured and astonished big men at the council, if she appeared there, the grinning contempt of Thomas Wells, her father's anger. She turned away again from the door.

Minutes passed. She went through stages of careless dullness, of unbearable suspense. At last, moved by an ungovernable longing, she left the room. She intended no longer to go to her father, but she would at least see the door behind which he was sitting with the others. She had an unreasonable certainty, which she could not examine, that waiting would be easier near the place where all was being decided.

She slipped along the corridor as softly as she could, ruefully aware that she did not usually move quietly and had often been reproved for it. But the intensity of her purpose helped her to avoid anything that could draw notice to her strange conduct. Soon the corridor was cut by another at right angles, which a few steps to the left led to the door of the Speaker's room. At the corner the Lady Eva paused and looked cautiously around. In this part of the ill-constructed house reigned a perpetual dusk, and any passer-by would be heard by her long before he could see her.

Her certainty was justified. Waiting was easier here; and the time slipped by less oppressively. She did not know how long she had been standing pressed close against the wall, when her father's door opened and two men came out and stamped up the corridor to the right. Even in that gloom she could see that they were strangers; and their odd looks and something odd in their manner, as though they were departing with a sinister purpose, increased her curiosity. She craned her neck to keep them in sight as long as she could, and drew back hastily when Henry Watkins came out. He was obviously distressed, and, as he went by her, following the strangers, he was rapidly clenching and unclenching his hands.

A long interval elapsed and left her still in suspense. Once she went a few paces in the direction of her own room, but she was ineluctably drawn back again. She stared desperately behind her, to the right, at the ground, anywhere rather than at her father's door, which had for her a fascination she felt she must resist. She was not looking at it when she heard the sound of the handle. When she looked, it was standing wide, and Jeremy and her father were framed in the opening, their faces lit from the windows in the room.

Her father's face wore an expression of exultation which she had never seen there before, and, with a hand on his shoulder, was stooping over Jeremy, who looked worried, sullen, fatigued.

"Then all will be ready in a week," the old man was saying.

"Yes, they'll be ready... so far as that goes," Jeremy replied in a heavy toneless voice. "But there's another thing we haven't thought of. They haven't been tested yet."

"They can't be tested now," the Speaker said firmly. "It would take too long, and besides, we mustn't have the slightest risk of the news leaking out before we first use them. And you say that you are satisfied with them, don't you?"

"Yes, as far as I can see," Jeremy muttered. "But there may be something wrong that I haven't noticed."

"No doubt there may," the Speaker agreed. "But if there is, it would be too late to remedy it; and we should certainly be beaten without them. We may as well disregard that."

"But if there is," Jeremy said with an air of protest, raising his voice a little, "we may be..."

"Yes, yes," the Speaker murmured, "you may all be blown up. But there..." He drew Jeremy by the shoulder into the corridor, and both their faces came into the shadow. The Lady Eva, seized by a sudden terror, picked up her skirts and ran, miraculously noiseless, back to her room.

CHAPTER IX
Marching Out

1

THE NIGHTMARE SETTLED AGAIN around Jeremy with a double darkness and bewilderment. Again he labored in the work-shops with his octogenarian assistants, but this time at first under a new oppression and a new hopelessness. Yet in some ways his mind was easier since he had understood that the frenzied haste which the Speaker urged on him was not urged without reason. After the council of war, the terrible old man, still jubilant, still strung up to the highest pitch of nervous energy, opened his mind to Jeremy without reserve. Jeremy, alarmed by his shining eyes, his feverish manner, his wild and abrupt gestures, still could not help seeing that his discourse was that of a sane man, a practical statesman, who was putting all he had on a single throw because there was no other choice.

"My family has ruled without dispute," the Speaker said, "for a hundred years—and that is a long time. We had no position, we merely stepped into the place of the old government, and the people let us because they were so tired. They obeyed us because they had been in the habit of obeying us, when there was no one else for them to follow. But we were not chosen, and we are too new to claim divine right. We cannot even look to our religion for support, because the country is divided. We here in the south are mostly by way of being Catholics, but though the Holy Father would give us his help, we have never dared to accept it. They are violent Methodists in Wales, and in Yorkshire and the north they are nearly all Spiritualists."

Jeremy inquired with interest what this new religion might be; but the Speaker could only describe it as it existed, and then but vaguely. He could not give the history of its growth. Jeremy gathered that the Spiritualists still called themselves Christians, but depended much less on the ministrations of any church than on advice received in various grotesque ways from departed friends and relatives. Their creed seemed to have degenerated into a gloomy and superstitious form of ancestor-worship. They had absorbed also, he guessed, some of the tenets of what had been called Christian Science; and the compound had produced a great many extravagant manifestations. The Spiritualists owned no law or discipline in the spiritual world, but acted on the latest intelligence received from the dead. Most of them held firmly that evil was a delusion, a doctrine which had come to have a strange influence on conduct. All of them believed without a question in the future life; and the absolute quality of their belief, the Speaker thought, had gradually changed among them the distaste for fighting which at one time possessed the whole country. It would further, he thought, make them formidable soldiers. The picture he drew of them, still living in the decay of an industrial system, packed close amid the ruins of the old towns in a bleak country, dismayed and repelled Jeremy. The Speaker's discourses did not fail of their intended effect. The listener began to believe that this enemy must be opposed at all risks.

"And you," the Speaker said earnestly, as Jeremy rested for a moment in the workshop, "you shall have your reward. I have no son and I have a daughter." He muttered the last sentence so much under his breath that it seemed he wished Jeremy not so much to hear it as to overhear it.

Jeremy's mind had been elsewhere; and it was a minute or two before the sense of these words penetrated to him. When it did, it brought him sharply back to the actual world. But he did not speak at once. His natural caution interposed, his natural diffidence bade him consider.

"What do you mean by that?" he asked quietly after an interval.

"What I say," the Speaker answered. "If you succeed in what you have to do, you shall be rewarded. If you don't succeed, I shall not be able to reward you, even if I wish to."

Jeremy desired very strongly to point out that this was unjust, that whether the guns would be a decisive factor in the coming battle depended almost entirely on chance. But he refrained. He refrained, too, from asking the Speaker precisely where the Lady Eva came into the scheme. Fortune appeared to him like a great, glittering bubble, which a miracle might make solid at the proper time for his hand to seize it. He dared not question further: he dared not think how much he was influenced by the Speaker's determination not to consider the consequences of defeat.

And as that crowded week wore on, his mind settled into a sort of calm, like the apparent quietness of a wheel revolving at high speed. That would be which was written. In his anxiety to be sure that there was an adequate supply of shells (he did not hope to have more than thirty for each gun) he quite forgot that one of them might suddenly blow him into eternity, together with all the Speaker's chance of success.

A great part of his time in the workshops was now spent alone— alone, that is to say, as far as the Speaker was concerned, for the old man was busy at the Treasury, mustering his army and making ready for it to march. As for the octogenarians, Jeremy felt little more kinship with them than if they had been a troop of trailed animals. Communication with them was so difficult that he confined it to the most necessary orders. But when he realized that these ludicrous old men would have to come with him to the battlefield to fire the guns, for want of time to train others, he began to feel for them a kind of compassionate affection. He regarded them rather as he would have done the horses of the gun-teams than as the men of his battery; but towards the end of the week he found himself talking to them, quite incomprehensibly, as he might have done to horses. It seemed to him pathetic that these witless veterans should be led out to war and set to the highly hazardous venture of firing off the guns they had themselves manufactured.

So, between the hours which he devoted to elementary instruction in loading, aiming, and firing, he gave to them his views on the situation in which he found himself. His views were, by reason of fatigue, strong emotions and bewilderment, of a confused and even childish sort. He told Jabez, the wizened expert in explosives, the whole story of Trehanoc's dead rat— a story which, brief as it was, covered more than a hundred and seventy years. He confided to Jabez his desire, his impossible craving, to see the rat again. It was perhaps a little ridiculous to hanker so much after the society of a rather unpleasant animal. Nevertheless he and the rat were in the same boat, and in his more light-headed moments he felt that he ought to seek it out and take counsel with it. He was sure that the rat would understand.

At other times he had a suspicion that it would have adjusted itself much more easily to the changed world than he could ever hope to do. Perhaps it had not even noticed that there had been any change. Jabez, wrinkled, skinny and toothless, listened complacently while he went on fumbling with his work, never letting a sign appear to show whether he did or did not understand a word of it. Jeremy reflected that it was perhaps better to be quite incomprehensible than to be half understood.

At the end of the week, on the afternoon of the sixth day, he decided that all was done that could be hoped for. He put the gun-crew again through its drill, and desisted for fear of scaring away what little sense its members still retained. Then, after overhauling the guns once more, he returned to the Treasury to report to the Speaker that he was ready.

As he entered the building he met the Lady Eva, who had just come in from riding. His mind was too dull and heavy to respond even to the sight of her vigorous, flushed beauty. He merely saluted her—he had queerly taken in the last few days to using again the old artillery salute—and would have gone on. But he saw her hesitate and half turn towards him; and he stopped and faced her. But when he had done so, she evidently did not know what to say to him. She stood there, tapping her foot on the ground and biting her lip, while he waited, bowed, lethargic, incapable of speech.

At last she said, with a jerky effort: "I do not know how my father is expecting you to save us... but I know that he is...."

He wondered whether this was the attempt of a frivolous girl to get news to which she had no right. He inclined his head gravely and made no reply.

She went on, still with an obvious effort: "I know he is... and I wanted to wish you success, and that—that no accident may happen to you."

"I hope for all our sakes that there will be no accident," he answered wearily, "but you never know." He waited a few moments; but she seemed to have nothing more to say. He saluted her again and left her, continuing his slow way to the Speaker's room. He did not see that she stood there looking after him until he was out of sight.

"We're all ready," he said tersely, as he entered.

"Then everything is ready," the Speaker replied from his desk, where, with his clerk standing by his side, he was signing documents with great flourishes of a quill. "And it's only just in time."

"Only just in time?"

The Speaker dismissed the clerk and turned to Jeremy. "Only just in time," he repeated, with an expression of gravity. "They have moved much quicker than I expected. They held up a train last week as soon as their messengers got back, and they've been bringing up troops in it nearly as far as Hitchin. Luckily it broke down before they had quite finished, and so the line is blocked. But the advance-guard I sent out met some of their patrols just outside St. Albans this morning."

"Then the fighting has begun?" Jeremy asked, with a little excitement.

"Yes—begun." The Speaker's face was dark and sullen. "A hundred of our men were driven through the town by a score or so of theirs. They are moving on London already, but now they are coming more slowly than they have been. I intend to set out to-night and we shall meet them to-morrow somewhere on the other side of Barnet. They will come by the Great North Road."

Jeremy was silent, and the Speaker came to him and took his arm. "Yes, Jeremy," he said, with almost tenderness in his voice, "by this time to-morrow it ought to be all over."

"But if they beat us," Jeremy cried, "they will be into London at once. Haven't you made any preparations? Won't you send the Lady Burney and the Lady Eva somewhere in the south where they will be safe? I met the Lady Eva just now—she is still here—" He stopped and gulped.

"I will not," said the Speaker, his voice deepening and taking on the resounding, the courageous, the mournful tones of a trumpet. "If we are beaten, then it is all over, and there is no need for us to look beyond defeat. If we are beaten, I do not care what happens to me or to you or to any one that belongs to me. For our civilization, that I have worked so long to maintain, would be dead, it would be too late to save England from savagery, and it would be better for all of us to die. Go now and see that your guns are ready to move in three hours. The horses will be there in time."

Jeremy hesitated, reluctantly impressed by the old man's solemn fervor. Then, without a word, he left the room and returned to the workshop.

2

As the end of the summer day faded and grew cooler, the Lady Eva sat with her mother and their attendants in a window of the Treasury overlooking Whitehall. The Lady Burney, who had long abandoned the practice of reading, was yet in the habit of hearing long stories and romances from clever persons who got them out of books; and she judged from what she had learnt of wars in the old times that it would be proper to her position to sit in a window and smile graciously on the army as it marched out to battle. It was an unfortunate thing that the Speaker, ignorant of her intentions and careless of the ritual of conflict, had appointed various places of assembly for the troops, and had taken no pains to make any part of them march through Whitehall. Detached bodies went by at intervals; and some of them, who chanced to look up, saw fluttering handkerchiefs. But most of them marched doggedly and dully with drooping heads, reflecting in their courage the prevailing spirit of gloomy anxiety which had settled on London.

Once a small erect figure on horseback clattered suddenly out of the Treasury almost immediately underneath, struggling with a wildly curvetting mount. The Lady Burney bowed and waved to it graciously. The girl Mary began and checked a sharp sigh of admiration. The Lady Eva sat motionless and expressionless. But Thomas Wells, impatient annoyance apparent in the line of his back, as soon as he had mastered the restive horse, trotted off, without once looking up, in the direction of Piccadilly, where he was to join the Speaker.

The light grew less and less, the sky became paler, with a curious and depressing lividity, as though the day were bleeding to death. The sound of marching troops, never very great or very frequent, came to the listeners in the window less often and less loud. A cloud of impalpable sadness fell upon the city and affected the Lady Eva like a spiritual miasma. The streets were not, in truth, quieter or emptier than was usual at nightfall:

there was no outward sign that the people guessed at an approaching calamity. But there rose from all the houses a soft, deadening air of gloom. It was as though London had the heavy limbs, the racked nerves, the difficult breathing of acute apprehension. The Lady Eva could feel, and dumbly shared, the general oppression. She wished to leave the window, to take refuge amid lights and conversation from the creeping chill. But her mother, obstinate and sullen, dully incensed by the failure of her romantic purpose, insisted on staying, and made the rest stay with her.

Just when the day was changing from a pale light shot with shadow into the first darkness of evening, they heard a loud clattering in Whitehall, a little way out of sight; and presently a long, slow procession came by, made up of obscure, grotesque shapes, hidden or rendered monstrous by the doubtful light. First there came a string of wagons, each drawn by two or four horses; and the men who walked beside them seemed to walk, or rather to hobble, with ludicrous awkwardness, all with bent backs and some leaning on sticks. At the end rolled two strange wheeled objects heavily swathed in tarpaulins, each drawn by a team of eight horses. The women in the window, tired of regarding the empty street for so long, gazed eagerly at these, but could not make out or give them a name. The Lady Eva alone sat back in her chair, hardly looking, until with a start she thought she saw a square, familiar figure riding beside the train on a horse as square and sedate as itself. Then she leant impulsively forward; but already Jeremy and his guns were swallowed up in the shades as they jogged along towards Charing Cross.

"Another baggage-train!" observed the Lady Burney, crossly and obesely, as she turned away from the window.

*

Jeremy had, in fact, looked up at the windows of the Treasury as he went by, and with a romantic thought in his head. But he, as little aware as the Speaker of the observances proper to the marching out of the army, had not expected to see any one there, and consequently saw no one. He merely reflected that the Lady Eva was somewhere behind those black walls;

and he strove to lift away his depression by reminding himself that he was going to fight for her. But this exhortation had no effect on his anxious mind. The circumstances did not in the slightest degree alter an extremely difficult situation. It was merely one, even if the chief, of the factors which compelled him to face that situation, however unwillingly. It would not assist him to change the issue of a good old-fashioned infantry battle by means of two very doubtful sixty-pounder guns.

But this depression occupied only one part of his mind. With another he had got his column together at Waterloo, had seen to the effectual disguising of the guns, had marshalled the old men in their proper places and set out without misadventure or delay. The collapse of other means of crossing the river sent them round by Westminster Bridge, which shook and rumbled ominously under the weight of the guns, and thence along Whitehall in the direction of Charing Cross Road. Jeremy's route had been indicated to him by the Speaker without the help of a map; but, to his surprise, he had been able to recognize the general line of it by means of the names. The column plodded slowly along a vile causeway that had been Tottenham Court Road into another as vile which was still called Euston Road, and, turning sharp to the right, made for the long hill which led towards Islington.

The mere marching through that shadowed and cheerless evening was depressing to Jeremy. He had chosen for his own use the fattest and least exuberant nag that the Speaker's stables could offer him; and on this beast he cantered now and again to the head of the column and back, to see that all was well and to urge haste on the leaders. The old men were bearing it well. There was no doubt that they looked forward with a gruesome and repulsive glee to the use of their handiwork in action. As he rode by, Jeremy could see them hobbling cheerfully, cackling and exchanging unintelligible jokes in high, cracked voices. The gathering darkness and the changing shadows made them seem even more ghostly and grotesque. Jeremy shivered. He felt as though he were leading out against the living an army of the dead. But he mastered his repulsion and cried out encouragement, now to one, now to another, bidding them when they were tired to take it in turns to ride on the wagons. They answered him with thin cheers; and a few of them, marching arm-in-arm together, like old cronies released for an airing from the workhouse, set up a feeble but cheerful marching song.

As they topped the rise of the hill, the moon came up and revealed the uncanny desolation of the country through which they were moving. Here all was ruin, with partial clearings, like those which had been made in St. John's Wood, only more extensive. The wide road had not been mended, yet had nowhere fallen into complete disuse, and was a maze of crisscrossing tracks and ruts, studded with pits which had here and there become little pools. Jeremy silently but fervently thanked the moon for rising in time to save his guns from being stuck in any of these death-traps. He rode by the first gun, watching the road anxiously; and he spent an agonized five minutes when one of the wagons in front slipped a wheel just over the edge of a pit and blocked up the only practicable way. The old men gathered around at once, cheering themselves on with piping cries, and at last heaved the wagon out. The column went slowly on—all too slowly, it seemed to Jeremy, who yet dared not make greater haste.

And then, in spite of his fears and his whirling brain, fatigue sent down on him a sort of numbing cloud. He drooped and nodded in the saddle, picking his way only by a still, vigilant instinct. Wild fancies and figures hurled themselves through his weary brain without startling him. Once he seemed to see the thin, animal face of the Canadian, teeth bared and a little open, painted on the darkness only a few inches from his eyes. Once as he lurched heavily it seemed that the arms of the Lady Eva caught him and steadied him and held him, and that he let fall his head on the delicious peace of her breast. He woke with a. start to see that the road forked and that the column was taking the road on the right. The moon was now high, and made his battery and the road and the few houses that were still standing here all black and silver. On his right stood a small ale-house, with open door, whence came the pale glow of a dying fire. It occurred to him that he must see to it that none of his old men straggled in here to rest or hide; and, pulling out of his place in the column, he rode towards it. As he did so he saw the sign on which the moonlight fell full and read with strange feelings the rudely-scrawled words, "The Archway Tavern." He looked, with hanging lip and staring eyes, for the busy swing-doors of the public-house which had been a landmark and which he had passed he knew not how many times. Though he had never entered it, this simulacrum, this dwindled vestige on the place where of old it had stood, opulent, solid and secure, affected him like a *memento mori*, a grim epitaph, the image of a skull. It was a sudden and poignant reminder of the transiency of human things and of the strange nakedness of the age in which he now lived. When he turned away he was sitting limp and dazed in the saddle.

In an alternation of fits of such drowsiness and of vigorous, bustling wakefulness, Jeremy got his column slowly over the undulations of the Great North Road. The moon at last went down; and as morning approached, the sky grew cloudy and every spark of light vanished from the world. Then, at the moment they entered on the first rise of what Jeremy supposed to be Barnet Hill, a thin breeze began to blow from the east and to bring with it a faint radiance. Jeremy felt on his right cheek the wind and the light at once, light like wind and wind like light, both numbingly cold. And, as they came to the top of the hill, the sun rose and revealed to them the assembled army.

CHAPTER X
The Battle

1

JEREMY'S ORDERS HAD BEEN TO meet the Speaker near the church on the hill; and thither he rode, not staying to look about him. By the long, cold shadow of the church tower stood a little knot of people whom he recognized for the Speaker and his staff. He rode up to them, dismounted stiffly, and saluted, as the old man came forward to meet him.

"You have come, then," said the Speaker, in his usual thick soft voice, laying an almost affectionate hand on his arm. "And are the guns safe?"

"Quite safe," Jeremy answered, shivering a little and stamping his feet for warmth.

"I knew I could trust you to bring them," the Speaker murmured. "Come over here and they shall give you a warm drink."

Jeremy went with him to the little knot of officers, who were standing just in the growing sunlight, and took from a servant a great mug which he found to be full of inferior, sickly-flavored whisky and hot water, highly sweetened. He lifted his head from it, coughing and gasping a little, but immediately found that he was warmer and stronger.

"All the army is assembled," the Speaker told him. "We continue the march in half-an-hour. The enemy pushed past St. Albans last night and they are camped between here and there. The battle will be two or three miles north of this."

Jeremy was now sufficiently revived to look about him with interest. Here, as almost everywhere in the farthest limits of London, the restorations of time had been complete. The little town had returned to what it was before the nineteenth century. The long rows of small houses had gone, like a healed rash, as though they had never been; and on all sides of the few buildings that clustered round the church and to the north of it, grazing land stretched out unbroken, save here and there by rude and overgrown walls of piled bricks. On this narrow platform, which fell away rapidly on the right hand and on the left, the troops were bivouacking, huddled in little clusters around miserable fires or dancing about to keep themselves warm.

Jeremy's eye ran from one end of the prospect to the other and back again, until he became conscious that somebody was standing at his elbow waiting for him to turn. He turned accordingly and found the Canadian, whose customary barbaric fineness of dress seemed to have been enhanced for the occasion by a huge dull red tie and a dull red handkerchief pinned carelessly in a bunch on the brim of his hat.

"What do you think of them?" asked Thomas Wells in his hard, incisive tones, indicating the shivering soldiers by a jerk of his head.

"I've not seen enough of them to think anything," Jeremy answered defensively. "I dare say they're not at their best now."

"Poor stuff!" snapped the Canadian, between teeth almost closed. "Poor stuff at the best. I could eat them all with half of one of our regiments. Yes…" he continued, drawling as though the words had an almost physical savor for him, "if I got among them with two or three hundred of my own chaps, I bet we wouldn't leave a live man anywhere within sight in half-an-hour. We'd cut all their throats. It'd be like killing sheep."

Jeremy shuddered involuntarily and moved a step away. "Where's all the rest of the army?" he asked.

"The rest? There isn't any rest. You can see all there is of it."

"But surely…" Jeremy began, and paused.

The Canadian laughed with malicious and evil amusement. "They're not great at fighting here," he said. "If they'd taken only those that wanted to come there'd be you and me and the Speaker. And they wouldn't take people from the fields—or not many at all events. And there's nobody come from Gloucestershire or the West, though the Speaker sent to them twice. The farmers over there are waiting to see what happens. They don't want to quarrel with the bosses that buy their wool. No, it's not a big army—eight thousand at most. And yet," he went on reflectively, "it's more than I had when I tore the guts out of Boston. I tell you, we got into that city…."

"Yes," Jeremy interrupted him nervously, not desiring in the least to know what happened in Boston, "but how many have the northerners got?"

"Oh, not many more, by all accounts," the Canadian answered airily. "Ten or twelve thousand, I reckon. Oh, yes, we're going to get whipped all right, but I've got a good horse, and I expect the Chairman will want to stand well with my dad. Yes—I've got a good horse, a lot better than yours." As he spoke he glanced at Jeremy's tubby nag, and his narrow mouth stretched again in the same smile of evil amusement.

Jeremy's heart sank. But, as he was wondering whether his dismay was betrayed by his face, a gentle bustle rose around them.

"We're marching off," cried the Speaker, as he strode by with the vigor of a boy of twenty. "Back to your—to your charge, Jeremy Tuft."

It was not until the whole army was well on the road that Jeremy found himself sufficiently unoccupied to examine it carefully. His old men resumed the march, with, if anything, a little too much enthusiasm. They were extravagantly keen to show the twenty-first century what their guns could do; but in their anxiety to take their place on the battlefield they behaved, as Jeremy bitterly though unintelligibly told them, like a crowd of children scrambling outside the door of a Sunday-school tea. Even Jabez, whom he had chosen to act as a sort of second-in-command, danced about from wagon to wagon and gun to gun like the infant he was just, for the second time, becoming. A company of the ordinary soldiers, who, in accordance with plan, had been attached to the battery so that they might help in man-handling the guns, watched the excited gyrations of the old men in solemn silence. The march northwards out of the little town was well begun before Jeremy could feel sure that his own command was smoothly and safely in hand. As soon as he was satisfied he left it and rode on ahead to see what he could make of the army.

He had had little enough time to make himself familiar with the new methods of warfare. He had, in his rare, idle moments, questioned everybody he met who seemed likely to be able to tell him; but he found much the same uncertainty as to the deadliness of modern weapons as he dimly remembered to have existed in the long past year of 1914. The troops with whom he was riding to battle were armed, and had, many of them, been drilled; but what would be the effect of their arms and how their drill would answer in warfare no one knew, for they had never been tried. He formed himself, this gray and early morning, a most unfavorable impression of them.

Their uniforms were shabby and shoddy, uncouth, loosely-cut garments, varying in shape and color. On their feet they wore rude rawhide shoes or sandals and round their legs long strips of rag were shapelessly wrapped. Their bearing was execrable. They made only the emptiest pretense at march discipline, they slouched and shuffled, left the ranks as they pleased, held themselves and their arms anyhow. The officers were for the most part young men of good family who had been appointed to commands only during the past four or five days. A few, those who had trained the army in times of peace, were soldiers of fortune, who had been drawn by the Speaker's lavish offers to them from the wars in the Polish Marches and in the Balkans, from every place where a living could be earned by the slitting of throats. They were old, debauched, bloated and lazy, low cunning peeping out from their eyes like the stigma of a disease. They looked much better suited to any kind of private villainy than to the winning of battles; and the contingents under their command had an appearance of hang-dog shiftiness rather than the sheepish reluctance of the rest.

Not much more than half the army was provided with rifles; and these, as Jeremy knew, were hardly to be described as weapons of precision. The rest had a sort of pikes; or some had cutlasses, some bayonets lashed to the ends of poles. The rifles reminded Jeremy a little of those of his earlier experience, but suffering from the thickening and clumsy degeneration of extreme old age. They had no magazines: the workshops were not equal to the production of a magazine that would not result in fatal stoppages. The breech-loading action was retained and was frequently efficient, so Jeremy learnt, for as many as twenty-five rounds. After that it was liable to jam altogether and, at the best, permitted only a reduced rate of fire. The range was supposed to be five hundred yards, but the best and most careful marksman could rarely at that distance hit a target the size of a man. Jeremy calculated that the effective range was not more than two hundred yards at the outside; and he thought that very little damage would be done at more than half that distance. As he rode along by the side of the marching regiments, he observed the pikes and cutlasses, and the sheathless bayonets which hung at the belts of the riflemen, and wondered what would happen when it came to close fighting. Neither the carriage nor the expressions of the men inspired him with confidence. Many of them, especially the new recruits, haled in at the last moment from field and farm, were healthy, sturdy fellows; but, unless he was mightily mistaken, an abhorrence of fighting was in their blood. He himself had only a blunderbuss of a double-barreled pistol, which reminded him of the highwaymen stories of his boyhood, and a most indifferent horse....

He reached the end of this train of thought, found it disagreeable, and paused, as it were, on the edge of an abyss. Then he drew in his horse against the roadside, halted, and let the column march past him. At the end came his battery, plodding along with more enthusiasm than all the rest of the army put together. Jabez, perched beside the driver on the seat of the first wagon, hailed his reappearance with delight, scrambled down and ran to him, putting one hand on his stirrup.

"Well, Jabez," said Jeremy kindly, as he might have addressed an affectionate dog, "and how do you think we are getting along?" As he spoke he tapped his horse lightly and began to move on again. Jabez hopped by his side, ecstatically proclaiming in cracked tones that he expected the beautiful guns to blow the damned Yorkshiremen to hell. The only thing that annoyed him was this great press of useless infantry in front of them. They might be useful enough, he felt, to drag the guns into position and perhaps to remove what was left of the enemy when he had done with them. But he certainly envisaged the coming battle as a contest between the army of the north on the one hand and two doubtful sixty-pounder guns on the other. Jeremy listened to him tolerantly, as if in a dream. Faint wreaths of mist were rising up from the fields all around them and scattering into the sparkling air. The tramp of the soldiers sounded heavy and sodden, a presage of defeat.

Far ahead Jeremy could see the column steadily but slowly following the slight curves in the road. Right at the van, as he knew, though they were out of his sight, were the Speaker and his staff—Thomas Wells, on the swift horse to which he trusted, close at the old man's right hand. Somewhere just behind them was Roger Vaile, who, like many of the clerks in the Treasury, had chosen to be a trooper in the cavalry and had obtained admission to the Speaker's own guard. Miles away in the rear of the army—was the Lady Eva, doubtless asleep; and around her, who was now to him the one significant point in it, London, asleep or waking, awaited the issue of the struggle. Jeremy felt terribly alone. This was very different from being in charge of two guns out of some five hundred or so bombarding the German front line before a push. An unexpected wave of lassitude came over him, and, defeat seeming certain, he wished that he could be done with it all at once.

As he sagged miserably in the saddle, a sudden check ran down the column, followed by an ever-increasing babel of whispered conjectures. The men behaved as infantry suddenly halted on the march always have done. They were divided between pleasure at the relief and a suspicion that something untoward had happened out of sight in front of them. They murmured to one another, unceasingly and eloquently, that their leaders were born fools and were taking them into a death-trap. But the check continued and no certain orders came down; and at last Jeremy rode forward, so that he might pass a slight rise in the ground and see what had happened. When he did so he found that the head of the column was already slowly deploying on both sides of the road.

"We've begun," he murmured sharply to himself, and stayed a moment hesitating. Then, as he remembered that he had not yet heard a single shot, he spurred his horse on to make further enquiries. He found the Speaker, Thomas Wells, and two or three others just leaving the road by a farm-track to gain the top of a little mound close by.

The old man greeted him with a boyish wave of the hand. "There they are!" he called out, while Jeremy was still some yards away; and, following the sweep of his arm, Jeremy saw on the forward slope of a hill, about half-a-mile off, a flurry of horsemen plunging wildly about together. It looked at first like a rather crowded and amateurish game of polo; but, while he watched, he saw the sun sparkling again and again on something in the crowded mass. Then a body fell inertly from the saddle and a riderless horse galloped off over the hill. A minute later a few riders extricated themselves and smartly followed it.

"There they are!" said the Speaker again, this time in a quieter voice. The greater body of horsemen was now cantering back; and, before they had covered half the distance, a few scattered parties of infantry began to appear on the low crest above. Shots were fired here and there. The reports came over, dull and vague, against a contrary breeze.

"I must go back to my guns," Jeremy gasped breathlessly. "I must go back." He turned his horse and began to gallop lumberingly along the fields beside the road.

"Goo-ood luck to you!" came after him in a high-pitched mocking yell from the Canadian.

In a minute he had reached the battery. When he pulled up there he had to spend the best part of five minutes calming Jabez and his men, who wished to drag the guns incontinently into the next field and let them off at random over the slope before them. By liberal cursing he subdued the enraged ancients and got them at a sedate pace past the infantry immediately in front, who were in reserve and had not yet received orders to proceed. When he reached the top of the rise again he found that the whole of the enemy's line had come into sight. It stretched out on both sides of the road, and its left flank seemed to be resting on a wood. It had ceased in its advance; and across its front a body of cavalry was riding slow and unmolested.

2

The sound of firing broke out again and increased rapidly. From the almost hidden line of the Speaker's troops, and from the enemy on the opposite slope, black puffs of smoke arose, looking solid and sharply defined in the clear air. They drifted away, melting slowly as they went. Jeremy suffered a spasm of panic and haste. The struggle was beginning; and in a minute or two he must bring his guns into position and fire them.

He dreaded lest the battle should be suddenly over and lost before he could let off a single round, lest he should never get even the slender chance, which was all that he could hope for. In that moment his faculties stopped dead, and he did not know what to do. But, as rapidly, the seizure passed, and he halted the battery while he rode out into the field on the right to find a position for the guns. Presently he came upon a little shallow dip, which would, in case of necessity, give cover from an attack by riflemen, while leaving to the guns a clear field of fire. He went back to the road and gave his orders.

Jabez and his companions began at once to behave like puppies unchained. They turned the gun-teams and urged them recklessly off the road with complete disregard of the ground they had to cover. "Steady, Jabez, steady!" Jeremy shouted. "Look out for that—" But before he could finish, the first gun had negotiated a most alarming slope, and the second was hard upon it. At the end of ten minutes' confused sweating and bawling, the two guns were standing side by side, twenty yards apart, in the hollow he had chosen; and the crews, panting loudly with their mouths wide open, stood there also, looking at him and eagerly expecting the order to load and fire.

He had early abandoned all hope of using indirect fire from any kind of shelter: for the technical equipment of his men was plainly not equal to it. He had therefore been obliged to decide upon the use of open sights; and from the lip of this hollow he could see, he imagined, a reasonably large area of the battlefield. It stretched, so far as he could make out, from the woods on his right, which, where the front line ran, were closer to the road than here, to a vague and indiscernible point that lay a somewhat greater distance on the other side of the road. The Speaker's men were some three-quarters of a mile in front of him, the enemy nearly half a mile beyond that. It appeared to Jeremy that the exchange of shots up to now had been no more than a symbolic expression of ill-will, since at that range it was obviously impossible for the antagonists to hit one another.

A feverish and exhaustive search during the week of preparation had not obtained for Jeremy the field-glasses which he had hoped might be lying in some corner, uninjured and forgotten; but it had at last brought forth a reasonably good pair of opera-glasses. With these at his eyes, he stood on the edge of his hollow, shifting uneasily from one foot to the other, and vainly searched the landscape for a target. His only chance, he told himself, was to catch a mass of the enemy somewhere in the open and to scatter them with a direct hit. If he could do this, he thought, the moral effect might be to dismay them, and to put heart into the Speaker's troops. But he did not suppose that he could rout the whole army of the north with fifty rounds of a very feeble and uncertain kind of high explosive, which was all the ammunition he had been able to get together for the two guns. "If only we had shrapnel—" he was murmuring to himself; but then Jabez's attempt at a time-fuse had been altogether too fantastic. "If only we had quick-firers... seventy-fives..." But things were as they were, and he must make the best of them.

But still no target presented itself. Neither line seemed to move; and, in fact, any considerable movement must have been instantly visible on that smooth, hardly broken stretch of pasture-land. This state of immobility continued for half an hour or so, during which Jeremy's anxiety increased, relaxed, and increased again, until the alternation of moods became almost unbearable. Once, quite suddenly, the firing, which had grown slacker, broke out again violently on the right. It began with an attempt at volleys, but after a moment or two fell into irregularity and raggedness. Jeremy, scanning the ground with his opera-glasses, could find no cause for it. He attributed it to panic and was beginning to believe that the formidable-ness of the Yorkshire army had been much overrated. He had just let fall the glasses when he was disturbed by a touch at his elbow. He turned and saw Jabez, a stooped, shriveled figure that looked up at him with shining youthful eyes in a face absurdly old.

"*Aren't* we going to let them off?" pleaded Jabez in wistful tones. "Aren't we *ever* going to let them off? Just once—anywhere…." He swept a claw-like hand round the horizon, as though it was immaterial to him where the shot fell, so long as it was discharged. "It would frighten those fellers," he added with cunning.

Jeremy reluctantly smiled. "We must wait till we can frighten them properly," he answered, "and just at present I can't see anything to fire at."

"We sha'n't ever get a chance," wailed Jabez; and he lolloped mournfully back to the guns so as to be ready for the first order.

Intense quiet descended again upon the battlefield. Both sides seemed to be lying down in their lines, each waiting for the other to make a move. Jeremy uttered a short, involuntary laugh. This, he supposed, was what might be expected from a people so incredibly unused to warfare, but it was nevertheless a trifle ludicrous. He determined to ride forward again and consult with the Speaker.

He had mounted and ridden a hundred yards from the battery, when a second burst of firing broke out, this time apparently upon the left. The road, which ran along the crest of a slight ridge, would give him a better view, and thither he hastened. When he gained it he saw that on the extreme left the battle had indeed begun and, to all appearance, disastrously. A great body of Yorkshiremen was advancing in close formation, and already the Speaker's troops were giving way, some throwing down their weapons, some firing wildly as they ran. Jeremy paused rigid for a second. It was as though what he saw touched only the surface of the brain and by that paralyzed all power of thought. Those scuffling, running, dark figures over there were fighting and being killed. They were fighting and being killed in the great contest between civilization and barbarism for the body of England; and barbarism, it seemed, was winning. But there was nothing impressive in their convulsed and ungainly actions. They were merely dark figures running about and scuffling and sometimes falling. Jeremy knew very well what it was that he saw, but he did not realize it. It did not seem real enough to make the intimate contact between perception and thought which produces a deed. Then suddenly his paralysis, which felt to him as though it had lasted a million years, was dissolved, and before he knew what he was doing he had turned and was galloping back to the battery at a speed which considerably astonished his horse.

"Get those guns out!" he yelled, with distorted face and starting eyes. "Get those guns—" His voice cracked, but already the old men were in a frenzy of haste, limbering up and putting in the teams. In a few moments, it seemed, they were all scurrying together over the field, Jabez clinging to Jeremy's stirrup, flung grotesquely up and down by the horse's lumbering stride, the guns tossed wildly to and fro on the uneven ground. They breasted the slight ridge of the road like a pack of hounds taking a low wall and plunged down together on the further side, men, guns, horses, wagons, all confused in a flying mass.

"My God!" Jeremy gasped to himself. "Any one would think we were horse-gunners. I wouldn't have believed that it could be done."

His own reflection sobered him, and, lifting himself in the saddle, he shouted to the insane mob around him: "Steady! Steady! Steady!" The pace slackened a little, and a swift glance round showed him that, by some miracle, no damage had been done. How these heavy guns and wagons, even with their double teams of horses, had been driven at such a speed over ground so broken and over the bank of the road was, he supposed, something he would never be able to explain; and this was least of all the moment for troubling about it. But the divine madness, which must have inspired men and animals alike, had now evaporated, and it was time to think what he must do. In another hundred yards he had made his way to the front of the battery and had halted it by an uplifted hand. Then first he was able to see how the situation had developed.

It had gone even worse than he had feared, and he had halted only just in time. So far as he could make out, the whole of the Speaker's left flank had been driven back in confusion and was fighting, such of it? as yet stood, in little groups. Some of these were not more than three or four hundred yards in front of him. Complete ruin had failed to follow only because the Yorkshire troops had attacked in small force and were for the moment exhausted. But over where their first line had been he could see new bodies approaching to the attack. When he looked round for help he found that the Speaker's army was engaged all along its length and that only a meager company of reserves was coming up, slowly and from a great distance.

His decision was rapidly made. Now, if ever, he had his chance of using his guns to demoralize the enemy, and if he could thus break up the attack, the position might yet be restored. It was true that here in the open he ran a mighty risk of losing the guns. The remnants of the enemy's wave were not far off; and hardly anything in the way of defenders lay between him and them. But this only spurred him to take a further risk. He led the battery forward again to a convenient hollow, a few yards behind one of the still resisting groups, which was lodged in a little patch of gorse. And, just as the battery came up, a party of the enemy made a rush, driving the Speaker's men back among the horses and wagons. There was a whirlwind moment, in which Jeremy was nearly thrown from his plunging horse. He had no weapon, but struck furiously with his fist into a face which was thrust up for a second by his bridle. Around him everything was in commotion, men shouting in deep or piping voices, arms whirling, steel flashing. And then miraculously all was quiet again and he calmed his horse. A few bodies lay here and there, some in brown, some in uniforms of an unfamiliar dark blue. They were like the line of foam deposited by the receding wave. Not far away, Jabez, surprised and bewildered, but unhurt, lay on his back, where he had been pushed over, waving his arms and legs in the air. Another of the old men had collapsed across the barrel of one of the guns and blood was spouting from his side. Beyond the battery a few of the infantrymen were standing, wild-eyed and panting, in attitudes of flight, unable to believe that their opponents had been destroyed. Further off still the company which had been attached to the guns, and which they had left behind in their wild rush, was coming up and had halted irresolutely to see what turn events would take.

Jeremy recovered his self-possession, and, with the help of the shaken but indomitable Jabez, got the guns into place and gave the order to load. Then himself he trained the first gun on a body of Yorkshire troops which was advancing in column over half a mile away. There followed a tense moment.

"Fire!" He cried the word in a trembling voice.

Jabez, with an air of ineffable pride, pulled the lanyard and all the old men at once leapt absurdly at the report. Over, far over! And yet the shell had at least burst, and through his glasses he could see the enemy waver and halt, obviously astonished by the new weapon. He ran to the other gun, trained it, and again gave the order to fire. It was short this time, and the smoke and dust of the explosion hid the mark. But when the air was clear again, Jeremy saw that the column had broken and was dispersing in all directions. Apparently the flying fragments of the shell had swept its leading ranks. The old men raised a quavering cheer, and Jabez, leaping with senile agility to an insecure perch on the gun-carriage, flourished his hat madly in the air.

Jeremy's first feeling was one of relief that neither of the guns had blown up. He examined them carefully and was satisfied. When he resumed his survey of the field there was no target in sight. But the firing on the right was growing louder and, he thought, nearer. It was not possible to drag these guns from point to point to strengthen any part of the line that might happen to be in danger; and his despair overwhelmingly returned. He swept the ground before him in the faint hope of finding another column in the open. As he did so he suddenly became aware that he could just see round the left of the ridge on which the northern army had established itself; and, searching this tract, he observed something about a mile away, under the shade of a long plantation, that seemed significant. He lowered his glasses, wiped the lenses carefully, and looked again. He had not been mistaken. There, within easy range, lay a great park of wagons, which was perhaps the whole of the enemy's transport.

Now, if it were possible, he exultantly reflected, fortune offered him a chance of working the miracle which the Speaker had demanded of him. He beckoned Jabez to his side, pointed out the mark and explained his intention. The ancient executed a brief, brisk caper of delighted comprehension, and together they aimed the two guns very carefully, making such allowances as were suggested on the spur of the moment by the results of the first shots. They were just ready when the noise of battle again clamorously increased on the right and urged them forward.

"It's now or never, Jabez," muttered Jeremy, feeling an unusual constriction of the throat that hindered his words. But Jabez only replied with an alert and bird-like nod of confidence.

"Fire!" Jeremy cried in a strangled voice. The lanyards were jerked, and Jeremy, his glasses fixed on the target, saw two great clouds spring up to heaven not far apart. Were they short? But when the smoke drifted away, he saw that they had not been short. Feverishly he made a slight adjustment in the aim, and the guns were fired again. Now one burst showed well in the middle of the enemy's wagons, but the second did not explode. Jeremy was trembling in every muscle when he gave the order to load and fire for the third time. Was it that he only imagined a slackening, as if caused by hesitation, in the noise of the attack on the right? He could hardly endure the waiting; but when the third round burst he could hardly endure his joy. For immediately there leapt into the air from the parked wagons an enormous column of vapor that seemed to overshadow the entire battlefield, and hard after this vision came a deafening and reverberating explosion, which shook the ground where he stood.

"Got their ammunition!" he screamed, the tears pouring down his face. "There must have been a lot!" He reached out blindly for Jabez; and the old men of the battery observed their commander and his lieutenant clasping one another by the hands and leaping madly round and round in an improvised and frenzied dance of jubilation.

When the echoes of that devastating report died away, complete silence stole over the battlefield, as though heaven by a thundered reproof had hushed the shrill quarrels of mankind. It was broken by a thin cheering, which grew louder and increased in volume till the sky rang with it; and Jeremy, rushing forward to see, realized that everywhere within sight the Speaker's men had taken heart and were falling boldly on their panic-stricken enemies.

CHAPTER XI
Triumph

1

THE BRIEF REMAINDER of the battle was for Jeremy a confused and violent phantasmagoria. Immediately on the heels of that triumphant shout he ordered the guns to be brought forward again and had the luck to plump a single shell into a body of the enemies' reserves before they finally melted out of existence. After that he could not find another mark to fire at. The northern army, struck down in the moment of victory by an overwhelming panic, crumbled all along its line and broke up into flying knots of terrified men, who were surrounded and harried by the jubilant and suddenly blood-thirsty troops of the Speaker. When he perceived this, Jeremy was overcome by a rush of blood to the head.

"We've done it! We've done it!" he muttered in a dazed way. And then this stupefaction was replaced by a wild and reckless delight. "Come on, Jabez!" he yelled, pounding with his heels the long-suffering horse. "Come on! We've got to see this!" Again they were off together, this time leaving the guns behind. Jabez, exalted to an activity wholly unsuited to his years, flung up and down at the stirrup, while Jeremy waved his whip in the air and shouted incoherently. Before they knew it they had shot into the rearmost of the scattered fighting, and had ridden down an escaping Yorkshireman. Jeremy saw for a moment at his bridle the backward-turned, terror-distorted face and slashed at it fiercely with his whip. The man fell and lay still; and Jabez with a convulsive leap passed over the body. Out of the corner of his eyes Jeremy half saw, only half realizing it, that one of the Speaker's men was jabbing with his bayonet at a wriggling mass on the ground beside him. Then they were through that skirmish, and for a couple of hundred yards in front of them the field was empty. But the gentle slope beyond was covered with small figures, running, dodging, stopping and striking with the furious and aimless vitality of the ants in a disturbed nest. Jeremy and Jabez had hastened into the midst of them before Jeremy was overtaken by a belated coolness of the reason. When the sobering moment came, he wished he had had the sense to keep out of this confused and murderous struggle, and at the same time he remembered that his only weapon was a pistol still strapped in its clumsy holster. He reached for it and began to fumble with the straps; but while he fumbled a desperate Yorkshireman, turning like a rat, pushed a rifle into his face and pulled the trigger. It was not loaded. Jeremy, trying to understand that he was still alive, saw in an arrested instant like an eternity the man's jaw drop and his eyes grow rounder and rounder, till suddenly the staring face vanished altogether. Jabez, shaken to his knees by the man's onset, had grasped an abandoned pike and had stabbed upward.

Jeremy reined in and quieted the almost frantic horse. A cold sweat broke out on his face, and he felt a little sick. He wiped his forehead with his sleeve and looked faintly from the dead Yorkshireman to Jabez, who stood with the bloody pike in his hand, an expression of complacent excitement wrinkling the skin round his eyes. The fighting had already passed beyond them; and Jeremy without moving let it roll away noisily over the crest of the hill. He made no sign even when Jabez shouldered his weapon with a determined air and began to trudge off defiantly in its wake. But when the queer lolloping figure had already begun to grow smaller, Jeremy put his hands to his mouth and shouted:

"Jabez! Jabez! Come back!" Jabez turned, shook his head, waved the pike with warlike ferocity, and shouted something in reply that came faintly, indistinguishably against the breeze. Then he resumed his march, leaving his commanding officer alone.

It was over half-an-hour later that Jeremy found the Speaker. By that time the fighting was all over, and the fields, hardly changed in appearance by being dotted with a number of corpses, so soon to be resolved into the same substance as their own, were quiet again. In the course of his search, Jeremy encountered much that he would rather not have seen. He saw too many men lying face downwards with wounds in their backs, too many with tied hands and cut throats. He realized that a battlefield can too literally resemble a slaughter-house; and these evidences of the ferocity of an unwarlike race appalled him. And he even found one of the mercenary officers, of the sort that he had observed earlier in the day and had disliked, in the act of dispatching a prisoner, preparatory to going through his pockets. He advanced angrily on the man, who did not know him and turned with a curse from his just accomplished work to suggest that Jeremy's throat would prove equally vulnerable. Held off by Jeremy's pistol, he strolled away with insolent unconcern. Jeremy continued his way and at last discovered the Speaker, a couple of miles beyond the line on which the battle had been decided. As he came up, he could see that the old man's dress was disheveled, and that his horse was lathered and weary, presumably from taking part in the pursuit.

By this time he was faint and exhausted, and he did not announce himself in the confident manner that might have been permitted him. He rode up slowly to the crossroads, where the Speaker and Thomas Wells were standing under a sign-post, and dismounted. They were deep in a conversation and at first did not see him. The Speaker's thick voice came in rapid jerky bursts. His reins were lying on the horse's neck, and he gesticulated violently with his hands. The Canadian, whose eyes seemed to Jeremy to burn with a fiercer red than ever, spoke more slowly, but there was a kind of intense richness and gusto in his tone. Jeremy felt too inert to make any sound to attract their attention; but as he came nearer Thomas Wells touched the Speaker's arm and pronounced deeply:

"There's your hero!"

The Speaker dismounted and, running without consideration of dignity to Jeremy, clasped the astonished young man in his arms.

"You have done it! You have done it!" he cried again and again. "There is nothing left of them!" Then, when his transports had abated a little, he went on more calmly. "We have smashed them to pieces. The rebel army has ceased to exist, and the Chairman has been killed."

"Killed?" cried Jeremy, in surprise.

"Yes, killed," the Canadian interjected, still in the saddle and leaning down a little to them. "There's no doubt that he's dead. I killed him myself."

"But was that wise—" Jeremy began. "Wouldn't it have been better to keep him? It would have given us a hold over his people."

"That's what *he* said," the Canadian answered drily. "He seemed quite anxious about it. But I always go on the principle that you can't be sure what any man is going to do unless he's dead. Then you know where he is."

"Yes, he's dead, he's dead," the Speaker broke in, in a rising voice. "The scoundrel has got what he asked for. He'll never lift his hand against me or my people again!" Jeremy, dismayed and sickened, saw in the old man's posture something of the inspiration, of the inhuman rage, of a Hebrew prophet. He dared not look at Thomas Wells, from whose grinning mouth, he fancied, as from that of a successful ferret, drops of blood must still be trickling.

"But it was you that gave him into our hands, Jeremy," the Speaker resumed, in a softer and caressing voice. "You did for him—you killed him. All the thanks is yours, and I shall not be ungrateful!"

The Canadian laughed, low and ironical. Jeremy's stomach for a moment revolted and a thick mist of horror swam before his eyes.

"Listen! Listen to the bells!"

Jeremy roused himself, cocked his head and listened. He was riding slowly beside the Speaker down the long undulations of the Great North Road that led them back to London. Sure enough, far and faint but insistent, that sweet metallic music reached his ears, a phantom of sound that stood for a reality. London was already rejoicing over its deliverance. A thin haze covered the city; and out of it there rose continuously the ringing of the bells.

"I sent messengers in front of us," the Speaker went on, with great content. "They will be ready to greet us—to greet you, I ought to say. This has been your battle."

Jeremy bestirred himself again. An urgent honesty drove him to do what he could to make the truth plain. It was pleasant, and yet intolerable, that he should be saddled with a victory that he had won only because he had been the instrument of fortune. He reasoned earnestly with the old man. He pointed out to him what a piece of luck it had been that the Yorkshiremen were fools enough to leave their transport exposed. He insisted that it was a mere chance that the destruction of their ammunition had thrown them into so disastrous a panic. When at last he was silent, the Speaker resumed, unmoved:

"It was your battle, Jeremy Tuft. You settled them. I was right to rely on you."

The Canadian, who was riding on the Speaker's left hand and had not yet uttered a word, breathed again upon the air a shadow of ironical laughter, which Jeremy felt rather than heard, and which the old man disregarded.

"They will come out to meet us," the Speaker murmured in a rapturous dream, "and you shall be toasted at our banquet. Ah, this is a great day, a wonderful day! England is restored. Happiness and greatness lie before us. I shall be remembered in history with the good Queen Victoria." He turned a little in the saddle and looked keenly at Jeremy. "Do you not ask what lies before you?"

Jeremy, staring straight in front of him, knew that he was reddening and swore inwardly. He wanted to be left alone.

"I'm glad you're pleased," he muttered, awkwardly and absurdly; and he began to calculate how far they were now from Whitehall and how much longer the journey would take. He supposed that he would be overwhelmed with undeserved congratulations at the end of it; but he reckoned that under them it would be his part to be dumb and that no disconcerting questions would be asked of him. The Speaker was too happy to do more than smile at the young man's moodiness. As they rode along he continued his murmurings, which rose now and then into loud-voiced rhapsody.

In the daylight Jeremy vaguely recognized the country through which he had passed, in darkness, on the previous night, for the first time for many generations. At the Archway Tavern, which looked even ruder and more squalid under the sun than under the moon, the innkeeper and his family threw flowers at them and shouted uncouth blessings. But as they passed through Holloway and Islington, deserted and ruined districts, only a few squatters appeared to watch the conquerors march by. These hardly human beings displayed no emotion save a faint curiosity. They stood by the roadside, singly or in little groups, here and there, and gazed on the triumphant cavalcade with enigmatic faces. They reminded Jeremy of horses which he had seen gathering at a gate by the railway-line to watch a train go past. Their thoughts, their expectations, their hopes and fears, were as much hidden from him as were the minds of animals. And, as he looked at them, he experienced a singular pang. What to these creatures was all human history? What did it matter to them whence he had come, what he had done, what his future fortunes might be? Their sort, oppressed and tortured, had risen and had smashed in pieces the vast machine that tortured them, destroying by that act all that made life gracious and pleasant, and accomplished for their masters. It mattered so little to them what their own ancestors had done: it could not much matter what had been or would be the deeds of Jeremy Tuft, what edifice the old Jew would erect on the foundation laid by the victory. They gaped a little as they stared. Their attention was fleeting: they turned away and spoke and laughed among themselves. Jeremy felt in a piercing instant the nullity of human striving; and his blood was chilled.

When they reached the crossroads at the Angel, they went through a more elaborate repetition of the ceremony at the Archway Tavern. A deputation of good villagers brought out hastily twined wreaths to them, waved cloths in the air and shouted loyally; and the Speaker, bowing his thanks and his gratification, urgently commanded Jeremy to do the same. So it went all the way, save that the demonstrations grew increasingly elaborate, and as they approached the city became continuous. The people were throwing down flowers from their windows and hanging out flags. At the doors of the larger houses crowds were assembling to receive free distributions of beer; and down some of the turnings off the main street Jeremy could see rings of men and women beginning already to dance and romp in the abandon of an unexpected holiday.

In Piccadilly the crowd had grown impenetrable; and by the spot where the Tube Station had stood they were brought to a halt and remained for some minutes. Loud and incessant cheering mingled with the noise of the bells. Daring young girls ran out from the crowd to hang the victors with flowers; and Jeremy saw with concern the profusion of blossoms covering first his horse's head and at last mounting up round his own. The mechanical bowing and smiling, which the Speaker had enjoined on him began to tell on his nerves. He was conscious of bright eyes persistently seeking his, as the lingering hands fastened garlands wherever there was room for them, on his saddle or on his coat. He turned his head uncomfortably this way and that, shifted in the saddle, sought shamefacedly the eyes of the Canadian for some sort of sympathy. When he saw that Thomas Wells had had few wreaths bestowed on him and was grinning with more than his usual malice, he looked away again hastily.

The noise and movement around him continually increased; and it seemed that every minute some new bell found its voice and the crowd grew larger. Jeremy felt crushed and stunned, felt that he was sinking under the weight of the people's enthusiasm. He felt so small and so oppressed that it seemed impossible that most of this could be meant for him. And yet vaguely, dully, he could see the Speaker at his side, pointing at him and apparently shouting something. He could not make out what it was; but he knew that every time the Speaker paused the continuous yelling of the crowd rose to a frantic crescendo, in which the whole world seemed to sway dizzily around him.

Suddenly, when he thought that he could bear no more, there was a wavelike motion in the press before them; and it broke open, leaving a passage through it. A carriage advanced slowly and stopped; and out of it came the Lady Burney, followed by the Lady Eva, each of them carrying in each hand a small wreath of green leaves. Jeremy, petrified, watched them walking through the narrow clear space. The Lady Burney moved very slowly with corpulent dignity and acknowledged the cheering as she came, while the Lady Eva seemed nervous, and looked persistently at the ground. When they reached the little group of motionless horsemen, the Lady Burney would have handed a wreath to the Speaker, but he signed her away, crying in a loud voice:

"Both to Jeremy Tuft! Both to Jeremy Tuft!"

The crowd redoubled its vociferations, while Jeremy, feeling himself at the lowest point of misfortune, leant over to the Lady Burney. She deposited both of her wreaths somewhere, anywhere, on the saddle before him and then, raising her arms, firmly embraced him and planted a kiss on his cheek, just underneath the left eye. He nearly yelled aloud in his astonishment; but before he could do or say anything, she had rolled away and the Lady Eva was standing in her place.

It seemed to Jeremy at this moment that the shouting abruptly grew less, and that as the noise faded the surroundings faded too, and became misty and unreal. There was nothing left vivid and substantial in the world but himself, numb, dazed, unhappy, and the tall girl beside him, her face bravely raised to his, though her cheeks were burning. She, too, seemed, by the convulsive movement of her hands, to be about to put her wreaths on any spot that would hold them, but, with an effort that made her body quiver, she controlled herself and placed one on his head, from which the hat long since had gone, and fastened the other on his breast. She did this with interminable deliberation, while the people maintained their astonishing quietude. Then, after a pause, she put her arms round his neck and placed her lips on his cheek. At this signal the crowd's restrained joy broke out tumultuously. Jeremy closed his eyes and swayed over towards the girl, then caught at his horse's mane to save himself as she slipped away.

When they began to move again, he had lost all control of himself. He shivered like a man in a high fever, his teeth were chattering, and he was sobbing ungovernably. He had afterwards a confused memory of how they proceeded slowly down the Haymarket into Whitehall, and how a dozen helpers at once sought to lift him from his horse outside the door of the Treasury.

2

Jeremy's next distinct impression was that of sitting in a small room while the Speaker poured down his throat a glass of neat smoke-flavored whisky. It revived him, and he straightened himself and stood up, but he found that his back ached and that his legs were unsteady. The Speaker forced him down again and bent over him tenderly, muttering caressing and soothing words at the back of his throat.

"You will feel better presently," he said at last; and he went out softly, looking back and smiling as he went. When he was alone, Jeremy rose again and walked towards the door, but was checked at once by a great fatigue and weakness. He looked round the room, and, seeing a couch, threw himself at full length upon it.

"I wish I could go to sleep," he murmured to himself. But his brain, though it was exhausted, was so clear and active that he gave up all hope of it. When, a minute later, sleep came to him, it would have astonished him if he could have noticed it coming.

He woke to wonder how long he had been unconscious. It had been about noon when they had arrived at the Treasury; but now the tall trees outside the window hid the sky and prevented him guessing by the sun what hour it was. He turned over on to his back and stared up lazily at the ceiling. The confusion which had at first overwhelmed his mind, and the unnatural clarity which had followed it, were both gone, and he felt that he was normal again, not even very much tired. The indolence and calm of the spirit which he now experienced were delicious: they were like the physical sensations which succeed violent exercise.

He looked down again with a start, as he heard the door quietly opened; and he saw the Lady Eva standing there. She had a mysterious smile on her lips, and her whole attitude suggested that she was bracing herself to meet something which frightened but did not displease her. Jeremy rose abruptly, his heart beating, and tried to speak; but he could not get out a single word.

"My father sent me to ask if you were better," said the Lady Eva in a low voice. As he did not answer she closed the door behind her and advanced into the room. "Are you better?" she repeated, a little more firmly. Jeremy took a step towards her and hesitated. The situation seemed plain, and yet, at the last moment of decision, his will was paralyzed by a fear that he might be absurdly deceiving himself.

"I am much better now," he answered, with an effort. "I only feel a little tired."

"There is a banquet at five o'clock. I hope you will be able to attend it."

Jeremy shivered slightly and his wits began to return to him. "Will it be like—like this morning?" he enquired with a faint smile.

She smiled a little in reply. "Don't you want us to be grateful to you?" she said. "You know what you have saved us from—all of us. How can we ever reward you?"

"That's my chance," Jeremy's mind insisted again and again. "That's my chance… that's my chance… I ought to speak now." But the short interval of her silence slipped away, and she went on gently:

"You must expect to be congratulated and toasted. Will you be strong enough to bear it? My father will be disappointed if you are not."

It was at that moment, quite irrelevantly and by a process he did not understand, that Jeremy took the Lady Eva in his arms. Afterwards he had no consciousness, no recollection, of the instant in which their lips had met. There had simply been an insurgence of his passion and of his loneliness, ending in an action that blinded him. The next thing he remembered was folding her bowed head into his shoulder, stroking her smooth hair with a trembling hand, and muttering hoarsely and helplessly, "Dearest… dear one…"

Then they were sitting side by side on the couch and their positions were reversed. His head lay on her shoulder, while her fingers moved gently up and down his cheek. He stayed thus for some minutes without speaking or moving. He had been in love before and had not escaped the mood in which young men picture the surrender of the beloved. He had even more than once, after a long or a short wooing, held a girl in his arms and kissed her. But he had never yet seen this sudden and astonishing transformation of a stranger, mysterious and incalculable, whose faults and peculiarities were as obvious as her beauty was enchanting, into a creature who could thus silently and familiarly comfort him. The moment before she had been some one else, the Lady Eva, a person as to whose opinion of himself he was uncertain and curious, that most baffling and impenetrable of all enigmas, another human being, divided from him by every barrier that looks or speech can put in the way of understanding. And now she was at once a lover, a part of himself, a spirit known by his without any need of words.

He adjusted himself slowly to the miracle.

Presently he raised his head and searched her eyes keenly. She bore his gaze without flinching; and something again drew their mouths together. Then Jeremy said.

"I must speak to your father at once. Do you suppose he will feel that I have presumed on his gratitude to me?"

"I know he will not," she answered. "I am sure he meant to give me to you. Do you think that otherwise..." She stopped, and there was a long pause. "But I wanted you... first..." Again she could not go on, but began to sob a little, quietly. Jeremy, helpless and inexperienced, could think of nothing better to do than to gather her into his arms and kiss her hair. His sudden comprehension of her seemed to have vanished with as little warning as it came. She was again a mysterious creature; but now the mystery was a new one.

When her face was hidden she continued with more confidence, but in a low and broken voice. "I wanted you to tell me that you... wanted me, before my father gave me to you. I thought... perhaps you did... I hoped..." She freed herself from his arms and sat up, looking at him with proud eyes, though her face was blazing. "It is better than being given to you only as a reward for winning a battle," she finished deliberately.

Jeremy experienced the most inexplicable feeling of the young lover—admiration for the beloved. He wished to hold her away from him, to contemplate the lovely face, the gallant eyes, to tell her how wonderful she was, and how he could thank Heaven for her even if he might never touch her hand again. And on the heels of this came a great rush of unbearable longing, with the realization that human tongue was not able to express, or human nerves to endure, his love for her. He turned dizzy and faint, his sight went black, and he stretched out his arms vaguely and helplessly. When she gave herself into them, he clasped her fiercely as though by force he could make her part of himself, and she bore his clumsy violence gladly.

"This hurts me," he said in the puzzled voice of a child, when he had let her go again. She gave him with wet eyes a sufficient answer. Then he went on with the same simplicity, "I have been so lonely here—I didn't know how lonely. Are we going to be happy now? I am afraid… of what may happen…" She kissed him once and rose.

"I must go now," she said steadily. "Oh, we shall be happy—this dread means nothing, it is only because we are so happy." He started and looked at her, made uneasy by her echo of his thoughts. "Good-by, my dear," she said. She left the room quietly without his raising a hand to keep her back.

When she had gone his feelings were too violent to find vent in any movement. He sat quite still for some minutes until his brain was calmer and he could at last stand up and walk about the room. It was thus that the Speaker found him; and Jeremy stopped guiltily and stood waiting. The old man was evidently still in good humor. He stroked his chin and regarded Jeremy with beaming eyes.

"I take it you are feeling better," he pronounced drily, after a moment's silence.

"I am quite well," Jeremy answered hurriedly, "very well. I must tell you at once, sir—"

The Speaker stopped him with a gesture. "I know. I passed my daughter in the corridor leading to her room. You want to tell me that you have taken my gift before I could make it. Nevertheless, I shall have the great joy of putting her hand in yours at the banquet to-night."

"I can't thank you…" Jeremy mumbled.

The Speaker made a benevolent movement of his hand. "What you and she have done," he went on, "is much against our customs, but we are not ordinary people, you and I and she. You will be happy together, and it will make me happy to see you so. And I think you are young enough to get from her the help that I should have had, if there had not been so many years between us. She has something of me in her that you will be able to use. You will need to use it, for you will have a great deal to do, both now and afterwards, when I am gone and you are the Speaker."

Jeremy inclined his head in silence.

"The banquet is in half an hour from now," the Speaker said, turning towards the door. "If you are well enough to attend it, you must go and dress at once."

CHAPTER XII
New Clouds

1

IT WAS IN A STATE of tranquil elation that Jeremy left his room to take his place at the banquet in the great hall. All day one emotion had been chasing another through his mind, like clouds hurrying across a storm-swept sky. Now it seemed that the last cloud had gone and had left a radiant evening serenity. He had been crushed by congratulations that morning. In the afternoon his love for the Lady Eva had exceeded his endurance. But to-night he felt himself able to bear the last degree of joy from either. He dressed with care, and, a minute or so before the hour, walked with a light and confident step through the corridors of the Treasury. He approached the hall by way of the private passages and turned into an anteroom, where, on ceremonial occasions, the Speaker and his family and his guests were accustomed to wait until the proper moment for taking their seats.

Here he found himself alone. After lighting an Irish cigar, he strolled jauntily up and down the room with his hands in his pockets, occasionally humming a bar or two of one of the songs of the nineteen-twenties—the last expressions of a frivolous and hilarious phase of society—or lightly kicking the furniture in the sheer height of his spirits. Not once since the moment of his waking in the Whitechapel Meadows had he been in such a mood. Something had happened to him of which he had no experience before; and its paradoxical result was to make him thoroughly at home in the new world for the first time. He felt like a man who in choppy water has been bumping up and down against the side of a quay and has at last succeeded in making himself fast. And, even in this gay and careless spirit, he was deeply conscious of what it was that had made him gay and careless. He continued, even through his light-hearted and somewhat ludicrous maneuvers up and down the room, through his tuneless but jaunty renderings of vulgar songs, to praise Heaven for having made the Lady Eva and for having given her to him. He knew that it was because of her that he was fit, as he told himself, reverting to earlier habits of phrase, to push a house over.

He did not, as he had hoped, get a moment alone with her before the banquet began. The Speaker beckoned him out without entering the room, and he could only catch a glimpse of her, by the side of the Lady Burney, as they entered the hall together. Immediately on their entrance the guests, who were already assembled, rose to their feet and began to cheer deafeningly. The sound had on Jeremy's spirits an effect contrary to that which it had had in the morning. It elated him; and when the Speaker, with a hand on his shoulder, drew him into a more prominent place on the dais, he bowed without self-consciousness. At last the Speaker raised his hand authoritatively and obtained silence. There was a shuffling of chairs; and it seemed to be supposed that the banquet would begin. But the Speaker cried in a thundering voice:

"My friends!" A profound and instant hush fell on the assembly. "My friends," he continued less loudly. "It is not our custom to make speeches before dinner or my custom to make long speeches at any time. I do not intend to say now what is in all our minds. But I believe that good news is the better for being soon told; and I have news to give you which I would like you to enjoy during dinner as well as after it. Jeremy Tuft, to whom under Heaven we owe our lives and our freedom to-night, has asked for the hand of my daughter, and she has consented to marry him." The hush continued, while he said briskly in a low but audible tone, "Your right hand, girl— your right hand, Jeremy." Then he went on again more loudly, "I put their hands together. I am the first to wish them happiness." In the uproar that followed, Jeremy had a confused notion that he and the Lady Eva bowed to the guests in the hall with equal composure. He was vividly aware that the Lady Burney had kissed him, this time on both cheeks. A lull followed, in which his condition of exaltation enabled him to express his gratitude and joy in a few words without faltering. And then suddenly it was all over. He was sitting next to the Lady Eva, saying something to her, he knew not what, in an undertone; and the banquet had begun.

When he was calm enough to look around him, he saw that the table on the dais at which he was sitting was occupied by all the most influential of the "big men" that were in the habit of attending the Treasury. The Speaker sat at the middle of one side. The Lady Burney sat on his right, and beyond her the Canadian, on whose face for once the ordinary expression of grinning malice had given way to one of sinister displeasure. On his left was the Lady Eva, next to whom came Jeremy. Jeremy's neighbor was the wife of a "big man" whom he knew but slightly, and who, to his relief, was at once engaged in conversation by the apparently still careworn and desponding dignitary, Henry Watkins. From this survey Jeremy turned with pleasure to the Lady Eva. Her mood chimed with his, and he was in high spirits. Her eyes were gleaming, her color was bright, and she talked lightly and without restraint. He noticed, too, with some pleasure that she showed a healthy appetite and took a sensible interest in good food. He was very hungry; and they talked for some time about the dishes. She did not drink, however. Nothing was served, indeed, no drinks were usual in England of that day, save whisky and beer, both of which were produced in good quality and consumed in large quantities. Jeremy, fearful of the effect either might have on him in his already stimulated condition, drank whisky sparingly, having weakened it with a great deal of water. So the banquet went through its innumerable courses to the last of them. At the end the servants cleared the table, and, with the costly Irish cigars, great decanters were brought in. These contained a kind of degenerate port which, for ceremonial reasons, was usually produced on the greatest occasions. But it was very nasty; and most persons confined themselves to a single glass of it, which they took because, for some inscrutable reason, it had been the custom of their ancestors.

The speeches, which began at this point, were excessively long and tedious. Jeremy gathered that a succession of hour-long speeches on every public occasion was one of the habits of the time, though it seemed to him as incomprehensible as seemed in the twentieth century the even longer sermons of an earlier period. Notable after notable arose and made the same remarks about the victory and the marriage, sometimes not even perceptibly varying the language. It was only in Henry Watkins's oration that he found any gleam of interest.

It began dully enough. The man looked gloomy, and his utterance was halting. Jeremy was at first soothed into sleepiness by the monotonous voice. He decided that this great and wealthy man was almost certainly a descendant of the charwoman from whom he had had the earliest intimation that "trouble" was really in the air. There was something unmistakably reminiscent both in his despondency and in his stupidity. But all at once a new resemblance struck his ears and stimulated his attention. Mrs. Watkins, in that fast fading antiquity, had brought him bodements of ill; and this latest scion of her line seemed to be playing the same part.

"This young man," said Henry Watkins in stumbling accents, "has delivered us all—I say, has delivered us all, from a great, a very great misfortune. If greater, yes, if much greater misfortune should threaten us, it is to him, it is to him, under Providence, and our wise ruler, that we shall look for help. And I say, my friends, I say and repeat," he droned on, "that we must not regard ourselves as safe from all misfortunes—"

The Speaker, one place removed from Jeremy, moved sharply, knocked over a glass and scraped his foot on the floor. He interrupted the flow of the speech; and the orator paused and looked round at him, half grieved, half questioning. The Speaker took the glance; and it seemed to Jeremy that it was in answer that he frowned so savagely. The melancholy expression on Henry Watkins's face deepened by a shade and became dogged. He continued with something of defiance in his voice.

"I say we ought not to think that we have seen the worst that can happen to us. This—all this unexpected danger which we have survived ought to teach us never again for a single moment to think ourselves in safety." He concluded abruptly and sat down. He had apparently spoiled the Speaker's joviality; and he had propounded to Jeremy a riddle very hard of solution. Jeremy felt certain that some purpose had lain behind his words, other than his usual pessimism, and that the Speaker's interruption had betokened something more than his usual boredom.

"Do you know what he meant?" he asked of the Lady Eva; but she shook her head. He glanced along the table to see if Thomas Wells's expression would throw any light on the matter. But he had left his place and had moved away to talk to a friend at some distance. Jeremy could not make out what it was all about, and gave it up. And now the formal part of the banquet was over; and the guests began to leave their places and to move about in the hall.

This was the signal for all who had ever spoken to Jeremy to come to him and congratulate him. He observed in their various manners a curious mixture of genuine homage and of assumed adulation of the man who might soon be their ruler. In the midst of it he saw on the outskirts of the crowd around him Roger Vaile, lounging with an air of detachment and indifference. He broke off the conversation in which he was engaged and forced a way to his friend.

"Roger!" he cried, taking him by the hand.

"Good luck to you, Jeremy," Roger replied gently. "I've reason to be pleased with myself now, haven't I?—even though it was an accident."

"Be sure I shall never forget you, Roger," Jeremy murmured; and then, feeling in his reply something of the manner of a great man towards a dependent, he blushed and was confused. Roger's answering smile was friendly; and before Jeremy could recover his tongue he had slipped away. Soon half the guests had gone; for it was an *early race*. When the hall was beginning to look empty he felt a plucking at his sleeve from behind him; and turning he saw the Lady Eva. He followed her into the little ante-room behind the hall and found that they were alone there.

She shut the door behind them and opened her arms.

"Only a minute," she whispered. "Oh, my dear, my dear, goodnight. I am so happy." He embraced her silently, and his eyes pricked. Hardly had he released her before she had gone. He went back into the hall and found the last guest departing, and the servants putting out the candles. He wondered for a moment why all great days must end with this flat moment; but the thought did not depress him. He walked away, slow and unaccompanied, to his own room.

When he was there he busied himself for some moments with trifles and delayed to undress. He wanted very much to lie awake for hours so that he could taste again all the most exquisite moments of the day that was just gone. He also desired with equal intensity to fall asleep at once, so that he might begin the new day as soon as possible. He had got so far as taking off his coat when there was a discreet knocking at the door. He opened it and found a servant, who said deferentially:

"The Speaker would like to see you at once, sir, in his own room."

"All right," Jeremy answered, picking up his coat. And then, when the man had gone, he murmured to himself in sudden dread, "What can it be? Oh, what can it be?"

2

Jeremy hastened down the stairs to the Speaker's room in a state of rapidly increasing agitation. He did not know, he could not imagine, what it was that he feared; but he had been raised to so high a pinnacle of joy that the least touch of the unexpected could set him trembling and looking for evil. When he reached his object he found the old man alone, seated sprawling in his great chair by the open window, his wrinkled, thick-veined hands spread calmly on the carven arms. Two or three candles stood on the table behind him, flickering and guttering slightly in the faint night breeze.

"I am glad you have come at once, my son," he observed, turning his head a little, in a tone which showed no symptoms of trouble. "You had not gone to bed, then? I wished to speak to you alone, before the others have come that I have sent for. Sit down and listen to me."

Jeremy drew up a smaller chair on the other side of the window and obeyed.

"We have yet another battle before us," the Speaker pronounced abruptly.

Jeremy started. "What—" he began.

"Another battle," the old man repeated. "Do not be distressed. I know this is ill news for a bridegroom, yet it is not so bad as it seems. When we returned this morning—it was after you had fainted at the door and while you were still unconscious—I learnt that the President of Wales had made up his mind, only a few days after the Northerners, to march on London.

I knew that there was trouble of some kind in the west, but I had got no trustworthy news to show me how far it had gone. But information came to me this morning that the President and his army had passed round the Cotswolds and were marching towards Oxford. The worst part of the news was that the Gloucestershire wool-merchants had joined with him. Of course, they were very much interested in what might happen to the Chairman. That was what that gloomy dullard, Henry Watkins, was hinting at in his speech to-night—I know you saw me frowning at him. I tell you frankly I thought nothing of it. It was only the Yorkshiremen that disturbed the others; and I took it for granted that our victory would settle all quarrels at once."

"Yes…" Jeremy murmured doubtfully in the pause.

"Well, I was wrong. It seems that a survivor got away to the west this morning, apparently just after Thomas Wells took the Chairman prisoner. I don't know how he went. I think he must have got on to the railway somewhere and found an engine ready to move. He could hardly have moved so fast otherwise. Anyway, he found the President, with the greater part of his army, at Oxford—and the President has sent a letter to me. It reached me only a few minutes ago." He stopped and ran a hand through his beard, regarding Jeremy thoughtfully with tranquil eyes.

"Go on… go on," Jeremy whispered tensely.

"That was quick work, wasn't it?" the Speaker ruminated. "He can't have started before seven this morning, because I'm sure the Chairman wasn't taken till then. The letter reached me here at a quarter to midnight—less than seventeen hours. The President was in a great hurry—I know him well, I can see him raging." He checked himself and smiled at Jeremy with a kind of genial malice. "You want to know what he said in his letter? Well, he warned me that he would hold me responsible for the Chairman's safe-keeping; and he summoned me to a conference at Oxford where the three of us were to settle our differences and rearrange the affairs of the country."

"And what answer will you make?" Jeremy managed to utter.

"I have ordered the messenger to be flogged by the grooms," the Speaker replied composedly. "I expect that they are flogging him now. The only other answer we have to give, Jeremy, will be delivered by your guns."

"But this is terrible," Jeremy cried, springing up from his chair. "You don't understand—"

"Rubbish, my friend," the old man interrupted with an air of serene commonsense. "It means only that the President does not know what has happened. If he still wishes to fight when he knows—why, then we will fight him. I hope he will wish it. Perhaps when he is broken we shall have peace forever."

Jeremy walked three or four times up and down the room, pressing his hands together and trying vainly by a violent tension of all his muscles to regain his composure.

"You don't understand a bit," he burst out at last, "what luck it all was. I tell you it was luck, merely luck…" He stopped, stumbling and stuttering, so much confounded by this unexpected and horrible menace to his happiness, that he was unable to frame any words of explanation.

The Speaker continued to smile at him. "You are not yourself to-night, Jeremy," he chided gently. "You are overwrought; and it is not to be wondered at. You will find your next triumph less exciting."

But Jeremy's agitation only increased. It was not only his own future that was at stake, but the Lady Eva's also and his future with her. "Can't you make peace with him?" he demanded wildly.

"Peace—" the Speaker began in a more vehement tone. But before he could go on the door was opened and two servants appeared, dragging between them a torn and disheveled man, whose bloodshot eyes were rolling madly in their sockets, and whose face was white and twisted with pain. Just inside the room they let go his arms, and he fell sprawling on the floor with a faint moan.

"Peace!" cried the Speaker, rising from his chair and pointing at the man. "*That* is the ambassador of peace I shall send back to the President! Peace between us, I thank God, is impossible unless he humbles himself to me!"

Jeremy took a step towards the prostrate figure and recoiled again, seeing that the torn garments had been roughly pulled on over lacerated and bleeding shoulders. He recovered himself and bent down over the unhappy creature whose breath came thick and short through the writhing mouth. He looked up with horror in his eyes.

"This is... this is the President's messenger?" he muttered.

The Speaker nodded.

"But you didn't do this to the men from Bradford. You let them go back untouched."

"I will make an end of these troubles!" Again Jeremy could see in the old man a reincarnation of one of the vengeful prophets of the ancient Jews. But the next moment the menacing attitude was relaxed, and the Speaker, turning to the immobile servants, said coldly: "Take this fellow out and lay him down in the courtyard. Tether his horse fast beside him. When he is able to move, let him go back without hindrance to his master and say what has been done to him."

The men bowed, stooped over the moaning wretch and dragged him roughly away. A profound silence followed his last inarticulate, half-conscious complaints as he was borne down the corridor.

"And now," said the Speaker, resuming his serenity of manner without an effort, "now we must make our plans. I propose that we shall march out at once and prepare to meet the President west of London if he wishes to attack us; and I have decided that you shall take command of the army."

"I?" Jeremy exclaimed. "Oh, but—" He was overwhelmed by an absurd confusion. Once again he was in the nightmare world, struggling with shadows, wrestling with an incomprehensible mind on which he could never get a grip. "I *can't* command the army! I know something about guns, but I've no experience of infantry. I shouldn't..." His protests faded away into silence before the Speaker's imperturbability.

"Guns are all very well... I don't mind... I can't..." These words jerked out and ceased, like the last spasmodic drops from a fountain, when the water has been turned off at the main. Then, when he himself supposed that he had finished, he added suddenly with an air of conclusiveness: "I know something about *guns*..."

The Speaker made no answer for a moment or two. When he did it was slowly and with extreme deliberation. "You won this morning's battle for us," he said, "by the use of guns. Our battle against the President, if it is ever fought, will have to be won in the same way. None of us properly understands how to do it but you. And, after all, wasn't there a great general in the old times, somewhere about your time, who began his career in the artillery? What was his name? I know so little of history; but I think it began with a B."

"Napoleon," Jeremy suggested with a half hysterical chuckle.

"Napoleon? Was that it? I thought it was some other name. Well, then, if he could—"

"I won't do it," Jeremy suddenly uttered. The door opened again, and the Canadian entered. He was wrapped in a great furred gown, from the ample collar of which his face hardly protruded, looking sharper and leaner than ever.

"You sent for me," he said in a colorless and slightly drowsy voice. "What has happened now?"

"Sit down," the Speaker returned. "Henry Watkins and John Hammond will be here in a moment." Without a word the Canadian sank into a chair and drew the fur of his gown closely round his ears and mouth. Over the folds of it his small, red eyes looked out with an unwavering and sinister expression. His arrival brought an oppressive silence with it; and Jeremy began suddenly to feel the uncanny effects of being thus wakeful in a sleeping world. He looked furtively at the calm, stern face of the Speaker, and saw how the thick lips were compressed in a rigid line. Outside a faint and eery wind persistently moved the leaves. Within, the great building was stonily silent all around them; and the flames of the candles on the table danced at a movement of the air or burnt up straight and still in the succeeding calm. The hush lasted until a servant announced the attendance of Henry Watkins and John Hammond, who had been fetched out of their beds and had reached the Treasury together.

"I told you, sir, I told you how it would be," said Henry Watkins at once in a voice like the insistent notes of a tolling bell.

The Speaker made an abrupt gesture. "You have heard then?" he asked sharply.

"We passed a man outside, sir, in the courtyard, lying on the ground beside his tethered horse," John Hammond interposed, "and we made inquiries while we were waiting to be brought in to you."

"I have made no secret of it," the Speaker said simply. "Every waking man in the Treasury may know all about it by now. Well, then…" And in his deliberate and unconcerned manner he repeated to them the same story that he had told to Jeremy. "Nor am I sorry for it," he concluded. "It is as well that we should be done with all this at once, as I think we shall be."

When he had finished the Canadian shifted slightly in his chair. "You say they are at Oxford now?" he asked, his voice a little muffled by the thick fur that brushed his lips. The Speaker assented. "And the Gloucestershire men have joined them?" Again the Speaker assented. "Ah!" murmured the Canadian enigmatically; and he seemed to sink further into the folds of his gown, as though he were preparing himself for sleep.

Henry Watkins and John Hammond made no answer, but looked at one another lugubriously.

"Come, gentlemen," the Speaker cried heartily. "We know now that we have nothing to be afraid of. I have determined that Jeremy Tuft shall take command of the whole army; and I am sure that the man who saved us this morning can save us again."

"Ah, that is a good plan," observed John Hammond sagely. He was a heavy man of slow speech, and he wagged his head solemnly while he talked. "Jeremy Tuft will command the whole army. That is a very good plan."

"We could not do better," said Henry Watkins with an approach to cheerfulness.

Jeremy fancied that he heard Thomas Wells sniff under his wrappings; and the justice of the implied criticism twitched horribly at his nerves. He stared out of the window into the blackness, a resolve taking shape in his mind. At last he stood up deliberately and spoke with a roughness, almost arrogance, that he certainly did not feel.

"I will not take command of the army," he said, letting the words fall one by one. "I am not fit to do it. I should only bring disaster on all of us. I have too much at stake to risk it. It would be better if Thomas Wells were to take command." He stopped and waited, defiant and sullen. The Canadian made one sharp movement, then folded his gown more closely around him, so as still further to hide his face, and sat on impassively.

Henry Watkins was at him at once, eagerly arguing that there was little hope, but that what there was lay in his hands. Jeremy looked around as though he were seeking some way of escape. He felt very weary and alone. He didn't want to argue: it was a waste of time and pains since his mind was made up, and neither the most urgent nor the most persuasive reasoning could change it. But while Henry Watkins talked and he countered in stubborn monosyllables, he was watching sidelong, with an unnamed, unadmitted apprehension, the Speaker's resolved and quiet face. Suddenly Henry Watkins ceased and threw up his hands in a gesture of despair. Then the Speaker rose, walked away, and, without a word, tugged sharply at the bell pull. A servant immediately answered the summons, and in his ear the old man delivered a long whispered order. The servant bowed and went out, and the Speaker returned to his seat. All the others looked at him curiously, but maintained the silence which had fallen on them.

Then Jeremy involuntarily broke out, "What have you done? What have you sent for?"

"I have sent for my daughter," the Speaker answered steadily. "It is time for her to be called into our counsels."

3

Jeremy's muscles jerked and quivered at the Speaker's announcement, but he said nothing. His mouth set more firmly, a frown came on his forehead, and his hands, thrust under his folded arms, were so tightly clenched that he had a sensation of pain in the knuckles. Behind this appearance of resolution his thoughts were plaintive and resentful. He repeated over and over again in his mind, "I will not give way. I must not give way. Why will they be such fools?" The more he considered it the more certain he became that he was not competent to command an army. He could not do it, he told himself, and at the same time look properly after his guns. Besides, he was modest in a hard-headed way; and he refused to believe that he had the qualities which are necessary in great military commanders. The fact that he most passionately desired that they should win the coming battle only made him more determined to refuse this absurd proposal. As he sat silent in the ring of silent men he felt injured and aggrieved, and his temper grew with every moment more obstinate.

The conversation did not revive after the Speaker's interruption, for a sense of expectation filled the room and kept it in abeyance. Presently the old man rose stately from his chair and, moving to the window, thrust out his head and leant his arms on the sill. By doing so he broke the tension a little; and Jeremy got up and went to the table to look for a cigar, walking self-consciously and feeling that all these people regarded him with dislike. When he had found a cigar and lit it, he shrank from going back to his seat and facing them again. He lingered at the table, where he had discovered some papers of his own relating to the guns; and these made an excuse with which he could pretend to busy himself. He was vaguely conscious somewhere just within the blurred edge of his vision that John Hammond had gone over to Thomas Wells and was talking to him in a subdued voice. The Canadian answered seldom and briefly, and their words floated past his ears in a faint confusion of sound. Then John Hammond grew louder and more urgent and the Canadian exclaimed morosely:

"I have no patience…"

John Hammond insisted; and, in spite of himself, Jeremy turned his head sideways to listen.

"It would be better to be beaten," he heard Thomas Wells say, almost under his breath but with a vicious intensity, "than be led by a vampire risen God knows how from the grave!" A disagreeable thrill passed through him; but before he could stir the door by his side opened softly and the Lady Eva stood motionless on the threshold. She was wearing a furred robe, like Thomas Wells's; but it was less ample and hung on her more gracefully. Her fair hair fell in two long plaits, loose at the ends, down her back, and her eyes, though they shone with excitement, yet showed that she had just risen from sleep. As Jeremy silently regarded her, she glanced down and pulled the hem of the robe across to hide her bare ankles.

When she looked beyond him and saw how many others there were in the room, she seemed to recoil a little. "Father," she said, speaking quietly but steadily, "you sent for me!"

The Speaker slowly drew his great shoulders in through the window and turned around. "Come in, Eva," he ordered in an equable voice, "come in and sit down. These are all friends here, and you need not be ashamed before them." She advanced with short steps, sat in Jeremy's chair, which stood empty, and arranged the hem of her gown about her feet and the collar about her throat. Then, before fixing her eyes on the old man, she cast a candid and ardent regard of affection at Jeremy. He was discomposed by it, and only with an effort could he compel his eyes to meet hers and answer them. She seemed for a moment to be troubled; but her face cleared to an expression of eager intentness as her father began to address her.

"This is the first time I have ever asked you to help me, Eva," he said with kindly and matter-of-fact briskness. "Perhaps I should have done so before; but now at least I think you can do something for us that no one else can do. There is another war in front of us: I need not tell you now how or why it has arisen. It will be nothing at all if we face it properly; and therefore I have designed that your promised husband here shall command the army. He refuses; I do not know why—perhaps modesty… perhaps…" He shrugged his shoulders, pursed his lips and spread out his hands, palms uppermost. "I sent for you because I thought that to-night you might be able to sway him, as I cannot."

During this speech Jeremy's anger had been rising fast, and now he interrupted. "This is most unfair, sir," he cried, coming forward from the shadows in which he had been hiding.

"Be quiet, Jeremy," said the Speaker, without raising his voice, but with a note of sternness. Then he went on smoothly: "My girl, I ask you to remember that the safety of all of us, of you and of your mother and of myself, no less than of the country, depends on our leaving nothing undone to protect ourselves. I am persuaded that Jeremy Tuft should be our leader, but I cannot convince him. I put our case in your hands."

The girl leant forward a little towards him, breathing quickly, her eyes wide open and her lips parted. A shade as of thought passed over her face; but Jeremy broke in again, still looking at the old man.

"You won't understand me, sir," he protested anxiously. "God knows I would do what you ask if I thought it for the best. But I know what I can't do and you don't. You exaggerated what I did this morning. You don't know anything about it, sir, indeed you don't. There's only one man here who ought to do it, and that is Thomas Wells. You ought to appoint him. I will serve under him and… and…"

He stopped, a little frightened by what in his eagerness he had been about to say. While he had been talking desperately, seeing no signs of help on the faces around him, he had discovered suddenly his deepest objection to the proposal. The Canadian, damn him! was the man for the job. He had the gusto for war, for bloodshed and death, which commanders need: he was the only true soldier among them. And he hated Jeremy. Jeremy continued his pause, shying at this last, this fatal argument. Then on an impulse he chanced it, concluding suddenly with a gulp, "And he won't serve under me." The ghost of a chuckle came from the Canadian bunched up in his chair.

The Lady Eva swung around to him impetuously. "Thomas Wells," she murmured, her voice thrilling with an intense desire to persuade, "you won't mind, will you? Help me to get him to accept."

"I won't make any difficulties, Lady Eva," pronounced the Canadian levelly, straightening himself and pulling the edge of his robe down from his mouth. "Any one who commands the army is at liberty to—to make what use of me he can—while I'm your guest here. I'm not stuck on commanding. I guess these little troubles of yours aren't any business of mine. Anyway, I ought to be going back home soon, since I can't go and stay with the Chairman of Bradford, as I promised him once. My word, sir, but it's getting on towards morning! I'm beginning to feel cold," he finished inconsequently, turning to the Speaker.

"It isn't fair," Jeremy begun again. He was very tired. His body ached all over, and his eyelids were beginning to droop. His determination was not weakened, but he dreaded the effort of keeping up a firm front much longer. He felt too weak now to force his own view on the stubborn old man.

But the Speaker ignored him. He stood up and, including the three other men in one confidential glance, said: "Thomas Wells is right, gentlemen, it grows very late. Let us leave them alone for a few minutes. We will meet again in the morning. Jeremy, do you hear? I will not accept your final answer until the morning." He moved with ponderous slowness towards his daughter and put out a firm hand to hold her down in her chair. "Goodnight, my child!" he murmured, as he stooped and kissed her on the forehead. "Do what you can for us." His accent in these words was pathetic; but his air as he led the way to the door was one of infinite cunning.

As soon as he was left alone with the Lady Eva, Jeremy, who had been staring out into the invisible garden, turned reluctantly around and faced her, in an attitude of defense. She came to him at once, and, kneeling on the great chair beside him, threw her arms around his neck.

"My dear," she said brokenly and passionately, "don't—don't look at me like that!"

His obstinacy and resentment melted suddenly away as he responded to the caress. "Eva!" he muttered, "I thought… I was afraid you were… you wanted…"

"You looked at me as though you hated me," she said.

He comforted her in silence for some time and she clung to him. Then he thought he heard her whispering something. "What is it?" he asked gently.

"I am so afraid, Jeremy," she repeated, in a voice that was still almost inaudible; and as he did not answer she went on a little more loudly, "You know, I dreaded something… this afternoon… and this must be it." Still he said nothing; and after a pause she resumed: "Nobody but you can save us, Jeremy. I am certain of it—you are so wonderful, you know so much of what happened in the old times. Weren't you sent here by the Blessed Virgin to save us? I know why you don't want to—but it will be all right. Oh, Jeremy, it will!"

A great wave of hopelessness came over him and, when he tried to speak, choked his utterance. He could only shake his head miserably. Suddenly the Lady Eva let fall her arms from his neck and sank down in a heap on the chair. He realized with an unbearable pang that she was sobbing wildly.

"Eva! Eva!" he cried hopelessly, trying to gather her to him again. But she drew herself away and continued to sob, breathing shortly and spasmodically. He felt afraid of her. Then she rose and with a last jerky sigh gave herself into his arms. He felt her body, slight and yielding, yet strong and supple, in his embrace, and he began to grow dizzy. Her face was wet and her mouth was loose and hot beneath his.

"Eva!" he murmured, torn and wretched, with a sense of ineluctable doom stealing upon them. He looked up over her head and saw that in the garden the lawns and flowers were now growing distinct in a hard, clear, cold light. A chilly breath came in at the window, and all at once the birds began drowsily to wake and chatter. Inside the room all the candles were out but one, that still burnt on, though sickly and near its end. The light seemed to Jeremy to be coming as fast and as inevitably as the surrender which he could no longer escape. "Don't, dear," he uttered hoarsely. "Don't, don't! I'll do what they want me to do. I'll go and tell your father now."

She hid her face on his breast and for a little while her shoulders still heaved irregularly like a stormy sea after the wind has fallen.

CHAPTER XIII
The Fields of Windsor

1

JEREMY SAT WITH the Speaker in the parlor of a rude farmhouse at the edge of the little village of Slough. It was now a week since the army had taken the field, and during that time they had not once come to grips with the enemy. The President of Wales had lingered unaccountably at Oxford, and Jeremy had pitched his camp in the neighborhood of Windsor, not daring to move further from London. He could not tell whether the Welshmen would follow the windings of the north bank of the river or cross at Reading and approach the capital from the south, or march by Thame around the top of the Chilterns. The Speaker, judging the enemy by his own strategical notions, had affirmed that they would advance towards Windsor if they supposed that battle could be joined there; and he wished to go straight on, as far as Oxford if necessary. But Jeremy, determined to be in truth what the old man had forced him to be, refused to move. They spent a weary week of doubt and anxiety, receiving every day a dozen contradictory reports, and occasionally moving out the troops to the west or the north on a wild-goose chase.

This state of affairs told heavily on them both. Jeremy ceased to be able to sleep, and he felt inexpressibly tired. The Speaker grew irritable and the ardor of his spirit, confined by delay, daily corroded his temper. The Canadian, who attended them faithfully, never refused to give Jeremy his advice; but he never suggested less than two possible courses of action, and he never failed to make it clear that either might bring success, and that either might involve complete disaster. On this day at last Jeremy's patience had worn very thin. He had just explained to the Speaker for the twentieth time his objection to moving up the river direct on Oxford, and a dissatisfied silence had fallen between them. Jeremy sighed, and let his hands fall on the table, across the crude, inaccurate maps which were all that he had been able to obtain.

The dispute between them had grown so bitter that he felt unwilling to encounter the Speaker's gaze, fearing lest his own weariness and disgust and resentment should show too obviously. But as he glanced cautiously at the old man he saw that he was leaning back in his chair, his eyes closed and his hands folded in his lap. In this attitude of rest he betrayed himself more than was common with him. The air of fire and mastery had gone out of his face, the lines of power were softened, the thick lips, instead of expressing pride and greed, drooped a little pathetically, and showed a weary resignation. Not only his features, but also the thick-veined old hands, seemed to have grown thinner and frailer than they were. He looked to Jeremy like a lamp inside which the flame is slowly and quietly dying. Jeremy's heart suddenly softened towards him and he felt more unbearable than ever the fate in which they were all thus entangled.

But his tired brain refused to grapple with it any more, and he fell to making pictures. When they had marched out he alone in the whole army had felt despondent. The people of London wished them good luck with as much enthusiasm as, a few days before, they had welcomed them home. The troops marched off down Oxford Street and along the winding valley-road, covered again with flowers, which they stuck in their hats or in the muzzles of their rifles, singing odd uncouth snatches of boasting defiance in curious cadences which had suddenly sprung up among them and passed rapidly from mouth to mouth. Most of these praised Jeremy and his guns: some of them exalted him as a necromancer and credited him with supernatural powers. Even the Speaker chanted one of them in a rumbling, uncertain bass, somewhat to Jeremy's discomfort. The discomfort was greater when Thomas Wells hummed another below his breath, with a satirical grin directed at the horizon before them.

The Lady Eva at their parting shared Jeremy's distress but not his doubts. They had a few moments alone together on the morning of setting out, before the public ceremony at which she and the Lady Burney were to wish the army God-speed. She clung to him speechlessly, begging him with her eyes and her kisses to confess that he looked cheerfully to the result. Jeremy, shamefacedly conscious of having felt some resentment towards her since he had yielded to her entreaties, comforted her as well as he was able, and yet could not bring himself to say what she wanted to hear. Their short time ran to an end: the minutes ticked inexorably away; below in the courtyard he could hear the servants bringing around the horses. A dozen times his mind framed a pleasant lie for her which his tongue would not speak. Then they parted with this between them, and Jeremy went down into the courtyard with a heavy spirit. A few minutes later he and the Speaker and Thomas Wells were riding up Whitehall towards Piccadilly, the Lady Burney and the Lady Eva going before them in a carriage. There, on the spot where once the poised Cupid had stood, the Lady Eva kissed him again before the cheering people, and the army set out. Jeremy rode dully with it, wishing that his obstinate fixity in his own opinion could have given way for a moment and let him part without reserve from his beloved. He wondered much whether he would ever see her again, and the thought was exceedingly bitter.

Then followed this week of confusion and wretchedness, a depressing contrast with the lightning brilliance of the campaign against the Yorkshiremen. Jeremy's resolution, braced for a swift and single test of it, withstood the strain hardly. It seemed to him that the moments in which good luck might carry him through were fast running away; he felt them like material things melting out of his hands. Still at Oxford, the President maintained his enigmatical immobility. Slowly the spirit of the troops faded and withered, like the trail of flowers they had left behind them on the march. Jeremy preserved the stolidity of his expression, grew slower of speech every day, and hid the bewildering turmoil of his thoughts. Only the Canadian went about the camp with an unaltered cheerfulness of demeanor. He behaved like an onlooker who is always willing to do what he can when the players of the game invoke his help. He talked with the officers, rode out often in front of the lines, seemed always busy, always in a detached manner interested in what was going on. Jeremy grew to hate him as much as he feared him...

"Jeremy! Jeremy!"

He started up from his meditation and found that the old man was speaking to him.

"Listen! Wasn't that firing… a long way off?"

He listened intently, then shook his head. "No, I'm sure it wasn't."

"Jeremy, how much longer is it going to be?"

He was seized with surprise at the pitifulness of the Speaker's tone. "God knows, sir," he answered slowly, and added in an exhausted voice. "We haven't enough men to go on adventures and force the business."

"No… no, I suppose not." And then, losing some of this unusual docility, the Speaker burst out: "I am sick of this hole!"

"Campaigning quarters!" Jeremy replied as humorously and soothingly as he could. He was sick of it himself. The Speaker had desired that they should establish themselves in Windsor Castle; but much of the old building had been burnt down in the Troubles, and what was left had been used as a quarry. It was not possible to go anywhere in the neighborhood without seeing the great calcined stones built into the walls of house or barn. Hardly anything of the Castle was left standing; and the poor remains, in fact, were used as a common cart-shed by the inhabitants of the village of Windsor. In all this countryside, which was held and cultivated by small men, there was no great house; and they had been obliged to content themselves with a poor hovel of a farm, which had only one living-room and was dirty and uncomfortable. Jeremy grew to hate it and the wide dusty flats in which it stood. It seemed to him a detestable landscape, and daily the scene he loathed grew intertwined in his thoughts with his dread of the future. His feverish brain began to deal, against his will, in foolish omens and premonitions. He caught himself wondering, "Will this be the last I shall see of England?" He remembered, shuddering, that when he had first joined the Army in 1914 and had complained of early morning parades, a companion had said, "I suppose we shall have to get up at this time every morning *for the rest of our lives!*"

While he was trying to drive some such thoughts as these out of his mind, he was conscious of a stir outside the farmhouse, and presently an orderly entered and announced, "A scout with news, sir."

"Bring him in," said Jeremy wearily. He hardly glanced up at the trooper who entered, until the man began to speak. Then the tones of the voice caught his attention and he saw with surprise that it was Roger Vaile who stood there, his head roughly bandaged; his face smeared with blood and dust, his uniform torn and stained.

"Roger!" he cried, starting up.

Roger hesitated. The Speaker, who was leaning forward, his elbows on his knees and his face between his hands, muttered sharply, "Go on, man, go on!"

Roger straightened himself a little, disregarded Jeremy's outstretched hand, and began again. "I went out alone, sir, three days ago," he said, looking at neither of his listeners, "and went on upstream as far as a place called Dorchester. I saw a patrol of the enemy there coming out of the village, and to get away from them I had to leave my horse and swim across the river. There's a hill on the other side that you can see the road from—"

"I know it!" Jeremy jerked out. "It's called Sinodun!" The mere name as he pronounced it almost took his breath away. How well, in old journeys up the river, he had once known Sinodun!

"Is it?" Roger asked indifferently. "I didn't know. Well, I stayed on top of the hill under a bush that night. The next morning about eleven I saw a lot of cavalry coming into the village from the Oxford road and soon after that infantry. It looked to me like the whole of the President's army. There must have been ten or twelve thousand men altogether. So I started off to come back as fast as I could. I had some difficulty because when I got across the river again at Wallingford I was right among their patrols, and I couldn't get away from them till they camped at Marlow last night."

"At Marlow!" Jeremy cried, starting up. "Are you quite sure the whole army came as far as Marlow?"

"Absolutely sure," Roger replied. "I was hiding just outside the village while they pitched their camp."

"Then God be praised," Jeremy breathed, "they've come past Reading and they're marching straight at us. They can't cross the river between here and there. Ten or twelve thousand, you say? Then we're about equal in numbers and I believe we shall be equal to them in spirit—let alone the guns. And, Roger," he finished, "are you hurt?"

"Nothing much—only a cut," Roger assured him with his gentle smile. "Luckily I ran into one of their scouts and got his horse away from him—or I might not have been here so soon."

"Come, Jeremy," growled the Speaker, rising. "The battle is on us. We must get ready." Jeremy would have stayed to speak to Roger and to see that he was provided with food; but the old man was insistent, and he found himself outside the house before he could protest.

It was about eleven o'clock of a fine, dry day, and the variable wind was blowing clouds of dust this way and that over the flat fields. All around them stretched the tents of the encampment in slovenly, irregular lines; and the soldiers, on whom, untrained as they were, the period of idleness had had an unlucky effect, were lounging here and there in careless groups. Jeremy's attempt to make use of this week in drilling them had been for the most part unsuccessful. Officers and men alike were too much flushed with victory for his orders or appeals to have any effect. They were not so much impatient of discipline as negligent of it.

Jeremy sighed a little as he looked at the camp; but his spirits immediately revived. The Speaker was taking short steps up and down, rubbing his hands together and lifting up his nostrils to snuff the sweet, dry air. A kind of exhilaration seemed to fill him and to restore him to his former self. Jeremy caught it from him, and his voice was lively when he shouted to a servant to fetch thither, the principal officers.

The council of war had hardly gathered when a new report came that the enemy were marching on Hitcham, following the main road that had once, crossed the river at Maidenhead and now came around by the north bank. Jeremy's plans were prepared, and he rapidly disposed his army, with the right wing resting on the slightly-rising ground of Stoke Park, the center running through Chalk Hill and Chalvey, and the left guarding the bridge, in the empty fields where Eton once had been.

As he gave his orders, with some show of confidence and readiness, he tasted for a moment the glories of a commander-in-chief; but when he detailed to Thomas Wells his duties as the leader of the right wing of the army, his heart unreasonably sank and he faltered over his words.

"I understand," the Canadian replied gravely, with an inscrutable expression. "I am to stand on the line between Stoke and Salt Hill until you give the word. Then you will send up the reserves and I am to advance, wheel around, and force them against the river."

"That's it," said Jeremy with a heartiness he did not feel.

"So be it… sir," Thomas Wells assented lingeringly; then, with an air of hesitation, he murmured: "I suppose you're quite certain… that they'll mass against our left… that they won't attack me and try to drive *us* into the river?"

"I'll take the chance, anyway," Jeremy answered stoutly; and, nodding, he rode off to look at the guns, which were under the command of Jabez, immediately behind the center of the line.

"We'll do them in, master," said Jabez reassuringly. "Never you fear. You leave that to us." As he spoke a sharp crackling of rifle fire arose by the river-bank near Queen's Eyot.

"Well, we've started, Jabez," Jeremy smiled at him. "I must go back." As he rode again towards his chosen point for directing the battle his breath came regularly and his heart was singularly at rest.

2

When the firing spread and became general all along the line, showing that battle had actually been joined, Jeremy began to feel a little light-headed with excitement. He stood, with the Speaker and two or three officers, on the western edge of the slight rise on which the village lay; and from this point of vantage he could see that the outposts were being rapidly driven in from Dorney and Cippenham upon the main line of defense. In the center the enemy seemed to be pressing towards the Beaconsfield road. On the right, where Thomas Wells was in charge, the firing was furious, and great clouds of smoke were drifting away among the trees of Stoke Park; but the attack had not the air of being seriously driven home. Jeremy regarded it for a few moments, biting his lip and screwing up his eyes, and then turned from it to scan with particular anxiety the flats on the right between Boveney and Eton Wick. Here it was, he hoped, that the enemy would concentrate his troops. Here, with luck, his masses might be caught in the open and broken up by the guns, while the Speaker's men remained safe in cover behind the ruins of the viaduct.

In spite of his doubts and the frequent monitions of his judgment Jeremy retained somewhere in his mind an obscure belief that the fear of the guns would, after all, hold the Welshmen in check and enfeeble their advance. All the time, as he stood beside the Speaker, something was drawing him towards the shallow gun-pit which he had established, close to the line, between Chalvey and the old disused railway-cutting. But the hugeness of the moment, the release of his tension, and the incessant rattling outbursts of noise combined in an odd way to exhilarate him. He grew so restless that at last, with a muttered excuse to the Speaker, he mounted his horse and trotted off to look at the guns.

He found Jabez and his ancients standing in a strained attitude of readiness. Their faces were absurdly grave, and Jabez greeted him with what he thought a ludicrous solemnity. He rallied the withered old creature, with exaggerated heartiness, on his anxious air.

"Let 'em come, master!" Jabez replied with a menacing expression, "and we'll see to 'em. Let 'em just put their heads out—"

Jeremy laughed loudly at this, clapped Jabez on the back, and directed his tattered opera-glasses towards the little church of Boveney. But no considerable body of troops answered the invitation. Still restless, Jeremy rode back to his headquarters.

He found that the Speaker had given orders for his armchair to be brought out for him from the farmhouse, and he was sitting in it, his elbow on the arm and his chin in his hand, regarding the unshifting line of smoke with an immobile but somber countenance. Like Xerxes, Jeremy suddenly thought, with a shiver for the omen, over the bay of Salamis!

"You are trembling," the old man said, without looking around, as Jeremy reached him.

"I'm excited," Jeremy explained. "It's all right. I'm quite cool." He was indeed so cool that he could sit down on the dry, short grass beside the

Speaker, light a cigar, and consider quite calmly what course of action he ought to take. The only thing he found lacking was an indication of any one course as better than another. The enemy might be, and very likely was, concealing troops among the houses of Boveney, Dorney, and Cippenham—it was impossible to tell which. The battle seemed to be hung in a state of miraculous suspension. The enemy's advance had been brought to a standstill, and neither of the lines moved or wavered. From the bank of the river to Stoke Place there stretched a thick woolly bar of smoke as though a giant hand had smudged ink with its thumb across the landscape. Jeremy searched vainly through the whole of the country before him for some mark, on which the guns might expend their few shells, and especially for the Welsh transport; but he could find nothing. It was only as the minutes drifted by and the fighting continued that Jeremy began to realize his own vagueness and impotence, to understand that, in spite of his protestations, he had been relying hopelessly on some such stroke of luck as had served him at Barnet.

The first half-conscious realization was like a cold draught, an imperceptible movement of chilly air, blowing upon his resolution and high spirits. In a moment full comprehension followed and gripped him, and he awoke as though out of a dream, alive to the danger and yet incapable of action. Nothing had changed: the line of smoke was as before, the sounds of the fighting had grown not louder or more terrible. But what had been to Jeremy a picture had become a real thing, a vast and menacing event, in the path of which he was an insignificant insect. Not a muscle of his face stirred under the shock. The Speaker, above him, mumbled deeply:

"What are you going to do, Jeremy?"

"We must wait a little, sir," Jeremy answered confidently, but with a trace of impatience in his voice. He wanted desperately to gain time. Under his mask he felt like a man who is about to be detected in an imposture, whom the turning of the next page will bring to utter ruin. He gazed here and there over the field, wondering how long he could control his expression. Perhaps the next minute his muscles would betray him and he would burst into tears. But suddenly the seizure was relaxed and he rose with a jerk to his feet.

"Time to bring the guns in," he exclaimed with an air of authority which surprised himself. As he cantered down the slope one voice was whispering in his ear: "Throw your hand down! Confess that you're stuck," and another was answering, "You can't do that. One doesn't *do* that sort of thing!"

In the gun-pit he was greeted this time with enthusiasm, and Jabez accepted delightedly the order to drop a couple of shells on Dorney and see what would happen. The first shell did not explode. The second burst clean in the middle of the village, and, though they could not see that it had discovered a concentration, it seemed to have acted as a cue for the climax of the battle. The rifle-fire on the river-bank doubled in volume, and a line of black dots appeared out of Boveney, rushed forward, and was succeeded by another wave. But by the time the guns were trained in that direction the movement had ceased, and two or three shells thrown into the houses whence it had come produced no visible effect. Jeremy ordered the guns to cease firing.

On the right the noise of the combat had suddenly grown irregular and spasmodic. Jeremy was puzzled and worried, and racked his sluggish brain to guess what this might portend. Was it the moment to order Thomas Wells to advance the right wing and begin the encircling movement? He had had no messenger nor any news from the Canadian since the battle had begun. His plan now seemed to him at once wooden and fantastic, drawn up by an amateur on the map, dependent on an accommodating enemy. Should he wait a little longer until the Welsh army had shown its hand more plainly? In his agony of indecision he gripped the gun-wheel at his side, as though he had been in need of physical support. If he had been left to himself he would have collapsed on the trodden earth of the pit and let the battle and the fortunes of the world roll over him as they would. He felt himself a poor waif beaten down by circumstance, a child called on to carry an unsupportable load. Only some kind of irrational obstinacy, a sort of momentum of the spirit, kept him upright. But things, both mental and physical, began to be blurred and to lose their outlines, and anxiety shed on him a sort of intoxication.

When he moved away towards his horse he was swaying in his walk and preserving his balance with the solemn care of drunkenness.

"Fire—fire on any advance you see!" he said unsteadily to Jabez, and he thought the old gunner looked at him queerly as he touched his hat in acknowledgment of the order.

"I've lost control of myself," Jeremy muttered under his breath, very seriously and carefully, as he rode back to rejoin the Speaker. "I've lost control of myself… I must be calm… I've lost control of myself… I must…" Nothing more seemed to matter but this: the battle came second to the struggle between his will and his nerves. He thought hazily that by one prodigious effort he might clear his brain again and see an answer to questions which now looked insoluble. He mechanically urged his horse up the rise; but the beast, fat, lazy, and sulky, did not respond, and Jeremy forgot it. When he dismounted he saw the old man still motionless in his chair gazing across the field, while behind him were the attendants, motionless, too, as though what was going on did not at all concern them. Jeremy half glanced at these men, and thought that they whispered to one another as he passed. He went on and stood silently beside the Speaker's chair. His lips were still moving as he muttered to himself, and some moments passed before he became aware that the old man had turned and was looking up at him dubiously.

"I'm all right," he began; and then suddenly a bullet whistled past their heads. It was as though the shrill sound had cleared away a thickening fog.

"Come out of this, sir," Jeremy cried violently. "They're too close. Some of them must have got into Chalk Hill. It's not safe for you up here." As he cried out, clutching at the Speaker with a convulsive hand, his self-possession and his resolution returned, and in that fraction of an instant he began to survey the field again with a new eye. The reserves were behind him in the village of Slough. He would bring them up, on the right, and make his push forward while the guns fired over the heads of the attacking wing. All these thoughts passed, sharp and distinct, through his mind, while he was frantically endeavoring to drag the Speaker into safety. But the old man resisted, foolishly obstinate it seemed to Jeremy, without giving any reason for doing so. He was staring open-mouthed towards the right flank of the army towards Stoke Park, and his face was contorted, crumbling, ravaged by the effects of astonishment and horror. It was a grotesque face, not that of an old man but of a man incredibly ancient: it might have been a thousand years old.

Jeremy ceased the effort to pull him away and followed with his eyes the direction of the extended, helplessly shaking finger. There, on the right, all firing had stopped, and the last clouds of smoke were drifting heavily to the north, leaving the fields quite clear. It took Jeremy a moment to realize what it was that he saw. Then he understood that, between the railway and the woods, the opposing forces had left their shelter in ditches and behind hedges and were mixing together, running, it seemed, in groups across the intervening meadows to unite. And among the moving crowds little rags of white danced and fluttered up and down.

"What!" he cried stupidly. "They can't have surrendered?"

"No!" the Speaker wailed in a thin and inhuman voice. "No! Those white flags are ours: I saw them raised. Thomas Wells has betrayed us. He has sold us to the Welsh." He let his arms fall by his sides and stood there limp, lax, shrunken, hopeless.

"It can't be—" But as Jeremy began to speak he saw the masses swarming in the meadows turn and move tumultuously towards them, cheering and waving their rifles in the air. He leapt to the emergency. "Come on down!" he shouted hoarsely. "We'll turn the guns on them! Come on to the guns!"

As they ran to their horses, Jeremy dragging the spent and stumbling Speaker after him, the firing on the river-bank rose sharply to a crescendo, and Jeremy guessed that a final attack was being made there. But he disregarded it, shoved the unresisting body of the old man into the saddle of one horse, leapt on to another himself, and galloped heavily down the slope to the battery. He found Jabez and his men working like demons, their faces black from the powder, bleared and puddled with sweat. They were firing in the direction of Boveney, and staring at the spot where their shells were bursting, he saw a regiment advancing to the attack of the village. They must have crept up in small parties and taken shelter in the houses. Now the rifle fire against them was weak and hesitating, and the guns, soon worn out, were shooting inaccurately and could not score a hit.

Jeremy abandoned that disaster. "Turn—turn them to the right!" he stuttered fiercely; but Jabez, with a blank look of incomprehension, pointed to his ears to signify that the noise had deafened him. Jeremy, made him understand by gestures what he wanted, but knew not how to tell him the reason. The guns were only just shifted when the mixed mob of soldiers, Welshmen and Speaker's men together, came pouring over the edge of the low hill.

"Fire on them!" he bawled at the top of his voice. Jabez trained one gun, quietly and coolly, on the advancing mass, while Jeremy trained the other. When they fired, the shells went over the leading ranks and burst beyond the hill. Shouts of anger were mixed with yells of pain, and after wavering for a moment the mob came on again. With no more concern than if they had been at the lathes in the workshop, with the same awkward antic gestures, the devoted old gunners loaded once more; but they had hardly closed the breeches when the first wave was upon them. Jeremy desperately snatched at the lanyard of his gun, and, as he did so, saw fleetingly the Speaker beside him, arms folded, shoulders sagging, head apathetically bowed. He pulled, and, with the crash, the nearest assailants vanished in a yellow, reeking cloud. The next thing Jeremy knew was that a breaker of human bodies had surged over the edge of the shallow pit and had fallen on him. He saw Jabez sinking grotesquely forward upon the pike that killed him, saw the still unstirring Speaker thrown down by a reeling man. Then he was on the ground, the lowest of a mass of struggling creatures, and some one, by kicking him painfully in the ear, had destroyed his transient sense of a pathetic end to a noble tragedy. He struck out wildly, but his arms and legs were held, and the struggle grew fiercer above him, choking him, weighing on his chest. Slowly, intolerably slowly and painfully, darkness descended about him. His last thought was a surprised, childish exclamation of the mind, "Why, this must be death…"

CHAPTER XIV
Chaos

1

THE AWAKING WAS SUDDEN and disconcerting. Without any interval, it seemed, Jeremy found himself staring up at the blinding sky, which looked almost white with the dry heat, and suffering miserably from an intolerable weight on his throat. This, he soon perceived, was caused by the legs of a dead man, and after a moment he threw them off and sat up, licking dry lips with a dry tongue. His ears still sang a little and he felt sick; but his head was clear, if his mind was still feeble. A minute's reflection restored to him all that had happened, and he looked around him with slightly greater interest.

He alone in the gun-pit seemed to be alive, though bodies sprawled everywhere in twisted and horrible attitudes. A few yards away lay Jabez, stabbed and dead, clinging round the trail of a gun, his nutcracker face grinning fixedly in a hideous counterfeit of life. Jeremy was unmoved and let his eyes travel vaguely further. He was very thirsty and wanted water badly. But apart from this desire he was little stirred to take up the task of living again. What he most wanted, on the whole, was to lie down where he was and doze, to let things happen as they would. The muscles of his back involuntarily relaxed and he subsided on to one elbow, yawning with a faint shudder. Then he realized that he would not be comfortable until he had drunk; and he rose stiffly to his feet. Close by the wheel of one of the guns, just inside it, stood an open earthenware jar half full of water, miraculously untouched by the tumult that had raged in the battery. Jeremy did not know for what purpose the gunners had used it, and found it blackened with powder and tainted with oil; but it served to quench his thirst. He drank deeply and then again examined the scene of quiet desolation.

One by one he identified the bodies of all the members of the gun-crews: none had escaped. Some had been bayonetted, some clubbed, some strangled or suffocated under the weight of their assailants. The feeble lives of a few, perhaps, had merely flickered out before the terror of the onset. Jeremy mused idly on the fact that all these ancients, who, if ever man did, deserved a quiet death, should have perished thus violently together, contending with a younger generation. He wondered if they would be the last gunners the world was to see. He found it odd that he, the oldest of all, should be the last to survive. He felt again the loneliness that had overtaken him—how long ago?—in the empty Whitechapel Meadows, when once before he had emerged from darkness. But now he suffered neither bewilderment nor despair. It was thus that fate was accustomed to deal with him, and something had destroyed or deadened the human nerve that rebels against an evil fate.

He sank on to the ground in a squatting position, propped his back against a wheel of the nearer gun and rested his chin on his hands, speculating, as though on something infinitely remote, on the causes and circumstances of his ruin. Thomas Wells, he supposed, had, in fact, sold them to the President of Wales, had very likely been corrupting the army for days before the battle. By that treachery the campaign was irrevocably lost and, Jeremy told himself calmly, the whole kingdom as well. There was no army between this and London, nor could any now be raised in the south. England was at the mercy of the invaders, and the reign of the Speakers was for ever finished. It was over, Jeremy murmured, with the death of their last descendant—for he took it for granted that the old man had been killed.

And then a sudden inexplicable wave of anger and foreboding came over him, as though the deadened nerve had begun to stir again and had waked him from this unnatural indifference. He scrambled to his feet and stared wildly in the direction of London. He must go there and find the Lady Eva. He found that he still desired to live.

With the new desire came activity of body and mind. He must travel as fast as he could, making his way through the ranks of the invaders and more quickly than they, and to do this with any chance of success he needed weapons. He would trust to luck to provide him with a horse later on. His own pistols had disappeared, but he began a determined and callous search among the dead. As he hunted here and there his glance was attracted by something white and trailing in the heap of bodies which lay between the wheels of the other gun. He realized with a shock that it was the Speaker's long beard, somehow caught up between two corpses which hid the rest of him. He looked at it and hesitated. Then, muttering, "Poor old chap!" he interrupted his search to show his late master what respect he could by composing his dead limbs. But as he pulled the old man's body free, the heavy, pouched eyelids flickered, the black lips parted and emitted a faint sigh. In an instant Jeremy had fetched the jar of water, and after sucking at it languidly like a sick child, the Speaker murmured something that Jeremy could not catch.

"Don't try to talk," he warned. "Be quiet for a moment."

"Is it all over?" the Speaker repeated in a distinct but toneless voice.

"All over," Jeremy fold him; and in his own ears the words rang like two strokes of a resonant and mournful bell.

"Then why are we here?"

Jeremy explained what had happened, and while he told the story the Speaker appeared, without moving, slowly to recover full consciousness. When it was done he tried to stand up. Jeremy helped him and steadied him when he was erect.

"It is all over," he pronounced in the same unwavering voice. Then he added with childish simplicity, "What shall we do now?"

"Get away from here," Jeremy cried with a sudden access of terror. "Thomas Wells will want to make sure we are dead, and this is just where he will look for us—he may come back any minute! And we mustn't be caught; we must get to London, to help the Lady Eva!"

"Get away from here. Very well, I am ready." And with a slow unsteady movement the Speaker began to pick his way across the battery, lurching a little when he turned aside to avoid a body lying at his feet. Jeremy ran after him and offered his arm, which the old man docilely accepted. When they had climbed out of the pit they saw that not only the village of Slough was burning, but also that every building for miles around seemed to have been fired. On the main road, away to their left, Jeremy distinguished a long column of wagons and mounted men on the march, accompanied by irregular and straggling crowds—the transport and the camp-followers, he surmised. But already most of the invaders were far ahead, making for London and, eager for that rich prize, not staying to loot the poor farmhouses, the smoke of which indicated their advance.

Jeremy turned and looked at his companion. The old Jew had paused without a word when Jeremy paused and stood waiting patiently for the order to move again. A sort of enduring tranquillity had descended like a thin mask on the savage power of his face, softening all its features without concealing them. His eyes shone softly with a peaceful and unnatural light. He stared fixedly straight before him, and what he saw moved him neither to speech nor to a change of expression. Jeremy regarded him with doubt, which deepened into fear. This passivity in one who had been so vehement had about it something alarming. The old man must have gone mad.

Jeremy shuddered at the suggestion. His thoughts suddenly became unrestrained, ridiculous, inconsequent. It was wicked to have led them into this misery and then to avoid reproach by losing his reason! How was he to get a madman over the difficult road to London? He felt as if he had been deserted in a hostile country with no companion but a hideous, an irritating monstrosity... That fixed, gentle smile began to work on his nerves and to enrage him. It was a symbol of an unreasonable and pitiless world, where the sun shone and the birds sang, and which yet turned wantonly to blast his most beautiful hopes. He cursed at the old man, cried, "It was all your fault, this!" madly raised his hand to strike— But the Speaker turned on him with a regard so quiet and so melancholy that he drew back in horror from his own intention.

"Come on, sir," he said with hoarse tenderness. "Give me your arm. We must keep to the right, well away from the road. We'll get through somehow."

2

Darkness was fast thickening in the air when Jeremy and the Speaker at last reached the western edge of London. During that tortuous and incredible journey the old man had not more than once or twice been shaken out of his smiling calm. He had walked or ridden, stood motionless as a stone by the roadside or crouched in hiding in the ditch, as Jeremy bade him, obedient in all things, impassive, apparently without will or desire of his own. Jeremy bore for them both the burden of their dangers and their escape, planned and acted and dragged his companion after him, astonishing himself by his inexhaustible reserve of vitality and resolution. Or, rather, he did none of these things, but some intelligence not his own reigned in his mind, looked ahead, judged coolly, decided, and drove his flagging body to the last limits of fatigue. An ancient instinct woke in the depths of his nature and took the reins. He was not at all a man, a lover, Jeremy Tuft, scientist, gunner, revenant, struggling, by means of such knowledge and gifts as his years of conscious life had bestowed on him, across difficult obstacles to reach a desired goal. He was a blind activity, a force governed by some obscure tropism; the end called, and like an insect or a migrating bird he must go to it, whether he would or not, whatever might stand in the way.

Once, when they almost stumbled on a ranging party of the President's horsemen, Jeremy pulled the Speaker roughly after him into a pond and found a hiding-place for them both among the thick boughs of an overhanging tree. When the old man felt the water rising coldly to his armpits he uttered a single faint cry of distress or despair, and Jeremy scanned him keenly, wondering whether perhaps it would not be better to desert that outworn body and altered brain as too much encumbrance on his flight. Afterwards, when the danger had gone by and it was time to emerge, they found that they had sunk deep in the mud. Jeremy's expression did not change or his heart beat a stroke the faster during the three or four minutes in which he struggled to draw himself up into the tree. Then he gazed down pitilessly on his companion, considering; but, seeing no signs of agitation or indocility on that dumb immobile mask, at last after much effort he drew him out.

Once they came sharply around a corner and saw ahead of them one of the Welsh troopers leading a riderless horse. It was too late to look for cover or to escape, and Jeremy, halting the Speaker by a rude jerk of his arm, went forward with an air of calm. As he came closer he cried out to the soldier in a raspingly authoritative voice: "I am looking for Thomas Wells. You must lead me to Thomas Wells at once."

The man, dark, squat, low-browed and brutish, paused and hesitated. He was puzzled by the unfamiliar speech of the eastern counties and was ignorant whether this might not be one of the deserters from the Speaker's army whom he ought to receive as a comrade. His uncertainty lasted long enough for Jeremy to come close to him, to produce a bayonet taken from one of the dead, and to drive it with a single unfaltering movement into his heart. He toppled off the horse without a sound, leaving one foot caught in the stirrup. Jeremy disentangled it, took the man's pistol and cloak, and rolled the body into the ditch, where he put a couple of dry branches over it. Then he beckoned to the Speaker to come up and mount. Thereafter they traveled more rapidly.

They had gone by such by-ways as to avoid for the most part the main track of the invading army, but they saw bands of marauders here and there and more often the evidences of their passage. As they came closer to London, in the neighborhood of Fulham, they slipped miraculously un-challenged through the advanced guard. Here Jeremy saw with a clear eye horrors which affected him no more than the faces of other people affect a hurrying man who jostles impatiently against them in a crowded street. The flare of burning cottages lit up the gathering twilight, and there were passing scenes of brutality… The invaders were pressing on to reach the city by nightfall and had no time to be exhaustively atrocious. But Jeremy heard (and was not detracted by it) the screams of tortured men, women, and children, and sometimes of cattle. Beyond the furthest patrols of the army they found the roads full of fugitives, hastening pitifully onward, though the country held for them no refuge from this ravening host, un-less it might be in mere chance. These, like their pursuers, were but so many obstacles in the way which Jeremy and the Speaker had to pass by as best they could.

When they came to the first cluster of houses it was dark and the full moon had not yet risen; but in front of them great welling fountains of fire softly yet fiercely illuminated the night sky.

"The people have gone mad," Jeremy muttered with cold understanding. "They are plundering the city before the enemy can plunder it. Come on, we must hurry." He urged forward the Speaker's horse and they plunged together into that doubtful flame-lit chaos.

No man raised a hand to stay them as they passed. The streets were crowded with hurrying people, both men and women, among whom it was impossible to distinguish which were escaping and which were looting. All carried bundles of incongruous goods and all looked fiercely yet shrinkingly at any who approached them. Many were armed, some with swords, some with clubs, some with the rudest weapons, odd pieces of iron or the legs of chairs, which they brandished menacingly, prepared to strike on the smallest suspicion rather than be unexpectedly struck down. Here and there in the boiling mob Jeremy distinguished the sinister, degraded faces, the rude, bundled clothes, of the squatters from the outskirts. Without slackening his pace he glanced around at the Speaker, who was moving through the turmoil with gentle smile and fixed, unseeing eyes. The time was already gone when he might have been affected by the agony of his city.

Out of the raging inferno of Piccadilly, where already a dozen houses were on fire, they turned down a dark and narrow lane behind two high walls, and as they did so the noise of the tumult became strangely remote, as though it belonged to another world. Here there was no sound save the terrifying reverberations caused by their horses' hoofs. At the bottom of it was a gate set in the boundary wall of the gardens of the Treasury. It stood wide open, and inside there was a mysterious and quiet blackness. They rode through and immediately drew rein.

Then the sense of these invisible but familiar walks and lawns quickened Jeremy's cold resolution to an intolerable agony of pain—pain like that which follows the thawing of a frozen limb. During the wild and hasty journey the only conscious thought that had possessed him had been that somehow or other he must get to the Treasury. It had excluded all consideration of what he might find, or what he should do when he got there. Now suddenly he understood that this place and all the people in it had been existing and changing, as places and people change, in reality as well as in his mind, that things had been happening here in his absence, all that week, all that day, during the time he lay unconscious in the gun-pit, during the last hour… It was as though he had carried somewhere in his brain, unalterable till now by any certainty, a picture of the Treasury as it had always been; this black and silent wilderness substituted itself with a shock like a cataclysm. For the first time Jeremy made a sound, a low choked groan of extreme anguish. Then, cold as he had been before, he dismounted and bade the Speaker stay by the horses, because the gardens here were too much broken up for riding at night. He hastened forward alone, staring through the darkness at the empty place where the lights of the Treasury ought to have been.

But there was no light in any of the windows, and Jeremy stumbled on, sinking to the ankles in the soft earth of flower-beds, catching his feet in trailing plants, running headlong into bushes, growing desperate and breathless. Suddenly he became aware of the building, a great vague mass looming over him like a thicker piece of night; and as he stared up at it, it seemed to grow more distinct and the windows glimmered a little paler than the darkness around them. He crawled cautiously along the wall, found a door, which, like the garden-gate, was wide open, and slipped into the chilling obscurity of a passage. Then he paused, hesitating, frightened by the uncanny silence and emptiness of the house.

It was plain that the Treasury had been deserted, though how and why he could not conjecture. He stayed by the door and rested his body against the wall, racking his wits to think what the Lady Eva and her mother might have been expected to do when the news of the disaster reached them—as it must have reached them. He now perceived his own weariness and that he was aching in every member. His head was whirling, perhaps from the delayed effects of the blow that had stunned him, and he felt as though he were flying, swooping up and down in great dizzy circles. His back was an aching misery that in no attitude could find rest. This last check, at what had been for hours and through incredible adventures his only imagined goal, sapped at a blow his unnatural endurance, and for a moment he was ready to fall where he stood and weep in despair.

It was to choke back the tears he felt rising in his throat that he called out, foolishly, in a weak and hoarse voice: "Eva! Where are you? Eva!"

Then most incredibly from the bushes in the garden a few yards behind him came a wavering low cry, "Jeremy, is it you?" and then, in an accent of terror, "Oh, who is it?" At the same time he saw a shadow moving, and the next moment that shadow was in his arms, crying softly, while he held her in a firm embrace.

Some minutes passed thus before the Lady Eva recovered her power of speech. Jeremy lost all sense of time and of events. He wanted first to comfort her and next to know what she had suffered. He had forgotten that he had come to take her away from impending danger.

At last her sobbing stopped and she murmured, her face still close against his breast: "Jeremy, mother is dead!"

"Dead!" They both spoke in whispers, as though the silent gardens were full of enemies seeking for them.

"Yes, dead." She straightened herself and withdrew from his arms, as though she must be free before she could tell her story. Then she went on in a low, hurried, unemphasized voice: "Roger—you know, Roger Vaile—brought the news that… that you had been defeated. He was with Thomas Wells and saw him give the signal to surrender, but he managed to get away, and when he realized it was all over he came straight here. He was badly wounded, I think—he stumbled and fell against me, and my dress is all covered with blood…" She stopped and caught her breath, then went on more firmly: "He was telling us and begging us to go away and hide, and we didn't want to go. Then a crowd of people came into our room—servants, most of them, grooms and stablemen—and told us that everything was over, that there was no more government, and we had to get out at once, because the Treasury belonged to them now. And I said we'd go, but mother said out loud: 'Then I must get my jewels first.'

"They got very excited at that, and when she went to her chest to get them, they went after her and pulled her away, not roughly really, and began rummaging in the chest themselves. Roger was standing, holding on to a chair, looking horribly white, and he told mother to come away and leave them. But she wouldn't; she went back to the chest and ordered them out of the room. They pushed her away again more roughly and laughed at her, and she lost her temper—you know how she used to?—and hit one of them in the face. Then he—then he killed her… with a sword…"

Her voice trailed away into silence. Jeremy took her cold hands and muttered brokenly. "Dearest— dearest—"

"When that happened," she went on in the same even whisper, "Roger called out to me to run away. He'd got a great bandage around his wound, and he looked so ill I thought he was going to faint. But he stood in the door and drew his knife to keep them from coming after me: I was just outside in the passage. I couldn't run away. Then one of them came at him, and Roger struck at him with the knife. The man just caught Roger's wrist and held it for a minute—Roger was so weak—and then pushed him, and he fell down in the passage, and blood came pouring out of his side. Then I—I think he died. And I ran away. I don't think they came after me… I don't think they did…"

She was silent again, and Jeremy took her into his arms in an inarticulate agony. She lay there limp and unresponsive. At last she whispered: "I ought to have stayed and looked after him… but I think he was dead. Such a lot of blood came out of his wound… it poured and poured over the floor… it came almost to my feet…"

"Eva!" said Jeremy, and could say nothing more. Several minutes passed before he exclaimed: "It doesn't matter. We must get away. You must try and forget it all, beloved. I'll look after you now."

"I will, oh, I will!" she cried, clinging to him. "But I can't now—I can see it all the time. I'm trying. And, Jeremy," she went on, holding him as he tried to draw her away, "afterwards, when I thought they'd gone, I went back… I went back to my room—"

"Yes, dear." Jeremy was still trying to draw her away.

"And I got this—look!" Jeremy peered at something she held up to him, but could not make out what it was. She thrust it into his hand, and he felt a small round metal box, the size and shape of half an egg. "I took it once, months ago, from that silly girl, Mary. She was pretending to be in love, and she said that if ever her lover deserted her she'd kill herself. Then she boasted that she'd got poison so as to be ready—Rose told me. So I made her give it to me, and I never thought about it again till to-day."

"Yes, dear," Jeremy murmured soothingly, "but it's all right now. You don't need it. Shall we throw it away?"

"No, no!" she cried agitatedly, snatching the box back; then calmly again: "Don't be angry with me, Jeremy. It's stupid, but you don't know how I wanted that box this afternoon while I was hiding in the garden, so as to be sure… And I couldn't get up the courage to go back and look for it. I must keep it for a little while now. I'll throw it away myself in a little while." She tucked the box into her dress and gave him her hand. Without another word they set off towards the Speaker and the horses.

CHAPTER XV
Flight

1

THE OLD MAN HAD NOT moved from the spot or the attitude in which Jeremy had left him. He still stood by the horses, holding the bridles, his head fallen forward on his chest.

"Don't say anything to him," Jeremy whispered hurriedly to the Lady Eva. "He's… he's strange." She nodded in reply. Her father, however, took no notice of her, if he saw her, but only turned mutely to Jeremy as though awaiting orders. It then first occurred to Jeremy to ask himself what they ought to do next. The inhuman power which had sustained him so far and had given him supernatural gifts of foresight and decision, now without warning deserted him. He found himself again what he had been before, an honest, intelligent and courageous man, placed by fate in a situation which demanded much more of him than honesty, intelligence, or courage. He felt like the survivor of a midnight shipwreck who loses in a flurry of waves the plank to which he is clinging and is abandoned to the incalculable and hostile forces of darkness and the sea.

He turned to the girl and asked her advice; but she shook her head dumbly. She had followed him there as a child follows its guardian, without questioning him, accepting his wisdom and his will as though they had been the inalterable decrees of Providence. In despair he addressed the Speaker as he would have addressed him a week or even a day before, seeking to learn if there was any well-affected magnate in whose house they could find refuge.

A change became visible on the old man's face. He seemed to be struggling to think and to speak, and in his eagerness he sawed the air with his disengaged hand. At last he ejaculated in a strange, hoarse voice, produced with effort, which jerked from fast to slow and from the lowest note to the highest, as though he, had no control over it:

"Can't make peace with the President now—can't give him up the

Chairman alive. Thomas Wells took the Chairman prisoner and cut his throat." Then he added with a sort of dreadful reflectiveness: "Thomas Wells always did say that he believed in making sure." And so, having delivered what was perhaps his ultimate pronouncement on statecraft, he resumed his former position, motionless, except that now and then a violent fit of shivering shook him from head to foot. Behind the little group the houses in Piccadilly burned up higher and painted lurid colors on the sky, and away on the other side of the Treasury a great fountain of golden sparks, dancing and gyrating, showed that one of the houses on the Embankment, apparently Henry Watkins' house, had now been fired. But in the garden the shadows only wavered and flickered feebly, and the noise of the flames, and of the looting of fleeing crowds, came incredibly thin and gentle. Jeremy and Eva and the Speaker seemed in this obscurity to have been sheltered away from the violence of the world in a little haven of miraculous calm, the walls of which, however, were yet as tenuous and unstable as those of a soap-bubble.

Jeremy pondered again, while his companions silently and expectantly regarded him. After a minute he said in a very gentle tone: "Eva, I know so little… if we could get down to the coast, do you think we could find a boat to take us over to France?"

"I think so," she replied doubtfully. "I know that there are boats that go to France, of course. But what shall we do when we get there?"

"I don't know. I shall find some way of looking after you. But anyway, we must do that because there's nothing else for us to do, unless we give ourselves up."

"I won't be taken by Thomas Wells," she said, with a catch in her voice.

Jeremy set his teeth hard to keep back his exclamation. "We'll do that," he assured her firmly. "But first of all we must go back to the house and get things to take with us."

They found their way in silence through the gardens, Jeremy leading one horse and the Speaker the other and Eva walking by Jeremy, holding his free hand. They searched the stables first, and there, to their delight, found two fresh horses, strong, ugly beasts, not elegant enough for the

Speaker's carriage or to go with the army, but very suitable for such a journey as was now proposed. They also found a lantern which Jeremy took with him into the Treasury. He returned after a while with a supply of bread and meat and some clothes. Then they went as quietly as possible around to the courtyard, there to make their preparations.

Eva helped Jeremy to pack the saddle-bags, while he explained his intentions to her. The coast round the mouth of the Thames, he thought, and probably as far as Dover, would be overrun at once by the Welsh invaders, and it would be fatal for them to go in that direction. He therefore proposed to double west, strike across Sussex, and make for one of the Channel ports there or farther on in Hampshire. He thought that he could find his way, and that if they made haste they would escape pursuit. His plans beyond that were of the vaguest: he supposed that in the end he could put his mechanical knowledge to some use. Perhaps later on they might even return to England, if the country remained unsettled, and assert the Speaker's claims against the usurpers. As he uttered this cloudy fragment of comfort he thought of the wandering Stuarts and chuckled to himself, sourly but half-hysterically, at finding himself in so romantic a situation.

Meanwhile the Speaker sat crouched, where Jeremy had placed him, on an old mounting-stone in the courtyard, muttering continuously under his breath. When all was ready for their departure, Jeremy went over to him, arranged a cloak to hide his conspicuous face and beard, and put a hand under his arm to raise him up. The old man stiffly acquiesced, still mumbling.

"What did you say, sir?" Jeremy asked gently.

"Thomas Wells always did say that he believed in making sure," the Speaker repeated with a terrifying evenness of intonation.

Jeremy twisted his shoulders impatiently, as though to shake off an evil omen, and led the stooping figure over to where the horses stood ready. The noise of the rioting and plundering came to them more distinctly here in the courtyard; but Whitehall itself was strangely quiet, as though the frenzied crowds had left the Treasury untouched in order to placate the fast-approaching invaders who were to be its new tenants and their new masters.

Jeremy had just seated Eva on one horse and the Speaker on the other and was preparing to lead them out, when they heard the clatter of hoofs coming furiously down Whitehall, rising loud and clear above the confused sounds that filled the air. There was something arresting, sinister, and purposeful in that sharp, staccato sound, and, as if by instinct, they drew together in the dark entrance to the courtyard, while Jeremy hastily blew out the lantern. Then the rider reached them, drew rein, and halted a yard or two away from them, peering into the shadow. They could see him only as a vague shape, thickly cloaked and muffled, while behind him in the distance little figures hurried aimlessly into or out of the dull glow of Henry Watkins' house. Jeremy put one hand on Eva's arm lest she should make a rash gesture, while with the other he grasped firmly the barrel of one of his pistols.

The horseman continued to stare at them without moving, as though uncertain whether what he saw in the gate was shadow or substance. But suddenly the flames opposite shot up higher and brighter and cast a red dancing reflection on their faces; and Jeremy felt like a fugitive whose hiding-place is unmasked. The horseman spoke at last, and Jeremy recognized with a shudder the calm drawling voice.

"Well, who are you?" he said. "What do you mean by looting here?" Jeremy clutched the girl's arm more tightly and made no reply, hoping that in the doubtful light they might still pass for stray fugitives. But the man urged his horse a little nearer, leaning over to look at them, and saying: "Speak up! It'll be the worse for you if you don't. I'm looking for the Lady Eva. Have you seen—" And then as he leant still closer, in astonishment, "By God!" Jeremy brought round his arm like a man throwing a stone and dashed the pistol-butt heavily in Thomas Wells's face.

The Canadian uttered a choked cry, sagged forward on his horse's neck, and slid free to the ground on the other side. Jeremy fumbled for the bayonet which he still carried with him; but Eva plucked agonizedly at his shoulder, crying: "Jeremy! Jeremy, come!" He hesitated a moment and heard a louder sound of galloping hoofs approaching. Then he jumped into Thomas Wells's empty saddle, turned the horse and rode out into

Whitehall, drawing the girl and the old man after him. A few minutes later they were fighting their way through the thickening crowd of fugitives that still poured southwards over Westminster Bridge.

*

When day broke they were well clear of the southern edge of London, and a little later they were crossing the broad ridge of the North Downs. They had made a dizzy pace during the short night, and Jeremy, who was no horsemaster, but knew that the horses must be nearly finished, called a halt and suggested that they should rest a little in a small grove which lay on the southern slope of the hill.

The old man, who was calm and indifferent again, and had ceased his muttering, rested his back against the trunk of a tree, his arms falling ungainly like the arms of a broken doll. He shivered violently at intervals, but still did not complain: he had not once spoken to his companions since their journey began. Jeremy after a doubtful glance at him, walked to the lower edge of the grove, and the girl followed him, treading noiselessly on the soft pine-needles. While he stared vaguely out over the misty chequer-board of the Weald, he felt her hand placed in his and dared not turn to look at her.

Presently, mastering himself, he cried: "Look, there's Chanctonbury!" For the mist had just rolled off that far and noble grove, showing it perhaps a little larger than he remembered it, but in every other respect the same. Then he added: "Go and sleep, Eva, while I keep an eye on the road." But he spoke without force, because he did not wish her to leave him alone, he did not wish to sacrifice these few quiet minutes with her.

"I can't sleep," she said. "I can't sleep again till we are safe. It won't be long now, will it?"

He shook his head and smiled as confidently as he could.

"I mean, it won't be long… one way or the other," she went on, dragging out the words and keeping her eyes with difficulty on his.

2

As they traveled on, through the tumbled slope of the downs and out into the flat country, a sort of quietude, a rigidity of expectation, descended on the little party. There had been so far no sign that they were pursued or that the wave of invasion was extending this way; and Jeremy began to believe that they had escaped from their enemies. But the news of fatal changes in the kingdom had gone before them. The sight of strange travelers on the road was alarming to the workers in the fields. Once, when they would have stopped a rustic hobbledehoy to ask their way, he ran from them, screaming to unseen companions that the Welsh had come to burn the village. Once they found the gates of a great park barricaded as if for a siege, and behind it two or three old men with shotguns who warned them fiercely away. The whole country, as yet untouched by that menacing hand, was in a state of shrinking preparation and alarm.

But they husbanded their provision and went on, independent of all help, striking towards the distant line of hills, which once crossed they would be able to find their way to the coast. From Portsmouth, Jeremy learnt, an inlet now silted up and almost negligible, the smugglers were said to cross to France and back; and a not unusual item in their freight was criminals escaping from justice. So at least Eva had gathered from the stories that used to drift about the Treasury, starting perhaps from some clerk concerned with the prevention or the overseeing of this abuse. Jeremy steered their course there for a little to the west, and trusted to heaven to see them straight to their goal.

Their progress was slow and fretted him, so that at first it was necessary for Eva to calm and console him two or three times in every hour. The Speaker, who had still not awakened from his dream, was manifestly very ill and sometimes kept his seat in the saddle with difficulty. His breath had grown short and stentorous; and he had fits in which he fought for air, while his face became black and the veins in his neck and temples congested. During the worst of these they had to stop and let him rest by the road-side, while Eva loosened his garments, bathed his forehead with water from the nearest ditch, and murmured over him the tender words of a mother over a child. At these times Jeremy would stride away, biting his lip and clenching his hands, muttering that every care Eva lavished on her father was a moment lost in the race for her safety. But before he had gone many yards in his indignation he would ask himself how much anxiety for himself and for his own future happiness with her had done to provoke this fury. Even while his brow was drawn and his lips were still muttering, some independent voice in his brain would be pronouncing judgment on his unworthy weakness and sending him back, quivering with self-restraint, to offer Eva, ungraciously but sincerely, what help he could.

Then she would smile up at him divinely, diverting to him for a moment the flood of loving pity she had poured on her outworn and helpless father. It seemed to him that she, who was the most terribly threatened of the three, stood most aloof, most untouched of all of them, from the cruel things of the world, a person infinitely wise and compassionate, who would comprehend at once the causes of his gusts of passion as well as their futility.

The country-side appeared to be, as Jeremy had indeed expected to see it, greener and richer and fuller than he had ever known it. The crops far and wide were already approaching maturity and promised a full harvest. The woods covered a greater space, but were better cared for; and everywhere men were working in them, tending them, felling trees, or burning charcoal. There seemed to be fewer enclosed fields of grass, while the open commons had grown, and now maintained sheep and cows, goats and geese, herded by ragged and dirty little boys and girls. Even on this journey Jeremy could not help watching curiously all they passed and noting the contrast with his own day, and he saw this rich and idyllic country with something of a constriction at the heart. Apparently in the mad turmoil of the Troubles, while lunatics had fought and destroyed one another, the best of the English had managed to stretch out a hand and take back a little of what had been their own and to restore a little of what had been best in England. And now... Jeremy wished they could have passed through one of the larger country towns to observe its reviving prosperity, but they dared not, and skirted Horsham as widely as the roads would allow them.

In the villages there seemed to be a more vigorous life but less civilization. Still, here and there, on ancient houses hung metal plates from which the enamel was not yet all gone, advertising some long-vanished commodity, or announcing that it was so many miles to somewhere else. But the old buildings tottered and flaked away even as Jeremy looked at them; and the new population was sheltered in hideous and rickety barns.

But all this progress through the Weald had the uneven quality of a dream, in which at one moment events are hurried together with inconceivable rapidity, while at another they are drawn out as though to make a thin pattern over the waste spaces of eternity. Sometimes Jeremy rode impatiently a yard or two in front of his companions, eaten up by a burning passion for haste, sometimes with them, or behind them, dull, patient, resigned, uninterested. When he looked at the Lady Eva with anxious or with pathetic eyes, he saw her still serene and controlled. On the first night after their escape they had covered only a little more than half of the distance to the hills, when weariness forced them to stop and rest in a wood not far from Slinfold. From the edge of the wood they could see the village, where one light still burned, perhaps that of the inn; and some desire for company made them rest in a spot where they could keep it in view. At first it was an intense and brilliant point in the soft, melting dusk and later, as the darkness grew complete, the only real thing in a country that had become mysterious and intangible.

Jeremy had wished to go on into the village and find a lodging there, so that the old man might be made comfortable at least during the night. But on reflection he decided that the fewer witnesses they left behind of their passage across the country the greater would be their chances of safety. It was not impossible that Thomas Wells or the President should send out scouting-parties after them; and the Speaker was a noticeable man. He therefore announced, as the leader from whose decision there was no appeal, that they would sleep in the open; and Eva, gravely nodding, acquiesced. They made a bed for the Speaker of dry leaves, such as still lay under the trees, and the saddlecloths, and disposed him on it. He was for once breathing easily and quietly, and obeyed them like a very young child. But no sooner was he asleep than his day-long silence and passivity gave way to a restless muttering and gesturing. Jeremy, bending over him, could distinguish nothing in the torrent of words that came blurred and jumbled from the blackened lips; but he recognized in the rise and fall of the voice a horrible likeness to those long and furious tirades on the future of England, of which he had been the recipient during his days in the workshops.

He covered up the Speaker with a shuddering tenderness, left him, and came back to Eva, who had settled herself with her back against a tree. As soon as he sat down at her side she slipped wearily into his arms and, looking up at him, said softly, "We love one another, Jeremy"—not an appeal or a protestation, but a simple statement of fact, of the last certitude which remained unassailable in this moving and deceitful world. She said nothing more before she fell asleep with her head on his shoulder; and in a little while in this cramped and uncomfortable position he too slept.

The next day they pressed on again; but they had not gone many miles before it became obvious that the Speaker was much worse, was in a high fever and was growing delirious. His eyes shone brilliantly and seemed to have increased in size and his cheeks were flushed with a deep red. Once, when from exhaustion and misery they had for a moment ceased to watch him and to hold him in his saddle, he checked his horse, slid off and made unsteadily for a wood which lay some distance on one side of their way. Jeremy had to dismount, go after him, and drag him back to the road by force. Now for the first time he began to speak aloud and intelligibly, to rave of what he intended to do for England, how he would strengthen her government and renew her civilization, how he would teach the people their ancient arts and make them again the most powerful in the world.

By this time Jeremy, persevering mutely and patiently, was conscious of the old man only as an intolerable burden on their flight. He even revolved plans of letting him escape or leaving him by the roadside, arguing furiously in his mind that to drag along with him a man so obviously past saving, a man who, at the best, all disasters aside, was anyway without doubt at the end of his life, was inviting destruction for himself and Eva, who were young and vigorous and hopeful, and had all their life and their love before them. But he knew very well that he could make no connection between his logic and the reality. He sometimes caressed the girl's shoulder with a clumsy gesture and she smiled at him in reply. All through that day hardly a word passed between them which was not necessary. To all appearance their only link might have been the ancient and insensible being with whose safety they were charged. But in their silent union to serve this end, in the accord moved and ratified by a look or a lifted finger, Jeremy recognized and was exalted by the inevitability, the invincibility of the bond that held them. Somehow he had been launched flying at random through the centuries and had fallen at the side of this one woman. Life might do with them what chance directed; but they had met, and out of that meeting had arisen their love, which was a stable and eternal thing, which he felt to be unmoved even in these death-throes of a world.

Amidst such delays they did not come until nightfall to the road which runs along the foot of the Downs, and at which Jeremy had been aiming. Just as they entered it from a deeply-rutted side-track, the old man uttered a heart-rending sound and collapsed on the neck of his horse in the worst crisis he had yet suffered. Jeremy reined in and stopped, his brow contracted, his heart sinking as he realized that it was impossible to push on. Then with a sigh he dismounted, and lifted the Speaker to the ground. As he did so it seemed to him that in this short time the old man's great bulk had wasted and grown frail, so that his body was no heavier than that of a child. Eva too dismounted, and, bending over her father, attempted to restore him, but without effect. It seemed every moment that his loud and labored breathing must cease from sheer inability to overcome the impediment that hung on it. His delirium had passed into a pitiful and not peaceful stupor; and Jeremy began to believe that death was at hand.

He contemplated the fact without emotion; but Eva grew agitated, caught him by the hand, and cried, "What shall we do? What can we do?" And then, before he could reply, she went on, "Look, there are some houses in front of us: we must be coming into a village. Let's try to get a lodging, whatever the risk may be. He mustn't die like this by the roadside."

Jeremy stood up and gazed where she pointed. A few houses were dotted among the trees, and lights flickered here and there. For a moment he was balanced between protest and consent.

"Very well," he said in a level tired voice, "I'll go on, and see what sort of a place it is. Will you not be afraid to be alone with him till I come back?" She shook her head, and he set off.

As soon as he entered the tiny village, dogs ran out from the yards, barking and snapping at his heels. He kept them off with his riding-whip, and stumbled along looking for the inn. Vague thick-set shapes lurched past him on heavy feet, and vanished here and there. Presently, after he had tripped over a rut and fallen headlong into a heap of evil-smelling refuse, he came upon a little ramshackle hovel which seemed, from the noise of conviviality issuing through the half-open door, to be what he sought. He paused outside for a moment, brushing the filth from his garments and listening.

Inside, the worthies of the village were rejoicing after the day's work. Jeremy could hear the slow, long drawn-out sound of Sussex talk, not changed by a couple of centuries (or rather thrown back by that interval into the peculiarity it had at one time seemed likely to lose) and the noise of liquor being poured and of pots being scraped on a table. Then a voice was raised in song, and all the laborers joined it, roaring and shouting in unison. Jeremy's momentary hesitation lengthened, continued, grew timeless... His tired brain was going round, the dark scene about him was melting and being built up again. He forgot why he was there or whence he had come. He could only remember, vaguely struggling still to realize that this was not it, one particular night, very black and wretched, when they had been hauling up the guns in preparation for the opening of the Battle of the Somme, and all the men of the battery had sung in chorus to keep themselves cheerful. This was like a shadow-show in which he could not tell the real from the fictitious. Who and where was he? Who was singing that familiar, that haunting or haunted melody? Was it those old comrades of the German wars who had suffered with him in the Salient, and at Arras, and by Albert, or could it be...? He could not hear the words until at last they came to him clearly in the emphasis of the last repetition, as the laborers shouted together:

Pack up my troubles in some owekyebow
And smile, smile, smile!

The recognition of the garbled words, the subtly altered tune, shot him back at once from that middle world of fantastic unreality to the immediate problem, the flight, the Speaker fighting to get his breath a few hundred yards down the road. His first start of surprise had carried his hand to the latch and he pushed the door open, and went into the low, brick-floored, reeking parlor.

His entrance produced an immediate hush. Pots were arrested halfway to thirsty mouths and every eye stared roundly at him. It seemed to him too that there was a slight involuntary shrinking away from him among all these hearty, earth-stained men, but he was too weary to do more than receive the impression without curiosity as to its meaning, without more than a flickering and uninterested recollection of the fact that he was unarmed. But immediately a relaxation succeeded the hush and the inn-keeper pushed forward, saying.

"Why, I did think as how you was one of them Welshmen come back again!"

This speech was to Jeremy as though a dagger of ice had been driven into his heart, and the room swayed round him. But he betrayed no trouble in his expression, took a firm grip on his mind and laughed with the inn-keeper at the idea. All the rustics joined in his laughter, nudged one another, went forward with their interrupted drinking, and murmured,

"That's a good'un!"

When the merriment had a little subsided, he asked as casually as he could manage whether the Welshmen had been there that day. All at once began to tell him how a party of soldiers speaking a strange, hardly recognizable tongue, had entered the village early in the morning. Their leader, who could just make himself understood in the eastern speech, had held an inquisition and had terrified the inhabitants almost out of their wits. They had also emptied a barrel of beer, and made off with a sucking-pig and a good many fowls before riding away. The villagers, it seemed, had been too much concerned in keeping out of their way to be certain what direction they had taken; but Jeremy gathered that they had scattered, some going towards Houghton Bridge, some towards Pulborough, some towards Duncton.

"Too bad," said Jeremy sympathetically, his wits working at high speed and warning him to be cautious. "What do you suppose they were looking for?"

"Some tale about an old man and a young man and a young woman," the inn-keeper grumbled. Jeremy nodded negligently in reply, and the inn-keeper went on, "And what might you be wanting yourself?"

Jeremy explained that he had been unexpectedly overtaken by darkness on the way to Arundel, and that he was looking for a bed. A friend, he said, was waiting just outside the village for his report: anything would do, he added, desiring to be plausible. He and his friend were easily served and used to roughing it: a truss of hay in a loft or a corner in a shed under a cart would be enough for them.

"We can do that for 'ee," replied the inn-keeper hospitably, and Jeremy, thanking him, said that he would fetch his friend and return at once. When they returned, he observed, as he slid through the door, he hoped the whole company would still be there to drink to their health. He left the inn a popular and unsuspected person. But when he was a few yards away from it he began to run, and he blundered desperately through the darkness till he came to Eva and her father, the old man still lying prone, the girl crouched by his side under the hedge.

"Eva—" he began, panting.

"Have you found a place, Jeremy?" she cried anxiously. "I think we could get him there now. His breathing's easier, and—"

Jeremy took her by the shoulder and spoke calmly. "Listen," he said. "We can't go into that village or any other. There's been a party of the President's men there to-day looking for us, and they're still about somewhere."

She turned her shadowed face up to him and listened attentively without opening her lips. "There's only one thing we can do," he went on with the same coolness. "We must get up at once on to the downs and leave the horses here. I used to know them pretty well and we ought to have something like a chance of hiding there if they chase us. We can crawl right along, never getting far from cover and only just crossing roads, till we're near Portsmouth. There's no help for it, Eva. They're looking for *us*: you know what that means."

For a moment it seemed that she would rebel; and then she bowed her head and put her hand in his. "Very well," she said in a quiet voice. "We must do as you think best." Jeremy had the impression that, from some divine and inconceivable height, she was humoring his childish attachment to this bauble of her life. Instinctively he took her in his arms and kissed her and felt the passionate response of her whole body. In the next second they were again practical and cold, taking from the saddle-bags and hanging about them such of their store of food as still remained. Then they lifted the Speaker between them and found that there was just enough strength left in his limbs to carry him along if he was strongly supported on both sides. A few yards away from them a narrow track, trodden in the chalk, glimmered faintly; and they turned into it, making a slow and labored progress up the side of the hill.

CHAPTER XVI

The Roman Road

1

THAT NIGHT WAS ONE of the cold and starry nights which sometimes fall on the downs in the middle of summer. As they began to climb up the slope, the earth seemed to be returning in warm, almost tangible waves, the heat it had received during the day from the sun. But when they got clear of the gloomy beech groves on the lower slopes, when the uneven track had failed them and left them in the middle of a great sweep of open grass, this ceased, and the air grew gradually cooler. Presently the wind, which had fallen at dusk, rose again, coming from another direction, faint but chilly. The motion of the air could hardly be felt, yet it had in it some quality which touched and stayed the blood and enervated the spirit. These hours of darkness promised, before they were done, to reduce the fugitives to a lower state of wretchedness than they yet had suffered.

When they had stumbled for some time up the steeply rising hill-side which bore only small and scattered patches of gorse and juniper, Jeremy realized that they were now as far from the road as they needed to be, and that it would be impossible for them to walk on much longer. He looked about him for some shelter in which they might pass the night and not be immediately obvious to any searcher when day broke. But he could see none; and he began to be troubled in his mind, for he dared not halt lest exhaustion should pin them in the open where they stood. He scanned eagerly every patch of bush that they passed; but all were too thin and too much exposed. At last on his left he thought he saw a line dark against the dark sky, which might perhaps be a wood. He pulled gently at the old man's arm and directed their steps towards it. When they came close it proved to be a thick grove of bushes and low thorn trees, running on either hand out of the narrow limits of their sight.

"This will do well enough," he said in the murmured voice of pre-occupation; and Eva assented with a single word.

They pushed their way through the close growth, and came suddenly on a steep bank three or four yards from the edge of the thicket.

"*This* will do!" Jeremy cried in a heartier tone; and he explained that he wished to be well hidden by bushes, but not so much shut in that in the morning they could not get a clear view of the country around them. But, while he was explaining all this, Eva was gently laying down the Speaker, so that his head rested against the bank, and making for his head a pillow out of her cloak. Jeremy silently gave her his own cloak, with which she covered the sleeping or comatose old man. When she had finished she stood up, shivered slightly, and folded her arms as if to retain the last vanishing sparks of warmth in her body. Jeremy, standing also, quiet and somber, felt a wave of inexpressible emotion rise in his heart at the sight of her slender and shadowy figure.

"Eva… Eva…" he murmured, and she came into his arms as though that had been the homing-cry. They had no words to use with one another. They kissed once, and then stood locked in his embrace, Eva's face pressed into his shoulder, one of his broad hands on her hair, the other at her waist. After a little while he pressed her head gently backwards, bent the supple waist and lowered her on to the ground as tenderly as she had lowered her father. She suffered what he did without speaking or resisting, and allowed him to move her head so that it rested on a thick tuft of grass, and to wrap her riding skirt tightly about her ankles. For a moment after he had done the silence endured, and Jeremy thought that, even thus, after the fatigues of the day, she would not find it hard to sleep. But when she saw him standing, square, black and aloof, between her and the stars, she called out to him softly.

"Jeremy! Jeremy! come down to me!" He knelt by her side, and laid one hand on her arm, conscious, as he made it, of the clumsiness and inexpressiveness of the gesture. "Lie down by me," she went on. "The night will be cold, and we shall keep one another warm."

After the first exquisite exhilaration of finding himself at her side, limb to limb, cheek to cheek, clasped in her arms as she in his, the faculty of reckoning minutes and hours vanished from his mind. This seemed to him an image of the eternal night which descends on all. He had a vision of a shrouded figure pacing an endless corridor and pausing for the length of a human life between one step and the next. Only the slow, unintermittent rhythm of the girl's breathing suggested to him that time passed. He stirred slightly in her arms: he wished to look up at the sky.

At their heads stood a low hawthorn, beaten, stunted, and misshapen by many fierce winds, which threw out its sprawling branches over them; and close to their side was a thick overhanging clump of gorse. Between the two swam vaguely the North Star; and his eyes strayed from this to the Great Bear, whence he found or guessed the other constellations, riding the night sky, remote, brilliant and serene. It seemed to him that what spirit he had left ceased to be human and was sucked up into the fellowship of those bright indifferent lights, and the vast spaces which separated them. He began to amuse himself by calling back to mind as much as he could remember of that ancient and ridiculous science, astronomy. Odd facts floated into his thoughts concerning the weight of the stars, the speed of a ray of light, the nature of gravitation. He recalled epoch-making and cataclysmic discoveries, all records of which were now very likely erased from the annals of mankind. He wondered idly what had become of So-and-so who had been forever busy with the perihelion of Mercury, and of Such-and-such who had exhibited strange frenzies when you mentioned to him the name of a noted Continental astronomer. He recollected queer empty wrangles about the relation between the universe we can see or conceive, and the infinite, inconceivable universe, of the existence of which our minds mysteriously inform us. He was fascinated by the recurrence in his thoughts of a theory that our system, and all the stars we can see, are but one minute and negligible organism, moving regularly through space… He was trying to form some image of what this must mean, when he felt himself recalled, as though to another life, by a voice that was infinitely distant, infinitely faint, and which had once held an infinite significance for him. It was a struggle to come back to this forgotten point in time and space: he struggled…

The girl was speaking. "Jeremy," she repeated, louder, "I am not asleep."

He came back, awoke into the real world with a shock like that of a diver coming out of the sea, and found that still the same night was in progress, that nothing around him had changed, and that he was very cold. They had both of them given up their cloaks to the old man and had nothing to cover them. The wind, so faint and tenuous that it was impossible to tell whence it came, crept insidiously through or over everything that might have served them for a shelter. The thin air surrounded and drenched them with its enervating chill, taking away from them almost even the strength for speech. But Jeremy answered,

"Nor am I, dearest. I was thinking."

They lay silent for some time. Then Eva began again, "Do you know where we are?"

"I don't at all. I didn't think to ask the name of the village. We must be somewhere on the downs between Bury and Duncton, but I couldn't see whereabouts in the darkness. Anyway, in the morning we must make towards the west."

Silence again.

But the effort of recalling these facts had drawn Jeremy back to human life; and presently he said with simplicity, "I love you... I love you..." She answered him, and they talked, telling one another of their feelings, exploring strange paths, making strange discoveries, each taking turns to draw the other aside, like two children together in a wood, one of whom points out the flowers, while the other, finger on lip, calls for silence to listen to the birds. As they talked in soft murmurs they forgot the cold and the passage of time: it was the longest converse they had ever held in intimacy. Thus it was not the gray light of morning stealing over the hill-side but the Speaker, who suddenly began to be restless and to cough and moan in his sleep, that first drew their attention from themselves.

Eva started hurriedly out of Jeremy's embrace and went to the old man. He was in the grip of another attack; and his contorted face showed that he was suffering deeply. Jeremy followed her, and stood helplessly by while she arranged more comfortably the folded cloak under his head and drew over his body the wrappings which, as constantly, with aimless violent movements of his arms he threw off again. Then, as suddenly as the attack had begun, it seemed to pass. The old man grew calm and allowed himself to be covered. He settled on his back, folded his arms across his breast and threw back his head; and his breathing became more gentle. Jeremy discovered with a shock that the sunken and brilliant eyes were open and were intensely fixed on his. He opened his mouth to say he knew not what, but the Speaker had begun in a faint but distinct whisper.

"Jeremy, we were beaten—"

It was as though he had returned to the last moment of the battle, as though the three days of his aberration had not been, and he was saying now what he might have said them. But to Jeremy there was nothing but injustice in this long-suspended comment. He forgot where they were and what was their condition; and words of hot anger rose in his mouth. He was deceived for a moment by the serenity and calmness of the Speaker's voice into thinking that this was indeed the man who had tyrannically driven them all into disaster by his ungovernable will.

"You—" shaped itself on his lips, never spoken; for the girl plucked in terror at his arm and at the same moment he stopped, jaw dropping, eyes starting and hands hanging as though the tendons of the wrists had been cut. For the old man was dead.

Eva threw herself down beside the body and pressed her lips on her father's cold forehead. Then realizing that what she had dreaded was true, that the final event had taken place, she slipped helpless to one side, sobbing violently with dry eyes and convulsed mouth. Jeremy looked from the dead man to the grief-racked girl, impotent and abased. This was the end of the old man's schemes and efforts, his life-long devotion, his last sufferings—this cold and miserable death, in the beginning of the morning, on a bare hill in the country that was no longer his own to scheme for. In the contemplation of the body Jeremy felt for a moment relieved of human desires, contemptuous of what demanded so much pains for so small a reward.

But while he stood thus he realized for the first time how light it had grown. All the down was dimly revealed, the sun was on the point of rising, and faint mists, curling off the fields, obscured the distances. But close at hand the grove in which they had hidden, and the bank against which they had rested, were plainly shown. Again a sense of staggering recognition invaded Jeremy's brain, and he did not know in what world or what time he was living. Then in a flash he was enlightened.

"The Roman road!" he exclaimed, forgetting the dead and living companions who lay at his feet. For the long bank, overgrown and almost hidden, extending into the mist on either side, was the Stane Street, running over the downs like an arrow to Bignor Hill. A pure wonder overcame Jeremy, and he went nearer to the road, touched the high unmistakable stony mound and followed its trace with his eyes. He remembered it, having tracked it without any difficulty from near Halnaker Hill through the Nore Wood, past Gumber Farm and past this very place, no longer ago than—no longer ago than the year 1913. The month had been September, and blackberries had been very thick in the hedges. He was bewildered and the waking earth turned dizzily round him, while the tragedy in which he had just taken a part and which was perhaps to continue, sank into the category of small and negligible things. It seemed to take its place with the road and everything else in a fantasy of idle invention.

He recovered himself when Eva touched him lightly on the arm. She was self-possessed again, save that she was trembling violently and that her beautiful face was drawn and pale. He wished to explain to her what had thus struck him dumb, but she whispered.

"Look! Look down there!"

The sun was now just up, the mists were fast clearing, and the open spaces and long shadows of the hill-side and the plain were very distinct. As he followed her pointing finger, he saw a line of little figures, a mile away, spread out as though they were beating the ground, advancing slowly up the hill.

"The Welsh!" he uttered, somberly and without agitation. This was what he had known and expected, and his heart did not beat a fraction the faster for it. When he looked at Eva, she too was calm, almost rigid, waiting for his next word.

"We must creep up through the bushes," he whispered, as though the enemy had been already within earshot. "Perhaps we can get away from them in the woods up there." She nodded, and while he unstrapped his pistols and saw that they were loaded, she bent over her father, disposed his limbs and covered his face with her cloak. Then she put her hand in Jeremy's, saying only.

"We must leave him. We could do nothing for him."

Without another glance at the dead man, they began to hurry, bending almost double, beside the bank of the road, stumbling over roots and avoiding the swinging-bushes as best they could. Once or twice they had to dash across open spaces where the ancient road had disappeared, gaps kept clear by old cart-tracks or a shepherd's path; and once, where the bushes clustered too thickly, they had to leave shelter and run for a hundred yards in the bare field.

2

As they ran, hand in hand, torn and impeded by the briars, growing more and more exhausted, Jeremy owned to himself, without a conscious shaping of the thought, that they were lost, that they had too small a start of their pursuers, and that these pursuers were acting in a careful and methodical way, which was an ill omen. But he was dazed and rendered distraught by the surroundings of their flight. With one part of his mind he felt no more than the animal's impulse to run for safety, carrying his mate with him. With the rest he was revolving loosely the odd chance that had landed them thus in familiar country and by the side of this great deserted causeway, a remnant of antiquity on which he had once looked with the feelings of awe and wonder that these people now bestowed on the vestiges of his own days. It was to this side of him that the landscape was growing increasingly familiar, seeming to drag him back into his own natural century, away from all the violent and incredible events of the last few weeks, away from the bravely struggling girl at his side... He felt her pull on his hand grow heavier, felt that she was stumbling more and more. Then the Nore Wood showed, obscure and gloomy ahead of them, and at the same moment Jeremy glanced through a gap in the bushes and saw, at the bottom of a gentle slope, Cumber Farm, the old weathered building with its small windows and the well in front of it, and a woman standing in a half-opened door, emptying out a bucket on the ground. Why run so painfully, he wondered, through a world that could not but be a dream? He halted suddenly and dragged Eva back. A few hundred yards in front of them, at the point where the Stane Street entered the wood, was a soldier on horseback, a dark, motionless, watchful figure, the long barrel of his pistol lying in the crook of his arm and shining in a stray beam of the sun.

"No good going on," he panted. "We must lie close somewhere for a bit." Eva said nothing and he saw that her face was white, her lips pressed together closely, her eyes half shut. Her free hand was clasped to her side, she was bending backwards from the waist, and her breath came and went in short convulsive gasps.

Near them, starting out of the growth on the old road and running down the slope of the hill, was another black hedge which seemed to lead to a little wooded knoll. Without speaking, Jeremy pulled Eva towards it, and keeping close in the shelter of the bushes they reached it without hearing any cry that showed they had been discovered. They scrambled to the top, which was some twenty feet above the level of the neighboring fields, and lay for a few moments, face downwards, exhausted and oblivious among the gorse and bracken. Then Jeremy recovered, sat up and surveyed their position. They were well hidden, and, by peering through the branches, they could watch all the country for some distance round. His hopes began to revive a little. They might even, with great good fortune, lie here unperceived while the trackers passed by: at the worst the cover was enough to help him to offer some encouragement to Eva. And his chief thought was to restore her, to see her breathe easily again, and the color come back to her cheeks, to stanch the blood that trickled from a deep scratch on her forehead, to kiss and hold her torn hands. If the very worst should happen and they were found— His thoughts broke off and he looked at her in agony, fearing to meet her eyes. She too had sat up and was fumbling in the bosom of her dress, as though looking for something.

When she saw that he was gazing at her she smiled faintly and said in a natural tone, "At any rate we can rest now." Then she began to rearrange her skirts, to put the tumbled folds into place, as well as the great rents in them would allow, and to smooth the disordered strands of her hair.

"Rest. Yes, we can rest," he answered somberly. And then he thought how adorable she looked and, bending over towards her without rising, took her in his arms and kissed her; and she returned his kisses. Presently they released one another, and Jeremy murmured, almost in a whisper.

"How quiet it is! You wouldn't think there was, any one in the downs but us." And as she made no, reply he went on, "Do you know what that bank was? It was a road built by the Romans more than two thousand years ago. Travelers and regiments of, soldiers used to march over it, though it's so lonely now." He broke off and stared abstractedly at the ground. "That seems a strange thing to talk about just now when we… when we…" He stopped altogether. She came closer to him, put her arm round his shoulder and drew his head down on her breast. Then she began gently to stroke his hair and there was infinite solace in her touch. He wondered whether he ought to discuss with her what they should do if they were discovered; but the pain of that thought was so great that it drove him back before he even felt it. He dared not… he dared not… he owned his cowardice. He let it go, closed his eyes and abandoned himself to the sweetness of her caresses.

Once more time vanished and became an unreal thing. It seemed an eternity before he opened his eyes again; but when he did so, lazily, it was to see the black remorseless figures of the pursuers spread out in a long crescent in the field below, half a mile away. Every muscle in his body stiffened, he felt his lips curling back from his teeth like those of a fighting animal, and he sat up abruptly and grasped his pistol. They were coming quite close, and they were searching all the hill-side with methodical care, advancing with regular and terrifying deliberation. Perhaps they had been led thus far by foot-prints and broken branches and rags left fluttering on the thorns, and now were casting about for further signs.

Jeremy turned and again took Eva into his arms, and pressed his mouth on hers. The kiss continued, seemed endless, was intolerably sweet and bitter, a draught not like any he had ever known. Then he broke away, saw with minute care to the readiness of his pistol, and bent forward, watching intently the approaching Welshmen. Eva, sitting a little behind him, again slipped her hand into his and held it with a firm clasp which, though he could no longer see her, conveyed to him all her sweetness and her love. Thus they waited without moving, they did not know how long, while the trackers advanced, vanished in a fold of the ground, began to emerge again. Then one of them uttered a harsh piercing view-halloo, that echoed horribly through the empty fields and sky; and in the next moment Jeremy felt Eva's hand tighten on his convulsively and then a weight behind it, dragging it back. He forgot the enemy, forgot his resolution to kill as many as he could of these hateful savages before he was himself destroyed. But when he swung round the girl had fallen on her back, and was staring upwards, her eyes and her lips quite peaceful, the pallor on her face no longer that of fear and exhaustion, but now the serene and even pallor of death. In her free hand lay open the little metal box which once she had taken from her foolish waiting-maid; and it was empty.

Jeremy did not rave or cry out, but an immense weariness overcame him, in which those who were approaching slipped altogether from his thoughts. Was it for this, he wondered, staring vacantly at the familiar English country around him, that he had come so far and done and suffered so much? All were gone now, all were enveloped in a common darkness, those friends of his earlier life and his new friends, the old, vehement Speaker, poor Roger Vaile, and, last and dearest of them, the Lady Eva, to find whom a century and a half asleep in the grave had been a slight and welcome preparation. What was he doing here? The Welsh were coming, the Welsh had sacked London, they had taken England in their ravening jaws. He had a vision of the world sinking further below the point from which in his youth he had seen it, still on a level with him. Cities would be burnt, bridges broken down, tall towers destroyed and all the wealth and learning of humanity would shiver to a few shards and a little dust. The very place would be forgotten where once had stood the houses that he knew; and the roads he had walked with his friends would be as desolate and lonely as the Stane Street of the Romans. Even all this story, his victory and his defeat, his joy and his sorrow, would fade out of the memory of man. But what did it all matter to Jeremy Tuft, who, wonder and portent that he was, strange anachronism, unparalleled and reluctant ambassador from one age to the next, had suffered in the end that common ill, the loss of his beloved? He raised the pistol to his head and fired.

THE END